KINNARA

Kevin Ansbro was born of Irish parents, and has lived in Malaysia and Germany.

He is married, and currently lives in Norwich, England.

BY THE SAME AUTHOR

The Angel in My Well (eBook)

KINNARA

KEVIN ANSBRO

2QT Limited (Publishing)

First Edition published 2015
Revised Edition 2018
2QT Limited (Publishing)
Settle, North Yorkshire BD24 9RH United Kingdom

The author has his own website: www.kevinansbro.co.uk

This is a work of fiction and any resemblance to any person living or dead
is purely coincidental. The place names mentioned are real but have no
connection with the events in this book

Cover Illustrations by Kevin Ansbro
Cover setting Charlotte Mouncey
Thai script supplied by Tanachai Sirimongkol

Printed in Great Britain by
Lightning Source UK

A CIP catalogue record for this book is available
from the British Library
ISBN 978-1-910077-54-2

For Julie, the perfect travel companion.

กินรา

QUOTES

Love, Loss, and Consequences

'T*is better to have loved and lost*
than never to have loved at all.
Alfred Lord Tennyson

When anger rises, think of the consequences.
Confucius

What would an ocean be without a monster
lurking in the dark?
Werner Herzog

CHAPTER ONE

The Mother Killer

Kaiserslautern, Germany, 2011

He acknowledged her beauty:

Perhaps, if circumstances were different, he could even have imagined dating her. But right now her neck was succumbing to the forceful pressure exerted by his strong, gloved thumbs. She did, however, put up a fight; her body initially bucked like an unsaddled mustang, but to no avail. Ulrika Kruger's flailing legs kicked with a desperate force, ripping away two of his shirt buttons which ricocheted off the kitchen floor tiles. Regardless of this onslaught, an abandoned tap continued to stream cold water into the sink. Ulrika's hands, now, were barely wafting the air, almost as if she were fanning herself on a hot day. The air was fragrant with the heady scent of the lilies that she had recently shuffled into a vase.

"*Schlafe liebe Mutter*," he soothed, watching the light disappear from her frantic eyes. Unseen by him, Ulrika's spirit had temporarily left her body; a butterfly escaping its chrysalis, and was floating on the periphery, not yet certain of its destiny.

It wasn't that he hated this woman *per se*, he just

despised what her pregnant stomach symbolised: a soon-to-be mother, with all the love in the world to share with her child; it sickened him to his core.

After tearing sheets of paper towel from a reel above the worktop, he dampened them under the running water; then packed the pulp through her mouth and into her throat, thereby ensuring that there would be no coming back. Her spirit expeditiously departed the scene, assured now of its duty.

****

For several months the newspapers had screamed headlines, in bold font, about a spate of murders, primarily in the Kaiserslautern area. The common denominator was that each of the victims was a woman, and that each was heavily pregnant: *Bild* newspaper coined the tag: *"Der Mutter Mörder"* (The Mother Killer) and almost every other daily then used the same epithet in their articles.

This was his fourth such murder in less than a year. In this instance, he'd spotted his victim at the local *supermarkt* and covertly followed her home, parking his car some distance from her house.

The Mother Killer looked down at the dead woman's belly in disgust. All that was left of her humanity was a posthumous stare.

He turned off the sink tap and casually retrieved his shirt buttons from the kitchen floor, a process slightly hindered by the gloves he was wearing. Ever the narcissist, he admired his handsome face in the hallway mirror before leaving by the front door. He called out a cheery *"tschüss!"* – waving goodbye to an imaginary person within the house, just in case a prying neighbour might be watching.

After that, he closed the door, adjusted his gloves, and walked for ten minutes to the road where his car was parked.

CHAPTER TWO

Schoolgirl Dreams

Norwich, England 2005

Hannah Cunningham stood pitch-side, supporting the school's football team. Her school, St John's, was playing against the Hewett's First XI, but fifteen-year-old Hannah was probably the only spectator who wasn't following the ball. Her eyes, instead, tracked each energetic movement made by her friend, Calum Armstrong. They were both in the same year and had known each other since their first gawky day at high school, at the age of eleven.

She studied Calum now, commitment written all over his James Dean face: those topaz-blue eyes and his lopsided smile had monopolised her daydreams of late. The teenage hormones, which invaded each and every cell in her body, had groomed Hannah to harbour a secret yearning that friendship alone couldn't satisfy. It wasn't just Hannah who had designs on him: *all* the girls, even the younger, more immature ones, fancied him.

"He's well lush," purred Imogen Gibson – who had already lost her virginity to Dylan Ramsey. "If you don't have him, I will."

Not if I can help it, thought Hannah, who considered

Imogen to be a total tart. Hannah was a popular girl, with innumerable friends at school; Imogen Gibson certainly wasn't one of them.

Hannah had a black Jamaican father; a big bear of a man, and an alabaster-skinned Irish mother. Their combined gene pool had bestowed on her a coffee-coloured skin, allied with Celtic-green eyes. Her face was undeniably pretty, each caramel cheek stippled with a daisy chain of freckles. Her eyes were actually chartreuse green, spattered with tiny brown flecks, and fringed with extravagantly long eyelashes. A slight gap between her two front teeth gave her voice a lispy smokiness that belied her youthfulness. The other girls looked for any excuse to touch her glossy black hair, which tumbled about her head in a bundle of loose spirals.

Hannah took her sport seriously: she was captain of the netball team, all athletic limbs and high energy, and currently held the school record for the 400 metres. Her white, knee-high socks accentuated the length of her colt-like legs whose smooth, lustrous skin glistened as if they were permanently moisturised.

Right from the outset, Hannah and Calum were destined to become the very best of friends.

Their inaugural meeting, on their first day at school, when every classroom smelled of gloss paint and floor polish, was purely by accident. Each was too proud to ask for directions to assembly, and both stumbled into the school canteen instead. Hannah found this far more hilarious than the situation warranted but, despite this, Calum was immediately struck by her sense of humour.

He liked almost everything about her, from the smell of Chupa Chup lollipops on her breath to the scent of apple shampoo in her hair. In addition, he loved the fact that she was always up for a practical joke. In their second week, they sneaked into the sports hall before assembly and placed a dead crow – which Calum had discovered in the playground – under the lid of the piano. Later, Mrs Fletcher, the music teacher, sat at the piano stool, not realising that some of the hammers were never going to hit their target strings. Then, as the entire school broke into the first chorus of *All Things Bright and Beautiful*, her piano issued a muffled *donk-donk* sound that swiftly halted proceedings. As the singing faded to a whispery silence, Mr Chalker, the deputy headmaster, was the first to figure out what might have happened. He strode over to the piano, lifted the lid and flamboyantly produced the crow in the manner of a magician plucking a rabbit from a hat. Of course the whole assembly erupted into laughter. Mrs Fletcher, ever the attention-seeker, splayed a quivering hand over her bosom in a show of distress that would have better suited an am-dram audition.

Hannah and Calum's *cool* credentials were unequivocally established from that day forward.

For Calum, the tedium of lessons was lessened by Hannah's willingness to goof around at every opportunity; she habitually crossed her eyes and poked out her tongue whenever he caught her gaze, and her face froze in comedic astonishment each time that she was scolded by a teacher.

Calum innocently only ever felt that they were the very best of friends but as far as Hannah was concerned, they were destined to become husband and wife someday. It wasn't as if she hadn't dropped him enough hints, but all of his passion seemed to be channelled into football and the karate classes that he attended after school. Calum, though, wasn't at all like one of those American high-school jocks who only hung around with the macho sportsmen. His best male friend was bespectacled Leo Griffiths, a boy who was – without wishing to be – the personification of geekiness. In fact, when Calum coerced him into taking an online geek test, he was an uncannily accurate match for most of its key indicators.

In cringe-worthy attempts to look hip, Leo would crowbar words such as "Yo!" and "Wassup!" into almost every conversation, inviting critical looks and rueful shakes of the head from Calum. But, despite their contrasting personalities, the two boys got on famously.

Even though he relished Hannah's company, there was never a time when Calum started to think of her in a girlfriend kind of way. They had become such close friends that treading into romance would have seemed downright awkward. So when Hannah occasionally dropped an, *'I'm going to marry you one day, Calum Armstrong,'* into a conversation, he self-consciously brushed it off as playful banter.

Calum would have been surprised to discover that she secretly liked to doodle his name, embellishing each letter with swirls and love hearts. In addition to this, he would have been astonished to learn that she often wrote her future name, *Hannah Armstrong,* just to see how good it would look on paper.

On the football pitch, Calum was fouled by one of the Hewett boys. He sprang to his feet like a Jack-in-the-box and shoved the boy hard in the chest, voicing his obvious displeasure.

Hannah was not in the least bit impressed. *When we're married, I'm going to need to work on that temper of yours,* she mused, wincing at the snarling mask of fury that spoiled Calum's otherwise handsome face.

In light of his anger-management issues, and because Calum was also highly protective of her, Hannah sensibly steered clear of mentioning any school incident where another boy had upset her. So, when one of the spiteful Adcock twins ground a large wad of bubble gum into her hair, she thought it better that he didn't know.

Instead, she calmly and carefully cut the sticky mess

out of her curls with a pair of scissors and didn't tell a single soul.

Less than one minute after being fouled, Calum, seeking retribution, deliberately scythed down the other boy in a clattering tackle which got him sent off. *So predictable* thought Hannah, shaking her head in resignation. Even so, she loyally applauded him off the field, before realising that this was wholly inappropriate.

Mr Bingham, the chubby Maths teacher, scuttled near to Hannah, wholly preoccupied with the time on an antique pocket watch. This caused him to trip clumsily over an opened sports bag and he crashed, arse over tit, into the turf, lying there embarrassed for a full two seconds. Clambering upright, he spat a blade of grass from the edge of his mouth and brushed a clod of damp mud from his wobbly chin. Mr Bingham was a chap who wore his trousers incredibly high, their waistband skirting the uppermost part of his belly, hoisted by braces that could have catapulted a flying acrobat. Because of this fashion *faux pas,* he was known throughout the school as 'Harry high pants' – and not just by the pupils. As a matter of fact, if he were daffodil yellow, rather than a pasty old-English pink, Mr Bingham would undoubtedly be the spitting image of Homer Simpson. What few hairs he possessed had flopped over his limpid eyes, so he stretched them back over the bare skin atop his head to resemble the strings of a banjo.

Hannah rushed to his aid, concerned that he may have hurt himself. Those assembled, including the teachers, found the incident hilarious and laughed loudly, like drinkers at a comedy club.

"Are you OK, Mr Bingham?" she asked, sympathetic to his wounded pride as much as to any physical damage occurred.

"Oh, you are so very kind Hannah … I think I

shall be fine, thank you," he mumbled, touched by her humanity and only too aware that Hannah Cunningham's thoughtfulness was in sharp contrast to the indifference shown by his colleagues – especially as he had only recently lost his dear wife to cancer.

Whilst it was easy for everyone to mock Mr Bingham, Hannah had always retained a soft spot for the guy. Yes, he existed in the wrong era and blundered through life like a bee trapped behind a curtain, but he was a sensitive, gentle soul and of absolutely no bother to anyone.

She efficiently brushed a clump of mud from his left knee and he quietly thanked her once more before continuing on his befuddled way.

By now, Calum had stepped from the field; he was still angry at being sent off, and hadn't seen Mr Bingham's fall.

"Why are all these idiots laughing?" he asked, thinking that their amusement was directed at him.

"Oh, it's because Mr Bingham tripped over and hit the deck. You just missed it."

"Poor guy. Is he OK? Does he need help?"

"Yeah, yeah, he's *fine*. I think his pride was hurt more than anything."

Hannah liked the fact that Calum was the only other person who seemed to care about Mr Bingham's welfare. *Considerate as always,* she thought.

Hannah clasped Calum's wrist to bring his attention back to her; she had been harbouring a matter of enormous significance which she needed to broach.

"Hey Calum, could we stop at mine straight after school? I've got something really important to tell you."

"Wow, sounds heavy. What's it about?" he probed, wiping sweat from his forehead with a muddy shirt sleeve.

"Tell you later, yeah?"

"OK," he breezed, breaking into the same engaging smile that even her mother often remarked upon.

Hannah felt a hollow ache in her heart as her eyes tracked his bouncy jog towards the changing rooms, his boot studs clattering against the tarmac like reindeer hooves. She bit her bottom lip and dug for the tissues in her satchel.

****

Hannah and Calum were met at the school gates, as per usual, by Leo. This was their fraternal routine every day after lessons. Together, they would take a slow, gossipy walk as far as Sainsbury's, and then Leo would peel off in the direction of his home, while the other two headed left into the Dussindale Park development.

On this particular afternoon Dean Gunt, the school shit-for-brains bully, was on hand by the pavement to engage in sparkling conversation with whomever walked or cycled past. Not only was Dean the heir to an unfortunate surname, he was also in possession of an overly large body and a potato head, one which only his roly-poly mother could ever have loved. In fact, apart from winning the school shot-putt event each year, he had absolutely nothing to be proud of. So instead his young life was devoted to tormenting people and setting fire to random objects.

Gunt was accompanied, as ever, by the Adcock twins, who shared a feral, rat-like quality: their mother's clumsy DIY attempts to clipper their hair made them look like the wretched convicts in *Les Misérables*.

"Hey Cunningham, come over here and suck my dick!" Dean hollered for everyone to hear.

Hannah ignored him, drawing the navy blazer across her chest and virtuously folding her arms. Calum, though, had other ideas and dropped his backpack onto the ground. "Don't worry, I've got your back," he assured her, not that Hannah needed or wanted him to protect her from idiots like Dean Gunt.

"Here, hold this," he said, removing his school blazer and passing it to Leo. Hannah and Leo both groaned as Calum sauntered over to the three cretins with a confident shoulder-rolling gait.

"Oooh, watch out lads, here comes pretty-boy Armstrong," Dean chuckled through moist lips that were overly pink and almost feminine. Dumb and Dumber gurned supportively by his side, like two lobotomised chimps.

"You talk to her like that again and I will punch your lights out," threatened Calum, who was a full year younger and twenty-five kilos lighter than Dean.

"What? *You*, you little shit?" Dean puffed, surprised at the kid's fearlessness. A rash of anger coloured his fat cheeks as he thrust a meaty hand towards Calum's throat. Quick as a flash, Calum punched him hard in the balls; the big kid made a noise similar to a dog's bark, and sank to his knees in agony.

The Adcock twins weren't sure what to do next; they were wholly unprepared for such an unexpected event but they directed their tough-guy stares at Calum anyway.

"You two twats got anything to say?" Calum said inviting, but not getting, a response. "Didn't think so, couple of wimps."

A hushed crowd of dumbfounded school kids had gathered to watch the excitement unfold. Looking every inch the coolest kid in school, Calum calmly strolled back to Leo and Hannah.

"Buggering hell!" spluttered Leo, nervously fidgeting with his spectacles.

Calum assessed Hannah's body language, working out if it was safe to approach, then placed a vigilant arm over her shoulder before walking her home, behaving almost as if nothing had happened. Hannah was prepared to overlook his hot-headedness on this occasion, especially as he had his arm around her, and gave the hand that cupped her shoulder an approving pat.

As agreed, Calum stopped off at Hannah's. They were greeted in the hallway by Marcus, her eight-year-old brother, who was a beautiful Down's syndrome child. His hair was more tightly curled than his sister's and it had mushroomed into a tidy afro.

"Hello, Calum," said Marcus, offering a shy handshake. He looked upon Calum almost as an older brother and loved it each time he popped round.

"Hiya, little fella," Calum schmoozed, moving in close for the customary tickle. Hannah knelt down to give her brother a squeeze amid a cluster of loud kisses that made Marcus chuckle with unabated delight.

Hannah's mother poked an inquisitive head from the kitchen, where she was baking blueberry muffins. "Oh, hi, Calum. Hi, honey," she said in her soft Irish brogue, waving slender arms that were attached to oven gloves.

At that point, Calum silently wondered why there were packing crates and large, labelled boxes crammed into every available corner of her house.

Before he'd had the chance to take his shoes off, Hannah's mother fixed him a reproaching stare. "Calum, I will allow you to go into my only daughter's bedroom, providing that you sit on your salacious little hands for the whole time you're up there."

"Umm, OK, Mrs Cunningham," Calum gulped, not having the faintest idea what *salacious* meant.

"Cal, she's joking with you. It's what she does," Hannah huffed, rolling her eyes as her mother laughed impishly at her own humour.

Upstairs, in her bedroom Hannah attempted to delay the broadcasting of her life-altering news by playing the Black Eyed Peas' *Monkey Business* album. Calum was amazed that, as usual, she knew every lyric to every track. It was he who eventually decided to confront the elephant in the room. "So what's this important *thing* that you're desperately trying not to tell me?"

Hannah gulped hard then suppressed a wave of tears, desperately trying not to look like a loser in front of her friend. "Well, you know my dad's a deputy manager at Sainsbury's?"

Calum nodded, listening intently.

"So, he's been offered a store manager's job in Peterborough…"

Calum was confused. "But, surely that's good news?" he suggested, totally missing the point.

"Well not really, Calum – it means my whole family moving away from Norwich!" she shouted, her voice sharper than she'd intended.

"Ah," Calum gasped, starting to understand the gravity of this development and also beginning to realise the significance of the packing crates.

Hannah couldn't maintain her composure any longer; her eyes puddled with tears and, as she averted her gaze from Calum, her lower lip started to tremble. When he moved in for a supportive hug, she erupted into a paroxysm of uncontrollable sobs.

****

At assembly the next day, the whole school was informed of the most dreadful news. Mr Bingham had taken his own life. Mr Dunkley, the school janitor, had discovered him hanging by a skilfully knotted rope in the sports changing room.

In the wake of such a grisly occurrence, the whole school descended into a collective stupor and those with the guiltiest of consciences seemed to cry the longest.

****

A large removal lorry arrived at Hannah's home just one week later.

By the time it was crammed with boxes and furniture, a posse of Hannah's girlfriends had come to say their goodbyes and neighbours had also nipped round to see the Cunninghams off.

Calum, though, was conspicuous by his absence. Hannah had explicitly told him that her family would be leaving around lunchtime and yet he was nowhere to be seen. She resisted the urge to text, hoping that he would come of his own volition. She had also gone to the trouble of making some of his favourite chocolate Rice Krispie cakes as an affectionate parting gift.

Even as her father closed the front door firmly for the very last time, she still hoped that her hero might suddenly appear to console her with his dreamy smile.

Whilst putting some bags into the back of her father's car, Hannah unwittingly knocked her phone from the seat, causing it to bounce off the kerb before it came to rest in the shadow of a tyre.

Meanwhile, the lorry's engine started with a throaty splutter. The removals men were travelling independently to the Cunninghams, who were all seated in the family car except for Hannah, who had rushed back into the house to search for her phone. She returned, empty-handed, with a look of desperation on her face.

"Has anyone seen my mobile? Please, I need it!"

"Let me call it," her mother offered, reaching into her handbag.

"That's no use, it's switched off!"

"Why is it switched off?"

"The battery was getting low. I had it in my hand less than ten minutes ago!"

"Honey, stop fretting about your blasted phone," her

mother urged. "It's sure to be in one of the boxes, we'll sort it out when we get there."

Hannah sat, despondent, in the back of the car as her father prepared to drive. He was hugely relieved that the process had run smoothly and that they were leaving ahead of schedule.

All hope had faded: Hannah's earlier optimism descended into a wounded, tearful anger. Her mother instinctively read the situation and dispensed tissues between the headrests to the back seat.

"Hey, I know that this is a big deal right now, honey, but a popular girl like you will make plenty of new friends in Peterborough."

Hannah's father drove the car in watchful silence, observing his precious daughter in the rear-view mirror. He knew not to involve himself with her teenage angst, as he had a habit of putting his foot in it when it came to such delicate matters.

"Don't be sad," encouraged Marcus, unable to understand why his big sister was crying so much.

Of course, this just heightened her heartache, she was leaving Norwich with an unfathomable emptiness that would be impossible to fill.

****

It was 12.15 pm. Calum and Leo had just left Sainsbury's after clubbing together to buy a bouquet of garish flowers. While they walked to Hannah's house, Calum busied himself by attempting to rub off the gluey residue that had been left by the price sticker.

"Oh no, look!" Leo howled, throwing one hand against his forehead and pointing a finger towards the big removals lorry that was thundering into the distance.

"You don't think...?"

Calum immediately tried to call Hannah but her

phone went unanswered.

He dropped his arms in disbelief. The cellophaned flowers hung by the side of one leg as an unnecessary embellishment.

The two boys were completely lost for words; Calum couldn't imagine what Hannah might be thinking.

One thing was certain. He'd let her down, badly.

CHAPTER THREE

Klahan Kinnara

The Andaman Sea, Phuket, Thailand: not far from the Patong beach shoreline.

Breaking open that human's head was the cruel justification for Klahan Kinnara's desolate underwater existence: he sits like this, cross-legged, alone on the sea bed, day after day, and has continued to do so, for more than two thousand years.

The Thai sun cast a rippling mosaic of forbidden solar, less than five fathoms above his weary gaze. He had, innumerable centuries ago, decided to ignore the taunt of the light's rhythmic dance as it undulated constantly, as amorphous as a jellyfish.

Oh how he wished to be back in that illuminated world above the waves. He had once walked and flown about that Earth, but since then had to endure two millenniums of abandoned isolation, trapped by a distant curse. He'd cried desperately for the first two years, but then couldn't sob any more. His groans of despair once echoed across oceans, at a pitch only heard by sea creatures; now he endured his watery incarceration through a meditative state where his mind was at one with the emptiness of the abyss. Despite being trapped on the sea bed, like a sunken chest, among sea urchins and plankton, he had somehow achieved a vulnerable kind of inner peace. That wasn't to say that he wouldn't have gladly swapped the poisoned chalice of eternal life for the sweet anaesthesia of death. If he were a human, he would undoubtedly have become insane in only a matter of weeks.

Boats, which were once simple vessels that slapped through the water propelled by human effort alone, passed overhead with a noise that was as clamorous as the wretched Crow People who trespassed the verdant borders of his former world.

Klahan felt that the death of the sun each evening represented a transient victory. He gladly welcomed the onset of each dark, claustrophobic night, when the torment of daylight could no longer be seen. Ancient wars once raged above his watery dungeon, but now the human world, for some reason, seemed to be at peace.

Despite being here for aeons, he had only ever been seen by a handful of submerged humans for Klahan was only visible if someone wished to see him.

In 1662, a drunken Dutch sailor had fallen overboard from a passing trade ship. The man was drowning right before Klahan's interested stare; he noticed that there was a fascinating poetry in the human's bulging eyes.

The sailor, wishing to God that someone, *anyone*, would help him, actually saw Klahan, serenely reposed, like a deity: But Klahan no longer possessed the power to help anyone. Excited that he was seen, though, he placed his hand upon the sailor's head and extracted every thought and every story from the dying man's memory.

As the sailor sank unconscious before him, Klahan assimilated the information that coursed through his luminous fingers and then into the neurons of his brain. He learnt that the human's name was Adrianus Bloemaert and that, until today, he had lived on Earth for more than thirty-seven years. Klahan was able to observe the man's first kiss, and he also watched Adrianus cry upon the death of his father. And at least he now knew what the huge claw was, the thing that one day attacked the seabed to his flank: it was called an *anker* in the Dutchman's language.

Occasionally – only a handful of times in each century – a human being would see him, usually by thinking they saw *something* and then believing it to be true. But even when they looked squarely at him, they were so instantly terrified that they hastily launched themselves back to the surface.

One recent occasion, though, remained entrenched in the forefront of his long memory: that day, the entire Andaman Sea was sucked right back to the horizon. Klahan suddenly found himself fully exposed on a vast desert of wet sand under the acid squint of the sun. For as far as his saffron eyes could see, there were legions of marooned fish that clapped and thrashed at the puddled sea bed in floundering applause.

Two inquisitive humans jogged out to his deep, waterless basin after scrambling down damp, sandy inclines. They wandered nearby, talking in strange languages that he didn't understand, completely oblivious to his existence.

But then the ocean returned with a spiteful vengeance. The noise was beyond thunderous. Klahan had seen this happen several centuries before, only then there were barely any humans in its destructive path. The water accelerated through him, leaving him unmoved: it rumbled above him, fifteen fathoms high, plunging him into temporary darkness.

In the airless calm thereafter, the bloated bodies of several humans drifted above his head – each one signalling a lost opportunity.

Klahan flared his nostrils at the iniquity of it all: if just one of these humans expected to see him and acknowledged his presence, he could finally become free from his lonely torment.

His fate, it would seem, was forever sealed – until such time that a mortal could conclusively offer him their forgiveness.

CHAPTER FOUR

Dumb and Dumber

Norwich, England: the day after Hannah's departure.

Now that Hannah wasn't around anymore, Calum realised just how much she had been an integral part of his adolescent life. Certainly none of the other girls at school were anywhere near as much fun.

He and Leo shared a mutual despondency as they traipsed in unified silence to their next lesson. Both friends felt diminished by her absence but neither possessed the emotional maturity to articulate their feelings. A burgeoning commotion up ahead, though, broke their quietude; small scrums of boys were jostling for position outside the science block, converging on its grimy windows like seagulls around a tractor. Clearly, something exciting was happening inside. Most of the lads were grinning as excitedly as spectators at a guillotining, while others, Calum noticed, were decidedly alarmed at whatever was taking place inside the building.

Francis Wong was one of those boys who fell into the alarmed category. He seemed somewhat reassured by Calum's sudden arrival on the scene.

"What on earth is going on?" Calum asked.

"It's Dumb and Dumber; they've got Saunders in there..."

Instinctively, and without hesitation, Calum forced his way through to the classroom entrance. Inside, one of the Adcock twins was pinning a squirming Lucas Saunders down on the floor, whilst the other was putting all of his wiry effort into writing something on the back of the boy's white shirt with a permanent marker.

Lucas had recently come out as being gay which, at the age of fifteen and still being at school, was an incredibly brave thing to do.

Calum hauled one of the twins off Lucas, and sent him sliding across the parquet floor; then he snatched the marker pen from the other one's determined grip. Lucas was fighting back hot tears. Dumb had written the word *FAGUT* in scratchy black capitals across the width of his school shirt.

"Just what the hell are you doing?" Calum yelled, protectively standing between Lucas and his two assailants.

"He's a faggot!" Dumb snarled, clearly assuming that this earth-shattering piece of information would justify their actions.

"You can't even spell the word, you moron!" Calum railed, shaking his head with disbelief.

Quickly, and without warning, he scribbled a black Hitler moustache under Dumb's nose, knowing full well that the ink wouldn't wash off any time soon. Dumber had quietly concertinaed himself from the floor and hoped that by creating some distance between him and Calum Armstrong it might exempt him from a similar reversal of fortune.

"You too!" Calum instructed, beckoning Dumber forward, like a passport control officer. The gathering tiptoed inside for ringside seats. Excited faces appeared at every window, pink noses were flattened against smudged glass. Dumber took a curious peek at his brother's embittered expression and saw that the moustache looked hideous:

"Punch me in the face instead," he offered, before closing his eyes and screwing up his weaselly features in readiness.

Oh, this is just fantastic, thought Calum, who was then afforded ample opportunity to draw another moustache, but with even greater accuracy.

Firecrackers of laughter detonated around the classroom. The twins tried to tough it out by walking to the exit with a deluded swagger. This attempt at damage limitation looked completely farcical, given the state of their desecrated faces.

Calum wrapped a comforting arm around Lucas's shoulder:

"I think that you and I need to go on a quick shopping trip straight after school. You definitely can't go home to your parents wearing that shirt. Me and Leo are gonna buy you a new one."

"I reckon I could have had them … you just beat me to it." Lucas smiled, with more than a hint of irony in his quavering voice.

****

Four hours later, Sharon Adcock, the twins' mother, phoned their dad, who was drinking pints of Stella with his deadbeat mates in The Griffin public house. Stephen Adcock was digging into his third bag of cheese and onion crisps when his wife's name flashed up on his mobile:

"It's me missus," he snorted, thereby immediately losing several man points. Steve thought he'd made it clear to his wife that his pub time was sacrosanct. His puerile beer buddies heckled him with throaty jeers and one started to crack an imaginary whip. Soon they were all cracking whips and making a *chushhh!* sound.

With all of his feathers well and truly ruffled, Steve brushed some crisp crumbs from his hands and gruffly answered the phone. "Yup, what do you want?"

"Steve, you need to get your arse back here, pronto!"

****

Once home, the sight that greeted Steve as he blustered into the living room was likely to live in his boozy memory until his dying day. Sharon had arranged their two apprehensive sons side by side on the sofa, like prize exhibits at a county show. She didn't utter a single word; instead, she presented their progeny in the manner of a game show hostess.

Each boy sported a Hitler moustache that even nail varnish remover had failed to eliminate.

"I'm going back to the pub," Steve grunted, without wanting to know the ins and outs. "*You* fucking deal with it!"

CHAPTER FIVE

Another Murder

Kaiserslautern, Germany 2012

Frankfurt Detective Lieutenant Otto Netzer presided over the latest *Mother Killer* murder. If, as he suspected, this *was* the work of the same man it would be the seventh such murder in just under two years.

Otto stood on the bank of the Nahe River, one of the Rhine's gentle tributaries. Earlier this year he'd been drafted in to help the local *polizei*, who were easily overwhelmed by an unstoppable avalanche of media attention.

Despite the pockmarked scars that spoke of teenage acne more than thirty years earlier, Otto had a ruggedly handsome face and an extravagant flop of silver-blond hair, which belied his forty-seven years.

The nicotine gum in his mouth was proving to be a futile gesture, as ineffective as his search for the perpetrator of these murders. He straightened the expensive *Brioni* silk tie that his wife, Kirsten, had recently bought for his debut on the TV crime show *Kriminalität Heute Abend*. He'd appeared on the programme to appeal for information that might lead to the eventual arrest of this serial killer but, despite several hundred phone calls from members of the public, there was still nothing in the way of solid leads. This inertia, and the absence of nicotine in his body, had pushed his buttons and frayed his nerves, making him even more irritable than usual.

Today there was quite a congregation of career professionals, either standing near the river bank or shuffling along its adjacent cycle path. Apart from the uniformed officers, almost everyone wore suits in a modest display of blues and greys. If it weren't for all the emergency vehicles and patrol cars at the scene, the collective would look like a group of businessmen assembled for a river cruise.

Otto envied the other detectives for their unpretentious ties. He doubled his chin to look at his own: *purple and pink, for Christ's sake:* He didn't even like the fucking thing; hated it, in fact. But because it was so expensive, and because Kirsten liked it, he felt duty bound to wear it as often as possible.

The huge claw of a crane had plucked the car from its semi-submerged position and was hoisting it towards dry land. As it did, torrents of brown water fell from every aperture. Much earlier, at approximately 5.30 am, a local man, cycling to work, had noticed the puddled roof of the car just about clearing the surface of the water, glistening like a beached porpoise in the dawn sun.

The man's original horrified thought was that someone had veered off the road and ploughed straight into the river, but when he supported an elbow on one knee to look at the driver's side of the vehicle, there didn't appear to be anyone inside. So, by the time he phoned the police to report his discovery, he had already passed it off as youthful vandalism.

Before Otto arrived at the scene, two police frogmen had entered the dark water to examine the vehicle. One of them pulled keys from the car's ignition and together the divers lifted the car's boot, pushing against the pressure of surface water.

Inside was the blanched, bloated body of twenty-eight-year-old Sabine Baumann. Her distraught husband had reported both her and the car missing the previous evening. He had also mentioned, in passing, that his wife was six months pregnant. The forensic pathologist later confirmed that Sabine's lungs were full of water, indicating that she was still alive at the point of submersion. Same *modus operandi*, acknowledged Otto: pregnant woman; husband at work; no evidence of sexual assault and no money stolen.

The *Mother Killer* had somehow managed to bundle this lady into the boot of her own car and then, without being seen by anyone, launched the vehicle into the river.

Frustratingly for Otto and his team, there were still no known sightings of the killer, not even a grainy image on CCTV. Amazingly, the guy hadn't left one molecule of DNA nor a single fingerprint.

Using only hand gestures to convey his request, Otto signalled for a lower-ranking detective to light him a cigarette; he was far too crotchety to engage in polite conversation. The younger guy hesitated at first; Otto had previously given clear instructions to everyone that he was not to be given cigarettes, *no matter what*. But the fierce look on his superior's face told him all he needed to know. He flared up a fresh one, catching the smoke in his own mouth, before passing it over.

Otto took a deep drag whilst he contemplated his invisible adversary. This bastard was either extremely smart, he reflected, or just incredibly lucky.

CHAPTER SIX

Sawat Leelapun

Patong beach, Phuket, Thailand: 26th December, 2004

The day started out like most others. By 7.30 a.m. the sun was already above the rooftops and Sawat Leelapun was tucking into breakfast at *Khun* Mae's roadside stand, just a few hundred meters from the beach. This is how he liked to start his morning, sitting on a low plastic seat as trucks and motorcycles thundered past. In a line among several others, Mae's food stand was intrinsically a two-wheeled cart, with a motorcycle attached. Sixty seven-years-old, she had a permanent smile on her face, even though there wasn't a single tooth in her entire mouth. Sawat had known Mae since he was a child and, although her food was the cheapest on the row, it was probably also the tastiest.

Patong, as ever, was infused with a clamorous energy that emerged from the first shuffle of dawn. The scattering of bare-footed monks had already vanished; each possessing a transcendental rhythm of slow calm somehow unaffected by the bustle of their surroundings. Each morning, at first light they fanned out amongst the street vendors, receiving gifts of food to take to their monastery.

In return, the stallholders were offered a brief blessing and a much-needed spiritual connection. Partly hidden beneath the folds of their saffron robes, the monks carried large, silver-lidded bowls which held the offerings. Both the giver and the receiver shared a mutual expectation, a synergy of Buddhism and capitalism.

Today happened to be Sawat's sixteenth birthday and his former school life was already a distant, carefree memory. Continuing his studies would have been a luxury that his small family could ill afford. Just two hundred baht meant food on the table for himself, his mother and his kid sister; anything less brought raw hunger and soul-crushing poverty to their door. Even small additional amounts of money meant that his family could begin to think about treats and unpaid bills. He had to hustle to eke out a living, and Patong beach was his workplace.

Sawat was a skinny boy with a kickboxer's physique: his waist was no bigger than the trunk of a young coconut tree and he approached life with a cheerful optimism, despite his meagre existence. As is true of most Thais, he was shorter than the average European of a similar age. His upper body was lean and ripped, similar to an anatomical diagram; his legs, particularly his calves, were disproportionately sturdy and capable of real damage.

He'd started Thai boxing at the age of eight, when Supanee, his diminutive mother, could still carry him under one arm. He trained at the Singpatong *Muay Thai* gymnasium along with an assortment of similarly undernourished kids. For the first few months, he was taken there by his father who was keen to encourage some outside discipline in his son's life. After this initial period, he cycled there willingly almost every day after school.

Just four desperate years ago Sawat's fisherman father, Boonrit, drowned during a violent storm whilst out at sea. This left a heartbroken Supanee as the only breadwinner in the Leelapun household.

His mother, though, couldn't afford to languish in the emptiness of her grief. To support her family, she worked six days a week in the back of a makeshift stall at the slow end of Chatuchak Market. Supanee was a trained seamstress and she altered clothes using a 1960s' Singer sewing machine that would break down at the mere mention of denim. On a good day she could earn over four hundred baht, which easily covered her household bills. Unfortunately, such days didn't come around all that often.

When he was born, Supanee and Boonrit immediately gave Sawat the nickname of *Mot* – meaning *ant* – because he was so tiny. Each parent held the traditional belief that, by giving their son the name of an animal, it would confuse any evil spirits who might then leave him alone.

Sawat was enjoying a breakfast of steamed rice with pork and omelette, to which he'd added a liberal splash of *prik nam pla*. This spicy condiment, made from fish sauce, lime juice, sugar and chillies, was his favourite and he used it to inject flavour into every single meal.

Mae smiled more than she talked, partly because her hearing had diminished with age, but also due to her innate shyness. She had always been exceptionally kind to Sawat. When he was a school kid, stopping at her stall whilst cycling to the beach, she would often give him free food, knowing that his family had no money. Even now she slackened her portion control to give him a little extra each time he dropped by.

Mae was something of a local institution and she was famed for owning an abundance of brightly coloured hats. Many people thought that this was just her particular eccentricity but she was a shrewd businesswoman who knew that the garish hats attracted people's attention and might tempt them to her stall. Her choice today was a wide-brimmed, fuchsia-pink sun hat, embellished with yellow butterflies.

Halfway through his breakfast, Sawat felt the ground tremble beneath him and looked at Mae to see if she'd also noticed. Shortly afterwards there was another, more noticeable, judder. This time the food stand shook like a rail track in the path of an oncoming train. Stacks of plates and sweaty pan lids rattled, as if disturbed by a mischievous spirit; bunches of fresh coriander leaves swung on their hooks like green pendulums.

The mini quake stopped almost as soon as it had started. Mae ignored its existence and served a steaming plate of food to a local businessman who was staring at the ground with nervous suspicion. Sawat looked toward a nearby temple for reassurance and it still rose majestically amidst grey concrete surroundings. High above the drabness of morning shade, a burnished glint of triumphant sunlight bounced off its golden finials, inspiring him to believe that nothing was going to spoil his birthday.

Many foreigners had celebrated their Christmas festival the day before. One of them, wearing a Tottenham Hotspur football shirt, had partied right through into the daylight hours and was only now traipsing back to his hotel. Sawat grinned as the man shambled past like an extra in a zombie movie. The guy walked as if he were holding onto an invisible zimmer frame. Searing sunlight clawed at his scrunched eyes and one of his unresponsive legs dragged along the hot pavement as if attached to a ball and chain.

Mae watched the man in silent amusement, and mirrored Sawat's grin; her toothless mouth a dark recess. "*Mow, mak-mak,*" she chortled, whilst waving some bothersome flies away from the food.

Sawat smiled and nodded in agreement: *yes, very drunk, indeed.*

After passing his empty plate back to Mae, he placed his palms together and lowered the bridge of his nose to his fingertips in a show of deep respect. Mae reached under her preparation area and handed him a Tupperware container that encased a banana cake baked the previous evening. Today, he was particularly delighted with such an offering; Mae would occasionally gift him with extra items of food, but the coincidence of being handed a cake on his special day was truly amazing.

He peeled back the lid to smell the container's contents, peering inside as if it held a rare antiquity. Despite wanting to eat it all, right there and then, he snapped the lid back into position knowing he would enjoy the cake even more in an hour's time. Seeing the unbridled gratitude on the boy's angelic face imbued Mae with a deep sense of satisfaction.

Tucking the box under one arm, Sawat offered Mae another, more exuberant, *wai* and cheerily thanked her for her gift, adding that today was his birthday.

Sawat didn't know it, but she had lost her only son twenty-eight years earlier. Distracted by his friends, he'd unwittingly stepped out into the path of a speeding police car. Another thing that Sawat could not have guessed was that Mae secretly loved him, almost as if he were her son and each time he visited her food stall he brought joy into her solitary life. Also, Mae had baked the cake especially, already knowing that it was his sixteenth birthday today.

Sawat had a small 110cc motorbike that he rode, helmetless, with the breeze in his hair. Because of his age, he could ride past the local police line that was regularly set up to catch anyone not wearing head protection. The main purpose of this trap was to elicit a bribe, normally an on-the-spot cash 'fine' of one hundred baht for locals and two hundred baht upwards, for *farang*. Perhaps, for sentimental reasons the police didn't want to extort money from a kid – or maybe they just figured he wouldn't have much money on him anyway.

He started the engine and rode his bike to the same local store where each day he bought cans of soft drinks and beer. The owners were two gay guys who adored young Sawat, but only in a virtuous way. He wasn't averse, though, to using his boyish good looks as he knew that this afforded him some small advantage in life. Every day – after some harmless flirting – he'd leave with free ice for his coolbox, plus they'd gift him some extra cans for good measure.

Sawat patrolled Patong beach each day with this frigid container. He could easily sell refreshment to any tourists who wished to avoid paying their hotel's high drink prices. This was to the mutual benefit of everyone involved: each can that he sold made him a small profit, plus the foreigners were more than pleased to have a cheap, ice-cold drink to accompany their beach walk. An added bonus for Sawat was that almost all of the *farang* – not just the English, Australian and American ones – spoke only English to Thai people. This made the business of conversing in a foreign language so much easier, and Sawat was an extremely fast learner.

He turned his bike into the narrow *soi* that extended down to the beach and parked it amongst all the other motorcycles, mostly belonging to the other beach vendors. Fixed to the coolbox was a frayed canvas strap which Sawat's uncle had attached to make it easier to carry. Sawat slung this over one shoulder and stepped from the shadow of the *soi* and into the full sunshine at the beach. His day's work was about to begin.

Each and every morning, when Sawat first strolled onto the sand, he felt a shudder of dread. Always, without fail, he stared out to that particular area of the sea where only he saw the demonic spirit who lived under the water.

This sighting, in 2003, was a taboo subject: his uncle made him promise to never speak of it again.

****

One year earlier, his uncle, Jao, took him out in his speedboat to the dark patch of water where the striped dolphins could sometimes be seen undulating in and out of the sea; despite his uncle's promise that they were highly likely to see them up close, they didn't. Instead, the two of them just sat there within sight of the shoreline, waiting for dolphins that never showed up.

Jao, understanding the need to make the trip more memorable, issued a sporting dare. Sawat loved a challenge and this instantly made him forget his disappointment at not seeing the dolphins. His uncle asked if he was capable of diving down and touching the sea bed: he remembered doing the exact same thing when he was a teenager. Hoping to turn it into an exciting escapade for the boy, he even teased him about the sea spirits who lived beneath the waves. Returning with one stone, a shell or even a clump of seaweed, would offer proof of his success.

Sawat couldn't wait to make his attempt; he was a strong swimmer and could hold his breath for a considerable length of time. Plus, he wanted to impress his uncle who was his only paternal influence since the death of his father.

Jao ensured his nephew donned a wetsuit. Despite the surface temperature being comfortable on such a hot day, the water was a great deal colder the further down you went.

Sawat dropped into the sea, clutching a dive torch. He took three shallow breaths then, on the fourth, inhaled as much air as his lungs could manage and disappeared below the surface. He found it incredibly easy at first and the seabed soon appeared in the torch's bright beam.

Going further, though, was more of a struggle; his ears were collecting unfamiliar sounds and the depths buoyed his body, resisting it with a hostile determination. *Perhaps it's the sea spirits pushing back at me,* he imagined nervously.

His fingertips had almost reached the bottom, when, unbelievably, he saw something large move.

Sawat redirected the torch: He hadn't imagined it; sitting on the sand was one of the spirits his uncle had warned him about, only this one seemed to be half-human, and half-bird! He had never been so scared in all of his life. Sawat yelped in terror, but only a bubble ballooned from his noiseless mouth. He recoiled and twisted his body so that he could return to the safety of the boat. The water roared against his eardrums.

His uncle, meanwhile, was beginning to worry whether he should have issued the challenge in the first place. Sawat seemed to be underwater for a disquieting amount of time. Jao was about to dive into the sea himself, when his nephew burst through the surface with cold fear in his eyes. The boy was shouting and babbling incoherently.

Jao dragged him from the water, fearing that some damage may have occurred or that he had been stung by jellyfish.

"Uncle, I saw the sea spirit! I saw the sea spirit!"

Jao was hugely relieved, realising that the kid had simply let his imagination get the better of him. He turned the ignition and allowed the engine to idle. Sawat, though, was still wide-eyed and had started to become a hyperactive irritation. Jao asked him to calm down and also to turn around, so he could unzip his wetsuit.

After releasing him from his suit, he was still rambling about the monster in the sea. Jao's patience had finally worn thin.

"Enough!" he shouted. He had never yelled at the boy before and the volume of his voice stopped Sawat in his tracks. "I don't want to hear anything more about spirits under the sea! And I do not want you to say such crazy things to anyone else. Do you understand?"

Jao knew from experience that such tales were met with derision in the neighbourhood, and he didn't want his brother's only son to become a laughing stock.

Sawat rolled the top half of the wetsuit down to his waist and sat dutifully in complete silence. He had never seen his uncle this angry before. Jao shifted the throttle and manoeuvred the boat in a tight circle, before powering towards the shoreline.

****

Walking on a soft sand beach with a heavy container of drinks was no mean feat, especially for a sixteen-year-old boy, but Sawat made it look easy. Plus, he reasoned that the more drinks he sold, the lighter his load would become: a win-win, in fact. He liked to hang around outside the Redford Patong Beach Hotel, which accommodated rich holidaymakers from around the globe.

The other beach vendors socialised in groups and mostly sold colourful sarongs and silk scarves to tourists. The trick was to spot the *farang* with the whitest skin. This meant that they had only just arrived and were easily seduced by the exotic goods on offer, not yet realising that they could buy the same stuff at the nearby night market for a fraction of the price. The group hailed Sawat as he headed in their direction. As usual, they were all smiles and sunglasses, each one unshakably optimistic at the beginning of each shift.

The busiest of them all was Chaiya, whose name meant *victorious* in Thai, which seemed appropriate, as he outsold everyone else on the beach. Chaiya carried a yoke on his shoulders, fashioned from bamboo, and hanging either side of him, like large weighing scales, were rattan baskets.

In one basket were fresh mangoes that he would slice, on request; in the other, he had ingeniously assembled a small charcoal grill, upon which he barbecued corn on the cob.

Foreigners couldn't get enough of his produce and he was besieged throughout the day. Even if a *farang* just wanted to use him as a photo opportunity, he would happily pose – but only on the condition that they would purchase something. The other vendors were hugely envious, but if any of them were to replicate Chaiya's idea for themselves, it would go against their unwritten code of conduct and would be seen as behaving dishonourably.

Resting his coolbox on the sand and taking a moment to stand in the shade of a beach wall, Sawat popped the lid from Mae's storage container and took his first bite of the moist banana cake. Viset, one of the other vendors, spotted the cake and scurried over, kicking up sand with every stride. Sawat happily broke off a large piece and shared it with him.

Ten minutes later, having just sold a cold can of Singha to a sunburned Scottish tourist, Sawat was suddenly alerted by a small commotion behind him. He turned to see that the seawater had retreated suddenly, as if the gods themselves had decided to move the ocean.

He could not believe his eyes. The entire Andaman Sea had retracted a long distance from the shoreline, causing curious tourists to come running from their sun loungers. Sawat was at a loss to understand what he was seeing: for sixteen years, the sea had always been a constant presence in his life and today it had decided to find a new home.

This sudden development scared him but the *farang* were totally beguiled, assuming that this was a common occurrence in these parts. They strolled out in ever-increasing numbers to marvel at the phenomenon. Sawat allowed himself a cautious smile as he heard the excited squeals of children as they tried to grab the floundering fish that were left stranded. Parents took photographs of their offspring on the wet sand, imagining that this would be a great conversation piece for years to come. Two young holidaymakers, keen to explore the previously hidden topography, jogged out as far as a deeper ridge and scampered down its incline before disappearing from view.

Sawat took stock of the reactions on the faces of his fellow Thais, like him, they didn't share the tourist's innocent excitement. Some of these guys had worked with the sea for most of their lives, either as fishermen or by selling water sports activities to foreigners. None of them had ever seen it behave like this before. Because these experienced guys were hanging back, Sawat decided that it would be prudent to follow their cautious lead.

Staff from the hotel congregated at its perimeter; their faces pinched with worry for the safety of their guests. A Thai family, enjoying a Sunday picnic at the beach, retreated to the hotel's retaining wall. Sawat asked Khomsan, the hotel's oldest security guard, what was happening, thinking that surely *he* would have seen this happen before, but Khomsan said that he hadn't, and looked as nervous as everyone else. Sawat's instinct was to attract people's attention, and call them back to the dry part of the beach but, being so young, he felt self-conscious about initiating such a plan.

Then he heard a distant rumble – louder than thunder.

Looking out to sea, Sawat saw a grey wall of water the width of the horizon, tumbling at high speed towards the shoreline.

Some of the foreigners acted quickly, snatching their children and running towards the hotel; others stood like statues, mesmerised, not yet knowing the danger they were in.

Sawat and most of the other beach vendors rushed to help the frantic tourists but before they had enough time, the demonic sea was upon them. Now it was white, and it was deafening. It swamped the screams of everyone in its murderous path.

An instant before the huge wave hit, Sawat recognised his own fear duplicated in the terrified faces around him. Those faces were quickly engulfed in a tide of unstoppable water that pulverised everything in its path. Sawat was propelled inland, like a leaf in a rapid, wherever the sea wanted to throw him. He swallowed salt water and was buffeted by unseen objects; he recognised that some of these were fellow human beings, whose skulls and knees collided with his bones.

Everything was happening too quickly. All of his thought processes accelerated and he realised that his life might be about to end at sea, in a similar way to his father. In a bizarre aberration of fate, he was going to die on the exact same day that he was born.

The darkness of the sea interchanged with daylight: one moment he was consumed by black water and drowning, and the next he was gasping for air, staring at blue sky. He pitched into a coconut tree that came at him hard, instantly breaking his collar bone and slamming his head sideways against his shoulder. Half-conscious and with all the strength he could muster, he clung on for dear life. Sawat adjusted to this new reality as if awakened from a bad dream. Lifeless bodies streamed past like small dolphins and a fatally wounded dog tobogganed through, its bloody jaw opened for one final, impossible howl.

Although he was in terrible pain, he gripped the abrasive tree bark, utilising both his arms and strong legs. The water was dark brown, with an overlay of churning white foam. It rushed him like a fast-flowing river. Debris continued to hit him, but with less velocity than before. He tasted blood in his damaged mouth and a hot pain from his fractured shoulder bayoneted the left side of his body.

Almost losing his grip, he suddenly vomited a copious amount of sea water which cascaded over his arms.

He identified his precarious position as being deep within the hotel grounds, a good two hundred metres from the start of the beach. He noticed that two of the hotel staff had managed to climb onto the roof of the pool restaurant and were clinging to each other, desperate not to fall into the ferocious water. Apart from them, he couldn't see anyone else who was alive. An upturned speedboat barrelled by at frightening speed and cannoned off the trunk of a large banyan tree. The stench of raw sewage was overpowering. A detached human head rolled around in the water, like a fallen coconut. It was hard to imagine that, more than two metres beneath this spiteful torrent, were the manicured lawns of the hotel grounds.

****

Sawat had no idea how long his cramped limbs had held onto the tree; he'd somehow relaxed himself into it, occasionally letting go with his left arm to ease the chronic pain in his shoulder. The sea level had dropped, so there was suddenly a healthy gap between his feet and the water line. This was the first time he had been able to see his legs since the giant wave hit; one bore a deep laceration which had opened like the peeled skin of a banana. A red stocking of blood began to spread out evenly across the wet surface of his skin.

At least now he felt it was safe to climb down from the coconut tree. He carefully shinned his way to the ground, rather than dropping, not knowing what might be hidden under the dark water. It was now only up to his waist and he was reassured when his feet found the unseen lawn. Naturally his flip-flops had been flushed away, so he shuffled forward, using his bare feet to probe and guide him through the murky water. The two guys on the restaurant roof didn't share his confidence that it was finally safe to come down and stayed where they were. Each, though, saluted him with a comradely wave.

Sawat didn't like the idea of wading through raw sewage, especially with open wounds, but he had little choice. His progress was painstakingly slow; he knew where the swimming pool was, and wanted to avoid a sudden plunge into that; he also didn't want to stand on any shards of glass.

As far as his eyes could see, the land was part of a foul-smelling ocean. Several drowned corpses bounced against the walls of the hotel building; he tried not to look, but he instantly recognised one as being Khomsan, the old security guard.

Sawat waded into the hotel building, which was awash with debris. It was incongruous to see sun loungers and vegetation floating around in the communal area of a hotel. Noticing dark water against some lift doors, Sawat was suddenly alert to the danger of electrocution, so he took the stairs to the next level.

The stairs delivered him up to the dry, marbled opulence of the lobby where the seawater hadn't reached. In one corner was a magnificent Christmas tree which seemed ostentatious, given the crudeness of the obliteration below. The multitude of people spread about the lobby fell into two distinct categories: those who were injured and in need of immediate attention, and those doing the attending. Echoing around the lobby were the heart-breaking wails of the injured and the newly-bereaved.

Sawat was amazed that his T-shirt had managed to stay on considering what he had been through. He needed to take it off as it was soiled with sand and shell fragments which scoured his raw skin. Removing his top was easier said than done, given that his left shoulder was useless. Even so, he managed to wrestle it off one-handed.

As well as the numerous lacerations that criss-crossed his skin, he was badly grazed from holding onto the rough bark of the coconut tree. There wasn't a mirror to hand but he could tell that his head, particularly his mouth, had taken quite a bashing. Some of his teeth felt badly cracked and his hair was gummed together with a tar-like substance that had set hard, like plastic.

There didn't seem to be any medics on the scene; hotel guests and staff members were fashioning splints from broken furniture and using torn bed sheets as bandages. Sawat walked to the nearest person, a tall *farang* with a goatee beard, who seemed to be orchestrating things, and offered his assistance.

The man looked at him as if he'd seen a ghost:

"Oh, my God!" the foreigner said with a grimace when confronted with a bedraggled kid whose torn, battered face looked as if it had been caught in a shark hook. "I think it is *you* who needs the help, young man."

The man with the goatee was a Norwegian pharmacist who holidayed in Phuket every Christmas. He cleaned the sand and dirt from Sawat's wounds with bottled water and wrapped them with makeshift dressings. "I think that you are a very lucky boy," he announced, placing a large, fatherly hand on Sawat's good shoulder.

****

Phuket's ambulance teams were overwhelmed, so several hours had elapsed before a paramedic could attend to Sawat. In the meantime, the hotel staff coped as best they could, providing fruit and bottles of water.

The medic attending Sawat cleaned his lacerations before an overstretched doctor anaesthetised and stitched them. A nurse swathed his arm in a sling, and he was instructed to get to a hospital – whenever that would be possible, given the scale of the disaster.

As he left via the slurried driveway at the front of the hotel, it was apparent that the destruction had extended further inland and into the town. Cars and minivans were upturned and crumpled like beer cans. Power line poles had fallen to the ground, leaving a cat's cradle of dangerously damaged wires. Going back for his motorbike seemed a futile gesture, but Sawat limped to the beach *soi* anyway. As he'd expected, his bike wasn't there anymore; only a few remained, each choked with silt and wedged into the unlikeliest of gaps. But on the way he at least managed to salvage two clashing flip-flops: one was blue, the other brown. The left one was tight and compressed his sore foot, whilst the other flapped on the ground like a wounded bird.

Outside the periphery of his vision he heard a familiar soft voice calling out: "Mot! Mot! Oh Sawat, my beautiful son, you're alive!"

His mother appeared on her motorcycle. Ignoring the puncture in her rear tyre, she weaved through debris to get to him. As soon as the cataclysmic news of a *tsunami* spread like wildfire through the market, she had shut up shop and rode to the beach end of town, frantically searching the ravaged coastline for her son. She dismounted and hugged Sawat tightly, tearfully relieved that she hadn't lost the only remaining man in her life to the cruel sea. He grunted in subdued agony, too polite to tell his mother that each squeeze of her effusive embrace caused him such raw pain.

Then, jolted as if struck by a small thunderbolt, Sawat suddenly remembered *Khun* Mae. She would also have been in the destructive path of the wave.

When he and his mother reached the pavement section that Mae always occupied, there was nothing but slurry and desolation. The area, which was normally buzzing with activity, had become ghostly quiet.

What Sawat saw next made him cry for the first time that day. On top of an upturned food cart, discordant in the sombre streetscape of browns and greys, was a flamboyantly pink beach hat patterned with bright yellow butterflies.

CHAPTER SEVEN

The Betrayal

Norwich, England: 2012

Seven years after her family's relocation to Peterborough, twenty-two-year-old Hannah Cunningham was back where she always wanted to be, in Norwich. Her father took up the job offer of store manager at Sainsbury's where he'd worked previously and, sentimentally, her parents even bought a house on the same cul-de-sac as before.

This was a dream come true for Hannah, who had always hoped to return to her home town one day. Still heavily into sport, she found a part-time job as a fitness instructor at the Norwich Fitness & Wellbeing Centre; this was in addition to a full-time position at Aviva, working as a claims handler.

On her first day at the sports centre, she was given an introductory tour of the complex by Nicola, the effervescent health and fitness manager. From outside, the building reminded her of an airport terminal, while inside it was bright, spacious and open-plan, with tiled floors that wouldn't have looked out of place in a Mediterranean hotel.

Hannah nodded politely whilst the manager went through her well-rehearsed spiel; manicured fingers caressed the air as Nicola recited banal explanations of each facility. Hannah wasn't paying that much attention and in any case, the purpose of the changing rooms and the goldfish-bowl gym were patently obvious. Comically, Nicola even went so far as to open a shower door to clarify the shower's mystical function.

The woman spoke in one of those artificial sing-song voices that drove sane people crazy and Hannah wondered if there was a training college where willing students were taught this particular affectation. The two wafted past clinical expanses of white walls, the austerity of which was made marginally more interesting by the enormous colour photographs that showcased the centre's range of activities.

One picture, though, grabbed Hannah's attention and triggered a fluster of excitement: There, prominently, was a sizeable shot of Calum Armstrong wearing a white karate *gi*. His graceful kick was frozen in time, his bare foot suspended in mid-air and at head height. She understood enough about martial arts to know that the two red bands on the tip of his black belt meant he had achieved the impressive rank of second Dan.

"Are you interested in karate?" Nicola asked, noticing that this particular photograph had caused Hannah to become lost in thought.

Hannah snapped out of her daze, "Uh … no, it's just … I used to know this guy."

"Ah, that's our Calum, one of our lovely instructors." Nicola nodded, giving the impression that he and she were close friends – which Hannah doubted. "He's going great guns at the moment is our Calum. He's even been selected for the England karate squad."

Mmmm, thought Hannah, dormant feelings suddenly reawakened. *I am definitely going to enjoy working here.*

Later, whilst fastening the seatbelt in her racing-green

Mini Cooper, Hannah cast her mind back to that last day when she left Norwich and remembered only too well those raw feelings of hurt and anger. She'd felt betrayed at the time and had made a conscious decision to forget about Calum Armstrong. But this same memory now brought a smile to her face: *What on earth was I thinking?* she reflected. They were both only fifteen years old. The thought that he would have wanted to pledge himself to her at such a young age seemed completely ridiculous now.

Of course she never forgot him. She dated a few guys in Peterborough but her first love still inhabited her daydreams on a regular basis, though less so with every passing year. Before she left Norwich in 2005, Hannah had hoped that it would be Calum to whom she lost her virginity. Sadly, it was a bit late for that now.

Turning the ignition of her car, she thought about the photograph she'd just seen. He looked more chiselled and had filled out and become more muscular. For her, this quantum leap into manhood seemed to have happened overnight, rather than over a period of seven years.

Hannah wiggled her slender arms in a shimmy of excitement: *Oh, my God, he looked so sexy,* she fluttered. *Please, please God, don't let him be married.*

****

Three days later, Calum was putting his Shotokan class through their final paces. He stood at the front, barking commands, like a drill sergeant; his students stood in the same precise stance, poised in linear rows, like a platoon in white uniform. Towards the end of class, Calum liked to push them to near-exhaustion with a series of triple-kick, triple-punch combinations.

He led by example, executing each sequence of movements in a snappy blur that caused his crisp cotton *gi* to crack loudly. As a precursor to each combination, he shouted the count in Japanese: "*Ichi … ni … san … shi … go … roku … shichi … hachi … kyu … ju!*"

As always, he was the quickest to complete each choreographed flurry, and did this to demonstrate the required standard. Each burst of simulated violence was interspersed with a move back to a fighting stance.

Only when his students were puce from their efforts, and had begun to flap their limbs like flippers, did Calum call them to *yamai*, allowing them to stand at rest. He asked them to tidy their belts, giving them time to draw oxygen back into their exhausted lungs.

As a teenager, when he was first involved in karate, it was expected that you would be yelled at from the very first bow of your head to the last. This old-school Spartan discipline didn't suit his modern sensibility; yes, he needed to play the hard taskmaster, but he also moderated this with words of encouragement. Plus, he was younger than many of his students and ridiculing someone two decades older than himself would seem downright disrespectful.

"OK guys, fantastic effort, you should all feel proud of yourselves. Warm-down and stretch to finish."

After showering, he changed into his street clothes, heaved his heavy sports bag over one shoulder and walked the curved corridor towards reception. The glass-walled lobby was bathed in the amber glow of late-afternoon sunshine making him squint like a prisoner released from solitary confinement.

As usual, he stopped by the reception desk to chat with Julie who always had a ready supply of wine gums to share with handsome young pups like Calum. This was their routine: they would engage in a bit of harmless James Bond/Miss Moneypenny flirtation, after which Julie would be left with a revitalised smile and Calum would depart with a handful of gelatine sweets.

On this particular evening, he hadn't even reached the part where Julie swiped him with a sheaf of papers before sending him on his way with confectionery, when a smoky female voice interrupted their pantomime. "Well, as I live and breathe … Calum Armstrong!"

When he span on his heels, Calum was thunderstruck. Standing before him was an older, sexier version of Hannah Cunningham. Despite her being backlit by harsh, low sunlight, he immediately recognised her cappuccino skin and green, feline eyes. Her corkscrew hair was straightened now and cut into a sleek, asymmetrical bob which left one ear exposed. She wore tight fitness pants and a matching cropped top that complemented her sporty physique.

Shading his eyes to take her in, she reminded him of the Halle Berry poster he used to have on his bedroom wall several years ago. Hannah still had the lithe limbs of her teenage years but firm curves had also appeared in all the right places. A composite of responses flashed through his mind including a long-repressed sense of guilt. Her sudden appearance rocked his self-assuredness: was this really the same schoolgirl with whom he had shared so many surreptitious glances? He hadn't felt this awkward for a long time.

Hannah placed her sports bag on the floor. "So, not even a hug?"

"God … yeah … of course," he spluttered, stumbling over his words.

He encased her in a tentative hug that didn't involve a kiss. She no longer smelt of Chupa Chup lollipops and apple shampoo: the fragrances were more sophisticated now, hints of cinnamon on the nape of her neck and a spritz of jasmine in her glossy black hair.

After their self-conscious embrace, she stepped back half a pace, letting him feast his eyes on her figure. She stood confidently, with both arms intertwined behind her back, the sport top displaying her bare midriff and the gentle definition of her abs. Then she fixed Calum with that familiar gap-toothed smile. "So, how're things with you?" she grinned, knowing that she'd hijacked his attention.

"Yeah, good thanks. How's little Marcus?"

"He's cool, not so little any more – he's fifteen now. Oh, and he would *love* to see you." She said this, knowing that a bit of emotional blackmail would help her cause.

"Yeah, yeah, I'd like that," Calum confirmed, feeling more comfortable in her company with each passing moment.

"So do you still see any of the old crowd?" Hannah asked, secretly hoping to learn his marital status.

"Well, you'll be pleased to know that I'm still good friends with Leo. In fact I was best man at his wedding recently…"

"Ooh, to anyone I'd know?" said Hannah, cutting in excitedly.

"No, he got hitched to a girl he met at work. Her name's Tilly and they both work at the Apple Store in Chapelfield."

"Well, there's a surprise," she chuckled. Without much difficulty she most probably could have guessed where Leo would be employed.

"…And I still see Imogen Gibson."

"Oh, you poor thing, that must be painful!"

"Uh – actually she's my girlfriend,"

"God, oh God! I'm so sorry! Seriously, I'm a complete idiot!"

Calum wasn't that offended; he could well remember Hannah calling Imogen a dirty slut in the school dinner queue, right in front of the dinner ladies – one of whom was Imogen's mother.

In a way, he was enjoying seeing Hannah squirm; it

helped assuage the guilt he felt for not saying goodbye to her seven years earlier. As it was, he could tell she wasn't really *that* embarrassed. Hannah and Imogen were not exactly the best of friends.

"Look, I'm sure Imogen is absolutely lovely and I hope that you're both idyllically happy," she gushed, with scant sincerity.

Calum shot her a Cheshire cat grin. "You know you don't mean that "

"Yeah, you're right. Never did like the stupid tart!"

Calum's smile stretched wider. *Same old Hannah,* he thought, *shooting from the hip.* She smiled back, mirroring his actions. They shared a moment.

Hannah was first to break the spell and pulled a business card from her purse; she'd had some printed to promote her new 'Legs, Bums and Tums' step class.

"Here's my number should you ever get bored with slutty Gibson. I haven't given up on you, you know?"

With that, she placed the elegant fingers of one hand in the centre of his chest and held them there for a full three seconds before stencilling a lipstick kiss onto one of his cheeks. As she sashayed like a pole dancer towards the changing rooms, she knew he'd still be checking her out. Before disappearing from view, Hannah stopped and looked over her shoulder, eyebrows raised as if to say, *What are you looking at?*

Then she flashed a coquettishly smile before continuing her slinky walk.

****

Whilst storing Hannah's phone number into his mobile, Calum was already trying to think of a way to break the news of their meeting to his girlfriend. He couldn't ignore Hannah now that she was back in town, and really wanted to see Marcus again. Considering that the two girls were sworn enemies, this was going to be tricky.

He also never got round to telling Hannah that the next day he and Imogen were flying to Thailand for a five-day holiday. Just as he was contemplating this unexpected dilemma, he received a text from his girlfriend: *hi hun, working late tonight, not free until 7:30, will come round yours to help with suitcases around 8? see u later, love & hugs, imogen xxx*

This was perfect timing. As a surprise, he'd secretly bought Imogen a Michael Kors watch that she craved; it had a white ceramic bracelet and small stones set in its rose-gold bezel – a perfect surprise gift for an exotic holiday. His plan was to leave it in the hallway of her apartment so that she'd see it just as soon as she returned home from work.

The sun's horizontal glare followed him to the old khaki Land Rover that he'd bought in a moment of madness. His lengthening shadow romped ahead like an enthusiastic companion. Immediately after slipping into his car seat, he reached over to retrieve Imogen's spare door key from a recess near the dashboard. He started to reverse but then paused to allow two of his students to continue their jittery walk behind his vehicle. They both waved at him as he left the sports centre car park, en route to Imogen's.

Calum was surprised to see his girlfriend's car in the parking bay outside her apartment. He double-checked; it was definitely hers – the white Fiat 500, with red and green Gucci stripes emblazoned along its sides. Suddenly, things didn't seem right. He rushed the two flights of stairs to her flat and unlocked the door.

A naked Imogen was the first to appear from the bedroom, clutching a bundle of clothes in a vain attempt to preserve her modesty. The next person to poke a terrified face from behind the architrave was Daniel, her friend from work.

Calum did his best to ignore Daniel. He clenched his jaw muscles and glared at Imogen, who was wet-faced with the tears of sudden regret. "Hannah Cunningham was right, Imogen, you really *are* a tart."

Without saying another word, he jogged back down the stairs, deliberately leaving the apartment door wide open, making it easier for her inquisitive neighbour to peer inside.

CHAPTER EIGHT

Mister Ponytail

On the day that he and Imogen were due to fly to Phuket, Calum rolled some T-shirts, and other clothes into his Samsonite suitcase. He'd decided to forge ahead with the holiday – but without Imogen, obviously.

He hadn't received so much as a text from her since he caught her *in flagrante delicto* the previous evening, trying like Botticelli's Venus to protect her modesty. Not that he wanted her to contact him; the damage was irreparable and, in retrospect, completely foreseeable. He was surprised to discover that he didn't feel any of the conventional human emotions, namely anger, sadness or even betrayal. In fairness, he couldn't shift all the blame on Imogen; he probably wasn't the best fit for her anyway. Imogen was needy and materialistic whereas he was self-confident and less inclined to worry about keeping up appearances.

He also accepted his own faults. He probably focused far too much on his karate training and teaching, without paying enough attention to his girlfriend. Sometimes he would look at her, nonplussed, when she burst into a tantrum because she'd broken a nail or her phone had lost its charge. To make matters worse, raspberries of suppressed laughter would often escape from him, like careless farts. His lack of empathy would enrage Imogen even further, resulting in her calling him a selfish bastard. Essentially, they had nothing in common – apart from the fact that they enjoyed great sex. He even conceded that smarmy Daniel might be a far better choice of boyfriend for her, in the long term.

He'd spent the remainder of the previous evening phoning some of his unmarried friends, thinking that they would jump at the chance of a free holiday to Thailand, but for all of them this was impossibly short notice, especially with work commitments. He even toyed with the idea of ringing Hannah, staring at her name on his phone screen for quite some time, speculating whether it would be too presumptuous to call. As it was, he decided to go it alone, and slid his burgundy passport into a large document wallet that contained this e-ticket, credit cards and Thai currency.

Before leaving his terraced house on Dover Street to start the three-hour drive to Heathrow, he stood in the doorway, ticking off a mental checklist. Satisfied that he had remembered everything, and that he hadn't left the iron on, he closed the door and walked to his car.

The only other thing that he had to remember was that, despite being twenty-two years old, he was still expected to ring his mother from the airport to say he'd arrived there safely; otherwise she would worry herself silly.

****

Thai Airways flight TG917 was scheduled to depart at 21.30. Calum was seated in economy, window seat 49K and contemplating which movies to watch: *Django Unchained*, definitely; *The Dark Knight Rises*, definitely; *The Expendables 2*, possibly (he knew it wouldn't matter that he hadn't seen *Expendables 1*).

He listened with interest to each inflight announcement: He loved the mellifluous softness of the Thai dialect, each consonant cushioned and the words spoken from the front of the mouth. It reminded him of the subdued *put-put* of his grandma's coffee percolator.

The last stragglers were shuffling along the aircraft's narrow aisles; some carried voluminous luggage bags and exhibited a total lack of spatial awareness. Calum frowned as these incoming passengers bashed and buffeted any seat that interfered with their progress. Air travel always brought out the fractious side of his personality. He absolutely understood that his was a primal reaction to being forced into sharing personal space with people you would normally avoid. So, mindful of this, before leaving home he had pre-decided not to let any trivial annoyances get to him. Calum was generally a tolerant person but conceded that he had absolutely no patience whatsoever with people's bad manners or thoughtlessness. His many bugbears included pushy sales staff who pestered you the moment you stepped into their store, loudmouths who swore in public and drivers who couldn't be bothered to indicate.

He was pleasantly surprised that the two seats next to him were empty, and began to look forward to a hassle-free flight. Unfortunately, the last passenger to board the plane was an elephantine middle-aged man who'd cultivated a ponytail to compensate for a hairless head. And, inevitably, guided by a slender stewardess, the man was lurching down the gangway in Calum's direction. His backpack swayed recklessly close to seated passengers' heads, his hands clung onto headrests as if they were banisters.

A small part of Calum died when he realised that this guy was going to be his travel companion for the next eleven hours. Mister Ponytail dumped his heavy carcass into aisle seat 49H, causing the entire row to shake like a fence in a hurricane.

Calum was thankful that at least there was a buffer of one vacant seat between them and hastily attached his Dr Dre headphones to secure some privacy.

Soon after the seat belt signs had illuminated, the flight crew demonstrated the on-board safety procedures. In common with the majority of passengers, Calum wasn't in the least bit interested but felt it impolite not to pay attention, so he dutifully nodded his head after each explanation and kept eye contact with one paticularly pretty Thai crew member. The girl smiled back at Calum, as if to acknowledge his audience participation. She and the other stewardesses elegantly moved on to the last-minute checks, before strapping themselves in for take-off.

Bang on schedule, there was a surge of engine noise and movement. The *Boeing* 747 began to accelerate causing overhead compartments to rattle like loose dentures. Calum peered through the window and watched the runway fall away beneath the huge wing. Beads of moisture tracked across the clear plastic, before disappearing from existence.

He had just selected a movie from the touch screen in front of him, when Ponytail tapped his arm and gestured for him to remove his headphones. "Have you been to Thailand before?" the man asked, spreading himself like a duvet into the middle seat.

"Uh, no, I haven't," Calum replied, noticing that the man's ears were pierced with enough earrings to grace a miniature curtain pole.

"Haven't you?" said Ponytail, expressing faux amazement. The guy was obviously glad that he'd found a newbie with whom he could regale his specialist knowledge of the country. "Oh, I've been at least twenty times," he bragged. "Name's Larry, pleased to meet you."

Oh God, this is going to be an awfully long flight, Calum thought, stuffing his headphones into the storage pouch, hoping for a chance to use them sooner rather than later.

****

One hour into the flight, a smell of food began to pervade the cabin. Calum congratulated himself on thus far enduring a relentless monologue from someone who was, essentially a globe-trotting pervert. Despite his attempts to steer Larry away from his sordid tales of debauchery and exploitation, there was to be no respite. Calum was concerned that any passengers listening in might think him guilty by association.

When the same pretty crew member who did the safety demo swished by with drinks, she intuitively sensed Calum's discomfort and conveyed her sympathy by discreetly grimacing at Larry before twinkling a knowing smile. She'd presumably seen enough amoral toe rags in her young life to be able to spot another a mile off. The stewardesses were all tiny, with onyx hair tidied into flawless chignons. Their violet uniforms were stylish and fashioned in tight silk; the diagonal sashes making them look like Miss Thailand contestants.

Calum's favourite flight attendant pulled up to their row with the food trolley and, noticing that Larry was too busy jabbering to be aware of her presence, raised her eyebrows at him in subtle disdain before sneaking Calum a collaborative smile. Enjoying every bit of her clandestine performance, she attracted Larry's attention. "Beef, or chicken, sir?"

"What?" he muttered, cupping a podgy hand to one jangling ear.

"Beef, or chicken, sir? We have beef noodles, we have

chicken curry."

"Beef," he grunted, turning his back on her to renew his one-way conversation with Calum.

"And how about you, sir?" she asked, turning to Calum with amusement on her face. "We have beef in black pepper sauce with yellow noodles, or we have red chicken curry with steamed rice." The spread of her glossy lips dimpled her flawless skin.

Calum returned her smile with interest. "I'd love the red chicken curry please."

"And how about some wine with your meal?"

"Some white wine would be great," he affirmed, realising that they were clearly flirting.

"Another Singha beer for you, sir?" she asked Larry, flatly. He said "yeah", without bothering to look at her.

She yanked the ring pull on a can of Singha, releasing a *psssht* noise and pulled a face behind Larry's back, causing Calum to grin from ear to ear.

"I will come back with your white wine, sir," she smiled, steering the cart sideways to allow a passenger to squeeze past. She returned a few minutes later with a half-bottle of Dom Pérignon and a plastic glass.

"I got this from the First Class cabin, special for you," she said, making space for the Champagne on his tray.

"Wow, thank you *so* much … that is amazing. What is your name?"

"My name is Noi, sir. And you?"

"Calum," he grinned, offering his hand. The softness of her grip accentuated her elegance. With a coy smile on her face, she returned to the trolley and continued on her way.

"Bloody hell, you got some specialist treatment there, dintcha?" Larry grumbled. "Now *that's* one thing about Thai women that I need to warn you about – they can be so bloody picky when they want to be."

****

Thankfully, once the cabin lights were properly dimmed and after necking yet another beer, Calum's flight buddy fell sound asleep. With his seat reclined and eye mask on, he was gone, splayed out like a slumbering walrus in one doughy expanse.

Every now and then, Calum caught sight of the guy's naked belly which had burst forth from his shirt. Disturbingly, on its surface, existed a hideous growth that Calum could only liken to a sow's teat. Despite telling himself not to glance at the man's blubbery stomach again, he was morbidly fascinated and, despite his better judgement, felt compelled to keep looking.

For crying out loud, stop staring at that damn teat, his inner voice scolded.

Calum seemed to be the only traveller in his section who wasn't asleep. The darkness of the cabin was only interrupted by the melancholic glow of entertainment screens. This created a twilight world where nothing seemed real, an artificial womb with a flickering bank of ultrasound scans. Calum noticed that each person was slumped, unresponsive, in their seat as if they all had been poisoned by an unseen gas to which only he was immune. He imagined translucent spirits stepping from their lifeless bodies, continuing a spectral march through the outer skin of the aircraft.

By the time he'd finished a third movie his bladder felt fit to burst, but common courtesy prevented him from disturbing his neighbouring Sleeping Beauty. A little later, an inquisitive passenger directly in line with them at the opposite side of the cabin, lifted her window shutter and allowed an eruption of blinding light to penetrate the darkness. This immediately caused Larry to wake up with a hoggish grunt. His eye mask had crept to the top of his head, like Mickey Mouse's ears. Seizing his opportunity, Calum asked to be let through and Larry sluggishly complied. He straightened his shirt and rubbed his eyes, before becoming entangled in an intricate web of headphone cables. Calum illuminated the display on his red G-Shock watch: *Five more hours to go.*

****

After a total flight time of just over eleven hours and having covered a distance of six thousand miles, flight TG917 landed at Bangkok's Suvarnabhumi Airport.

With military precision, the aircraft exited the runway and taxied towards its designated gate. Calum gazed through the window as a flurry of ground personnel and baggage trams appeared on cue. The captain announced that the ground temperature was thirty-seven degrees centigrade and that the local time was 2.46 in the afternoon.

No sooner had the craft come to a standstill than there was a cacophony of clicking sounds as innumerable seatbelts were unfastened. Larry, like most of the other passengers, was already out of his seat and foraging for his backpack in the overhead locker. It didn't come quietly, he had to tug at it, as if it were a bulldog reluctant to see a vet.

Calum was perfectly happy to loll in his seat for a good while longer; the aisles were claustrophobically packed with people, who couldn't go anywhere until the doors were opened anyway. Despite this, the passengers all shared the same look of impatient determination. Each person focusing on the exit door, overeager greyhounds in their starting traps.

Larry held his passport in his teeth and began to tighten the hair band at the base of his ponytail when there was a sudden surge of progress. He bid farewell to Calum with a flaccid flap of his hand, and proceeded to scuff every seat in his ponderous path to the exit.

Calum was one of the last to leave. Noi was stood near the door with another flight attendant, keen to see the blue-eyed *farang* about whom Noi had rhapsodised throughout the flight. Both girls were in full uniform and Noi was clutching a small soft elephant mascot in her fingers.

"*Khun* Calum, I would like you to have this present. Maybe remind you of Thai Airways, maybe remind you of your friend with the horse tail." She held a hand to her mouth to hide a giggle.

"Noi, it will always remind me of you," he said charmingly. He wasn't sure if it was appropriate to kiss her, so he held her hands instead. Her friend smiled, fully approving of Noi's interest in this man.

Calum sensed in that moment that Noi was reluctant to see him leave; if this were playing out in England, he would have immediately asked for her phone number but didn't know what the local protocol was. So instead, he steepled his fingers into the respectful *wai* that he'd seen in a guidebook. The two girls each responded with a more refined *wai*, pressing supple palms together in a prayer-like fashion.

"We hope to see you again, *Khun* Calum, next time you fly on Thai Airways."

Noi looked desperately sad, so Calum threw caution to the wind and placed a modest kiss on her cheek. He said goodbye to the girls and stepped onto the jet bridge, offering a final cutesy wave of the silk elephant.

Before disappearing from view, he took one last look back. Amazingly, the girls still stood by the exit door of the aircraft with their palms held in precisely the same position.

CHAPTER NINE

Pointing at Rainbows

Patong, 1965

Nearly five decades ago, when he was young and his tongue could hold a conversation and his eyes could still focus, Wuttichai Pookusawan, the drunk, was a proud fisherman. With time on his side, and a small amount of money in the Siam Commercial Bank, his life back then was ticking along nicely.

But his world turned from light to dark on one ill-starred day.

The fourth of March, 1965, was the very first Saturday of the month. Even fifty years of putting Mekong whiskey to his lips had failed to expunge the haunting memory of that awful day. Around that time, the US army had sent the first wave of combat troops into Vietnam and rumours about the possibility of American servicemen coming to Phuket for rest and recuperation were rife on the island.

Even though there was no certainty that the Americans *would* come, the other fishermen were already hatching plans. Foreign visitors meant money, so they fantasised about the ramshackle bars that they could construct along the beach. *Easy money*, they thought, *far easier than taking boats out to sea each day for very little reward.*

But twenty-six-year-old Wuttichai, who was Ghandi-thin and as ungainly as a new-born foal, wasn't the sort of person who would welcome an influx of foreign soldiers: he was an anxious, nervous soul who wanted things to stay just as they were. Life was fearsome enough, he thought, without trained killers being let loose on the island.

It was a surprise to everyone – including his own family – that Wuttichai had even become a fisherman. In addition to the danger of the oceans, he had to overcome his dread of storms, an aversion to open spaces and even his morbid fear of fish. He didn't know it when he climbed off his rattan mattress on *that* Saturday morning it was to be the last day that he would ever venture out to sea.

Wuttichai's home was no more than a crudely-constructed shack held off the ground by stout bamboo stilts. It was sited in a small wood near the south end of Patong beach, its rusty, corrugated iron roof sheltered from the searing sun by a cluster of tall coconut trees. This makeshift house, with rice sacks fashioned into window blinds, was shared by his mother, his father and one surviving grandmother. They kept chickens that scrabbled in the dirt outside and a black ridgeback guard dog that slept under the house.

Unlike the other fishermen, Wuttichai's morning routine did not involve trying to appease malevolent spirits or getting involved in anything faintly superstitious. He felt that such rituals would only intrigue the more evil-minded ghosts and therefore make you a target. Far better, he thought, to ignore their treacherous existence altogether. Each day, on his walk to the beach, he passed a large hopea tree which the locals had designated a spirit house. The villagers tied colourful strips of fabric around the circumference of its buttress roots to protect the heavenly creature that lived within its mystical trunk. Scattered around the base were gilded images of the Lord Buddha and some smouldering incense sticks that permeated the damp, woody air with their heady fragrance.

Nang Takian was the benevolent female spirit who was said to live in the tree.

The other fishermen and their families even left offerings of food, should she ever feel hungry, and drink should she become thirsty. Nang Takian was said to be a beautiful wood nymph who was predisposed to be kind to humans: It was rumoured that she occasionally appeared from the tree to offer fruit to passing monks; it was also widely believed that a terrible retribution would befall anyone who tried to cut down her abode.

Wuttichai was extremely wary of the tree and was terrified that Nang Takian might one day jump out at him. He could swear he heard the tree creak each time he walked past it. His father didn't help matters by telling him the story of a fisherman who was foolish enough to urinate against her trunk, only to wake the next day with blisters covering the length of his penis. So each day, Wuttichai sensibly gave the sacred hopea tree a wide berth.

There were times, even now, when he winced at a memory of childhood recklessness. As a five-year-old, his mother warned him never to point at a rainbow; if he did, he would lose his finger. So, of course, the next time a rainbow appeared in a watery sky he couldn't help but point at it. Although his index finger remained firmly attached to his hand, he considered this a lucky escape. He reasoned that because he was so young – and therefore knew no better – the gods had shown generous leniency.

The idiom 'scared of his own shadow' suited Wuttichai to a tee, because he genuinely was scared of his own shadow, especially at night-time. He was suspicious of the way it grew beneath him and then followed him around, like a dark spectre that he could never shake off.

Despite being as skittish as a deer, he still loved the romanticism of scary folklore. His absolute favourite was his mother's retelling of the story of Mae Nack:

****

Mae Nack was a village girl married to a soldier who was posted to a distant part of Thailand. She was pregnant when he left, but unbeknown to him, while he was away she died with their baby still inside her. Such an unfair death made her bitter and she immediately returned as a pernicious spirit, capable of vengeful cruelty. She terrorised all of her former neighbours and even killed some of them, before drinking their blood.

However, she still held a deep love for her husband. When he eventually returned, she hid the fact that she had become a spirit and continued with the pretence of being his wife. The other villagers tried desperately to warn him, repeatedly telling him that she was actually one of the walking dead. Naturally, he chose not to listen, until one day a lime fell from her grasp and dropped between a gap in the floorboards. He was shocked to see her arm extend freakishly through the wooden floor, as if it wasn't there, reclaiming the lime from the dirt below. Suddenly acutely aware that his beloved wife really was a ghost, he fled to the sanctuary of a nearby monastery. A senior monk went to the house and succeeded in capturing her spirit in a glass bottle, which he subsequently tossed into the sea.

Four years later, a crew of prawn fishermen found this bottle in their net. Without realising what they were doing they opened it, thus allowing Mae Nack to escape. With hatred in her black heart, she returned to the marital home and killed her husband and his new wife.

****

After dawn had broken, Wuttichai headed for the beach. His father had already left home before 2am to catch the truck to the rubber plantation where he worked as a tapper. Wuttichai saw him tiptoe past his mosquito net each morning, his kerosene lamp flickering like fireflies in the dark.

As usual, on Wuttichai's walk to the beach he evaded the hopea tree, which was swathed in brocade like a bride at her wedding. A platoon of red ants had already swarmed over the small bowls of rice that villagers had placed near its roots. The wood was alive with noise at this time of the morning: laughing thrushes chuckled high up in the canopy and a thousand cicadas shook their maracas each time the sun slanted through the cathedral of trees.

Even though Wuttichai lived in these woods, he found most of its noises sinister and most disturbing, and it was far worse at night, when the tree branches formed dark cages that huddled together to whisper amongst themselves. In his imagination, owls were the harbingers of night demons; he had come to believe that their sinister hoots heralded the appearance of black ghosts who could slide into homes after dark, in the guise of unattached shadows. One unforgettable night, when he was a teenager, a bat flew through the open window of their shack. At first, it fluttered around the room, piercing the *noir* with its echo-locating sonar but then it became entangled in Wuttichai's mosquito net. In the pitch blackness he was terrified by the vibrations he could feel and the awful noises he could hear. Things considerably worsened when his father fired up the kerosene lamp to investigate the clamour. There, staring Wuttichai squarely in the face, was a creature sent from hell. The veins of its large ears were x-rayed by the bright lamplight and its hideous face was frozen in a fanged scream.

Wuttichai was beyond fear that night. The event had

a profound effect on him and every evening thereafter, he ensured that the rice sacks were pulled tight over each window opening and securely held in place by wooden pegs.

His indulgent parents, who would have much preferred the cool breeze that these simple windows previously afforded, charitably complied and instead, they relied on an electric fan whose running costs were a further drain on their meagre budget.

Closer to the beach, the humidity of the woods petered out and the green scrub of vegetation gave way to sand. The other fishermen were already out to sea but Wuttichai wouldn't dream of taking his boat out while the sky was still dark; plus he found the other men's boisterousness highly intimidating. In fact, the last time he arrived in their raucous midst, they swung him by his arms and legs and hurled him into the sea, like a startled starfish.

Because of his innumerable idiosyncrasies, he hauled in far fewer fish than any of the other men. Most of his catch was for family consumption; the remainder, which he sold at the market, was hardly worth the trip. Even a lame cat, who hobbled to the beach every day in search of discarded fish scraps, had learned to ignore Wuttichai's boat. If it wasn't for the fact that his father was working and still happy to keep him under his roof, Wuttichai wouldn't have been able to sustain any kind of living for himself. He even felt it fortuitous that the local girls weren't remotely interested in him, because he knew that his chances of being able to support a wife and family were hopelessly slim.

His longtail boat was moored in the shallow water by the shore, anchored in the sand and tethered to a large rock. His father had adorned the vessel with coloured lengths of material which hung like ragged scarves from the neck of its bow. Yesterday's flower garland had already turned brown in the merciless heat and had curled up on itself, like a scorched snake. The banana-shaped boat was powered by a car engine, mounted on a rotating turret at the rear. It also had a plastic canopy at one end to shield him from the sun.

Wuttichai wrapped a large triangle of cotton fabric onto his head and tied it into a crude turban, then paid his daily respects to Lord Buddha.

After freeing the vessel from its mooring, he clambered on board. The boat wobbled from side to side before finding its balance. He hand-cranked the engine into life, throwing a cloud of diesel fumes into the air. The engine drove a propeller which was attached to the end of a long pole. He dipped the propeller in the water and it churned up an angry froth of seawater as he steered the boat out into open sea.

Patong, in the 1960s, wasn't the hedonistic sprawl that it is today; at that time there were only dirt tracks down to the beach and certainly no international hotels.

On this day in 1965, all Wuttichai could see as he scanned the shoreline was a long swathe of straw-coloured sand, punctuated by the occasional beach shack with lines of wet laundry waving in the breeze.

His longtail boat bumped the waves as he patrolled the coast, sending a pleasant aerosol of sea spray into his eyes. He steered the tail of the boat and headed out to the darker strip of water where the sweep of turquoise capitulated to a patch of dense ultramarine. Because he was fearful of almost everything, he constantly checked the clear sky for angry clouds, even though this period in early March was usually free from monsoon storms.

After reaching the darker water, he powered off the engine and executed a low, crouching walk to the front of the boat to fetch the anchor. Unfortunately, because of his inherent carelessness, he'd managed to tangle it up with his fishing net. Whilst fumbling with its chaotic folds, he accidentally jettisoned his machete which plopped into the sea. Because this was his father's knife, Wuttichai threw his customary caution to the wind and, after taking a deep breath, he dived in after it.

The knife was heavy and dropped at a quicker rate than he'd anticipated, always just out of reach of his flailing fingertips. The further down he went, the more difficult it was to see. He sensed an undisturbed melancholy here above a forest of dark weeds and the sea began to taunt him with oceanic whispers. Finally, as his throat began to constrict, he spied the dull glint of the machete in the murky darkness. He couldn't understand why, but it seemed to have halted its descent and, impossibly, it was floating in the water a good few feet above the seabed.

Then, when he grabbed it, the machete resisted his effort; the more he yanked on it, the more it pulled against him. His lungs were virtually depleted of oxygen and he was about to abandon his failing attempt to retrieve the knife; it was almost as if an unseen spirit was wrestling him for ownership. At that precise moment, he saw a dead man's hand gripping the handle of the machete. Except the hand had a living strength and was fully-functioning. Attached to the hand was an arm; he could see a shoulder, a head, a body mass. This was a dark apparition – a ghost!

Wuttichai recoiled in horror, expelling a few precious bubbles of air. Apart from its inky silhouette, he could make out the ghost's inhuman eyes. It was still holding his machete but was not making any attempt to use it against him. Even so, Wuttichai was sure that the ghost intended to eat him.

Why didn't I stay in the boat? he thought, hysteria gripping him like a bear trap.

An airless pressure groaned within Wuttichai's chest; he was at the stage where his misguided body wanted him to breathe in a lungful of water. He forced his way upwards, the water fought against him and he was petrified the sea ghost would grab his ankles and drag him down. He emerged through a wave, spat saltwater, and noisily gulped at the air.

Wuttichai's teeth chattered from the spiteful cold of the deeper water. Panic started to take hold, as he was now an impossible distance from his unanchored boat. Petrified by what lurked beneath him, he was also caught in a riptide that was dragging him out towards the horizon.

****

Perhaps only five hours had passed but to Wuttichai, it seemed like forever.

He'd managed to tread water for a while but each swell sent a slosh of brine into his gasping mouth. A passing log of crumbling driftwood offered him some buoyancy but all around him there was only grey, sparkling water for as far as his terrified eyes could see.

And the ocean wasn't his only enemy, the searing sun had desiccated his skin and the effort of staying afloat left him severely dehydrated. He was beginning to hallucinate and mistook some curious dolphins for sharks. He also began to imagine that he could drink the sea water after all.

Ready to relinquish life, and on the verge of abandoning all hope, he shouted out to Suvannamacha, the Siamese Queen of the sea. Whether or not she heard his desperate prayer will never be known, but the crew of a tuna boat spotted Wuttichai and hauled his exhausted body from the water.

****

Patong 2012

Forty-seven years on, Patong has changed beyond recognition. The beach is crammed with makeshift restaurants and foreign visitors. The dirt tracks have been replaced by tarmacked roads teeming with the noisy grunt of traffic. Wuttichai is just one of many local drunks; his near-death experience on that March day in 1965 had a disastrous and lasting effect on his already capricious nature.

Back then, as soon as he was able, he told everyone and anyone about the man-eating ghost who lived under the sea. But, to his consternation, no-one took him seriously. Even his normally supportive parents advised him to resist this alarming new development in his personality. His concerned grandmother looked at him with pity, wishing there was something that she could do to ease his troubled soul. Already something of a loner, he became ever more isolated from society.

To this day, his tortured mind remains in turmoil. His thoughts so intense they tumble from his mouth like apples from a basket.

"Why does nobody believe that I saw the evil spirit that day? They make offerings to phantoms, and yet when I offer them actual proof of one, they laugh in my face!"

In 1965, immediately after his escape from the jaws of death, he took to drinking cheap local whiskey in an attempt to exorcise the nightmare from his thoughts. His longtail boat had disappeared on the day of his near-drowning, never to be seen again. Not that it mattered; he didn't set foot on Patong beach ever again. His drinking spiralled out of control and descended into full-blown alcoholism by the time he was thirty. In those days he tried to hoodwink his family by pouring the whiskey into half-full Pepsi-Cola bottles but they could see the booze in his drizzly eyes, and they could smell it on his stale breath.

And now, at seventy-three years old, Wuttichai funds his drinking habit by collecting unwanted plastic bottles and containers from the chaotic streets of Patong. He pushes a simple two-wheeled cart, upon which he slings sacks of crumpled plastic. These, he sells to recycling plants for a pittance.

Without the first alcoholic drink of the morning, his hands shake uncontrollably. For decades he has suffered from stomach ulcers and gastritis and now he has a cancer in his mouth, for which he has no money to treat.

As a young man Wuttichai was hyper-vigilant; now he flounders in a permanent state of confusion, disoriented by a booze-induced amnesia. His hearing is shot and he is way past the age at which he could ever again hear the bugling whine of a mosquito in flight.

Having lost any remnants of self-esteem a long time ago, he isn't ashamed to shamble into local bars and restaurants to beg for food and drink. Some of the owners are kind and exhibit the Buddhist spirit of generosity by offering food; others have spitefulness in their hearts and see him off the premises with a succession of kicks and punches.

And now – almost five decades after that day in 1965 – he still stops people as they head towards the beach, to warn them about the evil sea spirit. But, without fail, they either laugh at him or ignore him altogether.

But today, someone was actually prepared to listen. A young man with a coolbox and a kind face appeared in the aftermath of a rainstorm. He stopped for a while and took an interest in what Wuttichai had to say. The young man took his hand, looked him in the eye and whispered, "You are not the only one who has seen the ghost in the sea. I have seen him too."

This was the first time that Wuttichai's leaden heart had been able to sing since that terrible day, nearly fifty years ago. He pressed his wrinkled palms together to offer a *wai* of gratitude. Tears began to drip from his viscous eyes.

"Thank you, thank you *so* much," he sobbed, gripping the youngster's hands, as if by doing this he could turn back the sands of time. "May I ask your name?"

"Sawat Leelapun," the youngster replied, gifting him a smile that enabled Wuttichai to momentarily forget his suffering. "And what is your name, sir?"

"Wuttichai, Wuttichai Pookusawan."

CHAPTER TEN

Affirmation

Sawat had often seen the rake-thin, drunken old man hanging about Patong, pushing his rickety cart and occasionally stopping to rummage in flyblown bins to retrieve plastic bottles. Whenever he was within earshot, he noticed that the man's voice was almost unintelligible, a gargled slur of words. So, when the drunk stopped him one day after a rainstorm on Bangla Road, he was pleased to finally meet this local institution face-to-face.

Sawat had just walked from the beach to buy some extra ice from a guy he knew at Scruffy Murphy's Irish Bar. At night, the street was the brassy epicentre of Patong's nightlife: a conglomeration of neon lights, go-go bars and sybaritic tourists. In the harsh light of day it was exposed for what it was, an unnatural cluster of tawdry establishments, each one subdued by the absence of nocturnal fluorescent embellishment. Black crows swooped down from the trees and scavenged the food-strewn pavement outside McDonalds. The old drunk stood in their midst, like a modern-day Francis of Assisi.

He offered a trembling hand towards Sawat, in the manner of a prophet trying to warn of impending doom, his sweat-stained clothes little more than rags. Sawat readjusted the strap of his coolbox and walked a few paces nearer. What the old man said next hijacked his attention. "I beg you, young man, do not *ever* go into that sea."

The words were indistinct and Sawat had to listen carefully to understand each distorted syllable. "Evil lives there … a ghost who sits under the water, I have seen this with my own eyes."

Sawat was thunderstruck. He was twenty-three years old now and had not dared speak of the sea devil since his own sighting eight years earlier. With the passage of time, he had even started to believe that he might have imagined the whole improbable episode and chalked it up as being a young boy's wild fantasy. Furthermore, to secure his silence, Uncle Jao warned him that if he ever breathed a word of his fanciful daydream, then the nocturnal demon Phi Am would visit his bedroom in the dead of night and sit on his chest.

But here, on an untidy pavement on rain-soaked Bangla Road, was the living proof that it wasn't an extravagant delusion after all. The old man had also undoubtedly seen the evil spirit at first-hand.

The dark brown skin on the man's hands was waxy and parchment thin, the texture of a deflated balloon. Sawat held them in his own palms and told him in hushed tones that he too had seen the ghost who sits on the seabed. The old man's relief was palpable; he clenched Sawat's hands stiffly, as if the young man was his godly saviour. Sawat understood the tears that streamed down the man's crumpled face. He realised that they were kindred spirits and that it was desperately hard for one person to shoulder such a secret for so long.

It felt cathartic for Wuttichai to have his story believed by this near-stranger, and as a result he had finally burst free from its kidnap.

From that day forward, Sawat wouldn't refer to the man as the old drunk who collects plastic bottles. The man, like every other man, had a name: Wuttichai Pookusawan.

Bright sunshine had burnt away any remaining rain clouds and the wet pavements steamed like griddles in the searing heat. Wuttichai raised a trembling finger to point wilfully at a colourful rainbow that had suddenly appeared across the wet, shifting sky. Then he triumphantly displayed this same finger, as if to emphasise its invincibility. He spoke with a croaky voice laced with pathos. "See, *Khun* Sawat, despite everything, my finger is the one thing that will always survive."

CHAPTER ELEVEN

The Hidden Mouth

Whilst exiled in Peterborough, Hannah kidded herself that she had almost forgotten Calum Armstrong and his ocean-blue eyes. But since their chance meeting the other day at the sports centre she was like a dizzy schoolgirl again, thinking about him all the time. He wasn't quite the same boy that she knew at school, but hadn't she also changed a fair bit in the past seven years?

His once-mousy hair was a few shades darker now, she'd noticed, and he had shrugged off a lot of his boyishness. In the blink of an eye, Calum's adolescence had absconded. His jawline was stronger, its skin now shadowed by light stubble, and he had packed on a fair amount of muscle without becoming bulky. Like her, Calum had grown taller but he *so* definitely retained that winning smile – the one that wasn't too showy, like a sexy grin. His smooth nose must have been on the receiving end of quite a few blows, as it had gained a rugged twist, which further-enhanced his masculinity. She was familiar with every nuance of that boy's face, even down to the creases which formed every time his lips widened. God, she could easily imagine kissing those perfect lips right now.

Hannah loved the way that he made her feel – even though it was almost certain that Calum himself was completely unaware of the hypnotic effect he had on her. Calum Armstrong had reignited a carnal desire in her body that had previously been extinguished. That familiar schoolgirl ache for him returned with a forceful vengeance.

And what the hell is he doing with Imogen Gibson? she frowned. While thinking this, she locked the Mini with a brisk press of her key fob. *Get a grip, Calum, you deserve far better than her.*

Hannah still lived with her parents and Marcus, an arrangement that suited everyone. She got on famously with her mother and father and, of course, Marcus simply adored having his big sister around. Living at home meant that she could boost her regular savings account so she would have enough cash to start a mortgage when the time was right.

As usual, it was sweet Marcus who was the first to greet her when she stepped into the hallway. "Hi Marcus," she said, engulfing him in a hug.

"Hello, Sis," he replied, handing her a piece of paper, on which he'd drawn a chaotic image of Hannah.

"It's *you*," he grinned, beaming with pride.

"I can see it's me! It's absolutely brilliant!" she gushed, seizing every opportunity to boost his self-confidence.

Marcus was fifteen years old now. The afro was gone; his hair was cut closer to his scalp these days and his weight had started to balloon, partly due to Down's syndrome but also because of his fondness for biscuits. What Marcus lacked in height, he made up for by the ever-increasing circumference of his body. His condition meant he had a lower metabolic rate than other boys, and the family were all complicit in ignoring medical advice by giving into his requests for food treats.

Hannah had decided that intervention was necessary to reverse this trend and she urged her mother and father to exercise stricter dietary control. It was made clear to Marcus that he could earn one of his favourite monster-sized chocolate cookies if he completed a gentle aerobic workout, which she devised especially for him. Hannah was determined that her precious kid brother was going to have as healthy, and as fulfilling, a life as possible.

She worried that Marcus might resist this ground-breaking new idea and stomp off in a sulk but he took to the exercise regime just fine and loved working out to music with his sister. Plus, he knew there was a gratifying reward at the end of it.

He gazed up at her with a heart-melting smile. "One cookie is better than nothing," he reasoned.

****

After his workout, Marcus went to lie down in his bedroom and Hannah immediately looked for the loft ladder pole which was stored in the airing cupboard.

"Mum! Dad! I'm just going up into the loft!" she yelled down the stairwell. Her mother, who had been watching *Strictly Come Dancing* in the living room with her father, appeared in the hallway.

"Were you calling me, honey? You do know that I can't hear you up there when we've got the TV on downstairs?"

"I was just telling you that I'm going up into the loft."

"What are you going up there for? The Christmas tree doesn't need to come down until December," her mother chuckled.

"I'm just getting some stuff down."

"*What* stuff?"

"Just stuff."

"Well, don't fall through the ceiling."

"I'll try not to."

Her mother returned to the sofa. Marvin, her husband, had thoughtfully live-paused *Strictly* for her. He didn't readily admit it but he enjoyed the show almost as much as she did, mainly because he fancied one of the female Russian dancers.

Hannah pulled down the loft hatch and tugged at the aluminium ladder with the hook end of the pole. Instead of coming down in incremental stages, it plummeted like icefall from a glacier and nearly hit her between the eyes. *Christ, that's dangerous!* she thought, steadying its flimsy base on the landing carpet.

Thinking of Calum earlier that day had prompted Hannah to search for the cardboard box which contained her school memorabilia. After scaling the wobbly ladder, she flicked on the light. The loft space wasn't a particularly healthy environment, the lighting strip lit up small particulates of fibre glass that floated in the stuffy air. Two large spiders near her feet scuttled for cover and a lone November wasp buzzed against the fluorescent tube above her head. Hannah's chances of putting her foot through the ceiling were lessened by the hefty sheets of chipboard that straddled the joists. There was a clear path to the water tanks, but the periphery was crammed full of boxes, rolls of carpet, pillows, lampshades and her father's reggae albums. Underneath and beyond the boards were swathes of yellow insulation that made her skin itch on sight.

Whilst sifting through pyramids of cardboard boxes, Hannah disturbed a tower of video cassettes that tumbled about her like Jenga blocks. She gathered them up, three at a time, and stacked them in a new pile out of harm's way. She looked at the videos with incredulity. You could tell by their titles that they all belonged to her father: *Die Hard; Lethal Weapon 1(*and *2); Schindler's List,* and *The Godfather* box set.

It wasn't just her father's hoarding of redundant video cassettes that baffled her. The entire loft was a monument to obsolescence. For reasons that only he could fathom, her father held onto stuff that no one on the entire planet could possibly ever need again.

There was a Hewlett Packard computer monitor from the 1990s encased within a sizeable chunk of pale grey plastic. She'd forgotten how bulky these units were; without a shadow of a doubt, this monstrosity would kill a man stone dead if dropped on his head from a bedroom window. Other items, which he kept as if they were valuable antiquities, were phones with curly cables and an office-sized fax machine. She even found the ancient video-cassette recorder that would one day rise like a Phoenix to reclaim its rightful place in the living room.

She knew how her father would react if she were to challenge him on this nonsensical compulsion: in his Anglo-Caribbean lilt, he would say, "I like to keep them just in case, Hannah, just in case."

The box that she was hunting for sat crumpled under a crate of china. The first thing she spotted was a school photograph which she unfurled as if it were a biblical scroll. This was first time she had looked at it in seven years. The photograph was a record of the entire school assemblage. In black print on its white border were the words: *St John's High School, 2005*.

Hannah recognised faces immediately. The first-year students sat cross-legged at the front, with the headmaster and all the teachers in the row behind them. Hannah realised that she was identifying each one of the teaching staff by their nicknames, rather than their real names. There was Mr Hussein, the geography teacher, who was called Saddam for obvious reasons. She spotted Jugs Jenkins, the school secretary, and Wanker Watling, the headmaster. The pseudonyms continued to jump out of the photograph: Fungus; Worzel; Slaphead, and SpongeBob. And then she saw poor Mr Bingham. Even in the photo, he seemed desperately alone, despite being in a crowd of people. He stood with his trousers up by his chest and his sad eyes pointed to the ground. It occurred to her that this photograph was taken only a month before his suicide.

Another thing that struck Hannah was that one of the teachers, bug-eyed Mr Pugh, or Gollum as he was better known, seemed to deliberately hold his hand over his mouth, almost as if he was stifling a yawn or speaking into a walkie-talkie. It seemed such a bizarre thing to do, especially if you were about to have your photograph taken. But then she remembered *why* he covered his mouth and giggled at the memory…

****

Calum had gathered Hannah and Leo into a huddle, then produced a white paper sweet bag from his trouser pocket. "Hannah, I'm going to need your help – but of course you don't have to do this if you don't want to."

Hannah agreed to whatever it was immediately, sensing that some devilish fun was about to be had.

"OK, in this bag are some sweets which I got from the joke shop in that fancy dress place." Hannah liked the sound of this already. "So, these sweets look and taste like normal boiled sweets, but they make your mouth go dark blue."

Hannah liked this even more, and threw Calum a conspiratorial smile as he continued with the finer details of his plan. "Right, you know how Gollum is always confiscating stuff, yeah?"

Hannah and Leo both nodded.

"Well, Hannah, if I offer these to you in the middle of his lesson, he's sure to confiscate them!"

"Genius!" exclaimed Hannah, who immediately

understood the intended outcome. Leo was also excited but at the same time relieved that he wasn't to be included in such a risky endeavour.

"OK, let's do it!" said Calum, initiating some high-fives. Leo always tried to add a fist bump, which Calum didn't approve of.

Five minutes into Mr Pugh's history lesson, Calum conspicuously offered the sweets to Hannah, who played her part like a pro. The trap was set. Mr Pugh stormed forward and snatched the bag from Calum's grasp. "I'll take care of those, my boy!" he barked, "What have I told you about stuffing your face in class?"

"Oh, but sir…" Calum whined, screwing up his face in mock anguish.

"Tough luck, Armstrong. You were careless, and you got caught. If your brain wasn't the size of a very small pea, you might have realised that handing out sweets when my back wasn't even turned was a very *stupid* thing to do."

"Can I have them back at the end of the lesson, sir?"

"You most certainly can't!"

Calum maintained the crestfallen look on his face until Mr Pugh returned his attention to the Franco-Prussian War. Hannah was in awe; it was a masterly performance. They exchanged a brief smile and smothered their laughter.

Later that morning, the whole school had assembled for the 2005 photograph. Mr Pugh, with his bug-eyed face looking like thunder, glared at Calum from a short distance. All around his lips, and on his teeth, was a dark blue stain, almost as if a fountain pen had exploded in his mouth.

****

Hannah searched the photo for herself; unsurprisingly, she was standing right next to Calum. She remembered tidying his school tie that day so that he would look extra smart. All her girlfriends were there, some of whom she had caught up with since her return. Hannah saved a silent scowl for Dean Gunt and the Adcock twins, but particularly for Imogen Gibson. *Just look at her, pouting for the camera and pushing her chest forward, as if she were a glamour model.*

Hannah had to grudgingly concede that Imogen was an attractive girl. Apart from Lucas Saunders, all of the boys fancied her. Perhaps it was inevitable that the two hottest kids at St John's would eventually get it together but Hannah was disappointed that, of all the girls Calum could have chosen in her absence, he had to choose Imogen. They were clearly so wrong for each other.

Before she rolled it back up, Hannah made a mental note to retain the photograph somewhere safe so that she and Calum could keep it with their wedding pictures, should they ever get married.

She shook her head in disbelief when she discovered school folders and books on which she'd written Calum's name umpteen times. Each entry was embellished with love hearts, and kisses swarmed the letters like small bees. *God, girl, you were infatuated,* she acknowledged with an amused smile.

Buoyed by her discoveries, Hannah placed a small pile of memorabilia near the loft hatch, intending to store it in her bedroom wardrobe. She switched off the light, said goodbye to the wasp and descended the shaky ladder.

By the time she entered the living room, her family were watching the *X Factor*. Her parents only liked the beginning of the series, when trashy families proudly pushed their untalented offspring in front of Simon Cowell.

Her father, Norwich's foremost collector of superfluous hardware, looked up from the television and said, "Hey, Hannah, sweetheart, I meant to tell you to be careful with that loft ladder. One of the catches is broken and it comes down a bit too quick."

CHAPTER TWELVE

Humidity and Humility

It didn't take long for Calum to realise that Thailand's Land of Smiles epithet didn't apply to Bangkok Airport's unpleasant passport control officers. While Calum dutifully stood on his yellow marker like an arrested felon, a sour-faced official scowled at him in the same sullen way he scowled at every foreign visitor with the audacity to enter his sacred country. He stamped Calum's passport with a series of hard thuds that could have tenderised a steak, and gestured for him to move on.

Because he was in transit, en-route to the island of Phuket, Calum's unseen luggage was already checked through to his domestic flight. This was a godsend, as his tired mind was now resolutely on autopilot.

Unfriendly immigration officials aside, Calum was impressed with Bangkok's Suvarnabhumi Airport. In particular, he admired the wave-like aesthetic of the cantilevered glass canopy which allowed diffused sunlight to flood the concourse. He also enjoyed catching his first glimpse of some Buddhist monks, who seemed somewhat incongruous as they padded through a throng of international travellers.

He soon discovered that sitting in a transit lounge, waiting for his next flight, was a tedious affair, especially as he'd been awake for the last twenty-four hours. Some of the transit passengers managed to sleep on the stanchioned seats with heads lolling at improbable angles, but Calum, yet to acquire this specific ability, remained awake. The travellers included a mix of Thais, who were returning home, and a pleased-as-punch English couple who needed the whole world to know that they went to Phuket every year.

Calum wondered if Thailand was going to be worth all this effort. Because of his sleep deprivation and the mind-numbing boredom of long-haul travel, he'd already made his mind up never to come here again.

****

By the time his Bangkok Airways flight touched down at Phuket's International Airport, Calum had lost almost all of his cognitive function.

Baggage reclaim showcased the usual jostle of inconsiderate passengers, who all felt the need to get as close to the starting point of the carousel as possible. One annoying oaf, who appeared to be prematurely dressed for the beach, barged in front, completely blocking Calum's access to the carousel. In a blameless world, Calum would have happily shoved the guy head first onto the moving belt, but he kept his fraying temper in check and moved to a less-congested section.

Compared to Bangkok's spectacular airport, Phuket's was a modest affair. As Calum passed through the green Nothing to Declare channel, a surge of unexpected happiness charged his flat batteries. The impatient beachwear guy had been stopped by two customs officials, who wanted to scrutinise his luggage. *Yep, karma can be a bitch,* he thought, as he shot the man an unsympathetic smile.

Once outside the airport terminal, he felt as if he'd wandered fully clothed into a steam room. Although it was late in the day, Calum had never before experienced heat and humidity like it.

A metered taxi became available on the rank, its bodywork was split into two colours, the top half yellow, the bottom half red – like a rhubarb and custard boiled sweet. Usually, Calum preferred to sit up front next to the driver, but he noticed that the passenger seat was loaded with stacked cardboard trays of eggs, resplendent with spatters of hen shit and feathers, so he sat in the back instead.

Things didn't get off to a promising start, the vehicle's gearbox offered up a noise similar to a goose being strangled. Happily though, despite guidebook warnings to expect Phuket taxi drivers to commonly ignore their meter, Calum was pleasantly surprised to see this one ticking slowly as they departed the airport.

The front of the cab doubled as a mini-shrine. Hanging from the rear view mirror was an amulet, which swung like a hypnotist's pocket watch. The driver had also superglued a figurine of Buddha to his dashboard. The more Calum looked, the more iconography he saw. In addition to the talismanic statuettes were artificial flower garlands and a photo of the King of Thailand, who Calum knew to be revered by his loyal subjects.

"Sir, what country are you from?" asked the driver. Only his eyes and nose were visible in the rear-view mirror.

"England."

"Oh, very good! What is your football team?"

"Um … Norwich City?" Calum said this as if it were a question, assuming that the driver wouldn't be familiar with his home town team.

"Ah," the driver mumbled, clearly having never heard

of them, "my team, Manchester United!" he exclaimed.

Calum hadn't yet realised it, but this would be a recurring theme whilst he was in Thailand. He was only surprised that the cabbie didn't also have a photo of the entire Manchester United squad plastered across his windscreen.

Calum's sunglasses were in his suitcase but thankfully the glare of the fading sun was diffused by the tinted glass of the taxi. The aircon was set a bit too cold for his liking, but he didn't want to make a fuss.

On first impressions, Phuket was not quite the *Shangri-La* he had envisaged; it appeared to be a mishmash of billboards, concrete buildings and roadside shacks, set against a Jurassic Park backdrop of viridian green jungle.

Each time they stopped at traffic lights, the symphony of sounds amazed him. Motorcycles appeared from every direction, weaving in and out of the gaps between cars, each one making a noise reminiscent of an angry wasp trapped in a jar. Bicycle bells rang incessantly and the drivers of the auto-rickshaws – the *tuk tuks* – called out to pedestrian tourists who might want to hop on board.

It surprised Calum to realise that Buddhist monks seemed to be an everyday sight, rather than the rarity he had imagined. A whole group of them were sitting indolently at a long table in an open-air restaurant by the side of the road. Some of the monks' robes were a drab saffron colour; others, though, were a bright tangerine hue, which made a vivid contrast to the dark green hills in the background.

Calum was curious as to why the monks weren't eating, despite being in a restaurant. "Excuse me," he said to the driver, talking to the back of his crepey neck. "Why aren't the monks eating?"

"Oh, cannot," the driver replied. "Monk, he must not eat at this time."

"Ah," said Calum, moving onto the subject of the Thai monarchy. "I can see that you love your King."

"Yes, *all* of the Thai people, we love our King *very much*. But the people right now are very sad. Our King, he in hospital but everybody hope he can be better soon."

Calum shifted forward in his seat. "And I hope so too."

He noticed, reflected in the mirror, a saddening of the man's eyes, so thought it best to change the topic. Just then, in the failing light, he spotted a monkey scurrying down a telegraph pole. *That's not the sort of thing you see every day in Norwich*, he thought to himself.

It took about forty minutes to reach the Redford Patong Beach Resort and day had suddenly become night. Shortly after passing a line of seedy massage parlours and a makeshift taxi rank, Calum's driver stopped at the hotel's security barrier where uniformed guards effected a perfunctory attempt at bomb detection, using a chipped mirror on the end of a pole. The sound of the road surface softened as the driver manoeuvred the cab up the Redford's pristine driveway, stopping by the lobby entrance where international flags hung limply in the warm, still air. Within an instant, a posse of hotel personnel descended on the vehicle, each with their palms pressed together in a *wai*. Calum was encouraged that the glittering opulence of the Redford was in sharp incongruity with its scruffy locale.

"Good afternoon sir. Welcome to Redfor' Patong Beach Resort, *kap*," said the head bell boy, who was wearing a uniform not too dissimilar to that worn by the crew of the Starship Enterprise.

The fare came to just over five hundred baht, so Calum peeled off six of the red one hundred baht notes and asked his driver to keep the change.

"*Kap Khun kap*," said the cabbie, offering a *wai* of his own, to add to all of the others.

Calum had learnt some basic Thai greetings before leaving the UK but was quickly realising that the average Thai man missed out the '*r*' in *Krab,* and pronounced the '*b*' like a '*p.*' Calum decided to pronounce the word phonetically, like the locals: *Kap* it would be from this day forward.

His suitcase and hand luggage were loaded onto a trolley and the guy with the Star Trek uniform escorted him to the reception desk. "What country are you from, sir?" he asked.

"England," Calum replied.

"Oh, England! Manchester United, my team!" the bellboy trilled, jerking two thumbs towards himself, assuming almost everyone in England would also be a fan.

The warm greetings just kept coming. The female receptionist, who was every bit as glamorous as the Thai Airways stewardesses, greeted him with an elegant *wai* and a fabulous smile, which instantly made him forget his tiredness.

"*Sawasdee ka,* sir," she gleamed. "You are checking in today? May I have your name please?"

"Mister Armstrong."

She tapped away, her perfect fingernails dancing above the keypad, like dragonflies on a lily pad. "And you have one other person in your party? Miss Gibson?"

"Um … no," spluttered Calum. He had completely forgotten to inform the hotel of Imogen's absence. "Miss Gibson is unable to come."

"May I please see your passport and booking confirmation, Mister Armstrong?"

"Sure… here they are," he mumbled, rifling through his document wallet. Fatigue was starting to get the better of him.

"Thank you, sir," purred the receptionist.

Calum peeked at her name badge. "You are welcome

Miss Panida," he grinned, not realising he had pronounced her name incorrectly, but she gave him a kittenish smile anyway.

"OK, we have the room you requested; high-floor, sea-view. The room, it is number four-zero-two, and *Khun* Nuay will show you the way. We hope you will enjoy your stay, Mister Armstrong." Again, she hit him with that fabulous smile.

Nuay handed Calum a luggage ticket and escorted him to the lifts, trotting ahead like a Thai Captain Kirk. For some reason he walked with his head cocked to one shoulder, as if he was listening to an imaginary parrot or cradling an invisible phone. Calum thought that this was probably a hotel brimming with funny walks; he'd already seen the concierge mincing around the lobby as if he was trying to kill a mosquito trapped between his buttocks.

In the lift, Nuay explained the main features of the hotel; Calum was too drained to pay proper attention, but nevertheless nodded politely. The lift doors opened onto a galleried walkway, lined with rooms on one side and open to the garden on the other. Beyond the balustrade Calum saw a floodlit tennis court and an unending succession of coconut trees. If he were to close his eyes, he could have easily imagined himself walking through a jungle, such was the tinnitus of the night.

The room was contemporary and comfortable, with mood lighting that was lost on Calum's failing senses. Apart from some artwork, depicting Thai mythology, the conker-coloured teak floor was the only indicator that they were even in the tropics.

Nuay sensed that Calum, like most of the European visitors at this point, just wanted to crash out on the bed. The luggage trolley arrived and Nuay helped the other bellboy with the bags. Calum handed them both a tip of one hundred baht. Whether this amount was an underpayment, or over the top, he didn't know; besides, he hadn't yet accumulated any smaller notes. In any case, the guys seemed pleased enough with the amount.

"*Kap Khun kap*, sir," said Nuay.

"It's Calum ... you can call me Calum."

"*Kap Khun kap, Khun* Calum," said Nuay, calibrating his response. The two bellboys departed quietly. As they left, Calum made a mental note to adopt the Thai habit of using the polite prefix of *Khun* before every person's name.

****

After showering to remove the grime of air travel and wrapping a white fluffy towel around his waist, Calum took only a few items from his suitcase, deciding that he would unpack properly the next day. He charged his iPhone via a travel adaptor and double-checked to make sure he'd turned data roaming to off.

The digital display on the bedside clock read 19:43, which meant that it was only a quarter to two in the afternoon back home. Using the room phone rather than his mobile, he made the call that his mother would have been waiting for from the moment she got out of bed.

Mark Twain once said that worrying is like paying a debt you don't owe. If that were the case, Calum's mother, Victoria, would have needlessly settled a lot of non-existent debts, for she worried about absolutely everything. She not only expected her son to phone from Heathrow to let her know he'd arrived safely, she also made him promise to call her the minute he arrived at his hotel. Gary, his father, was the polar opposite: a boisterous, self-employed gas heating engineer who didn't worry about anything.

Two days before Calum left for Thailand, Gary committed a serious error of judgment by making light of their son's forthcoming flight. "Vicky, I don't know why Calum has to ring you, just to let you know he's got there safely. Look, if a jumbo jet drops out of the sky and crashes into the Himalayas, killing four hundred people, don't you think it'd be all over the news?"

Rather than having its intended effect of allaying her fears, this only fuelled them. Gary looked at his son and shrugged his shoulders extravagantly as if to say, *I tried my best, son.*

After looking up the dialling codes Calum called his mother, who seemed very near to tears with relief. He suppressed a chuckle, when he heard his father in the background – tactless as ever – say, "Oh, his plane didn't drop out of the sky then?"

No sooner had he put the phone down, than the doorbell sounded. On the threshold stood two hotel employees, one male, one female. The girl nursed an arrangement of orchids as if she were cradling a new-born baby, the guy balanced a cling-filmed plate on his spindly fingertips. Upon this plate sat a small chocolate cake. Both staff members beamed expectantly, waiting for his delighted reaction. Calum, though, was completely nonplussed and assumed they had come to the wrong room. His indifference was definitely not the reaction that they had envisaged and he saw mild panic in their eyes, but they sustained their Siamese smiles nevertheless.

Then, like a thunderbolt, it dawned on him: he'd emailed the hotel a week ago to announce Imogen's birthday – and today was her twenty-second birthday. He didn't have the heart to tell these two the sordid truth.

The girl was first to speak. "Good evening Mister Arm-trong," she said, having trouble with the middle part of his surname. She spoke so softly, her voice was almost a whisper. "Complementary cake and flower for you, sir."

"Thank you so much … please, come in."

They wore brassy name badges on their uniforms and Calum surreptitiously read them as they removed their slippers and tiptoed past.

The guy was even more feminine than the girl. He made space for the gifts, then placed two sets of cutlery, which were wrapped in white linen napkins, next to the cake. The girl presented Calum with a card, holding it ceremonially in both hands. The card boasted a photograph of the hotel on the front and on inside someone had typed: *Happy Birthday Imogen. Best wishes from Rudolf Breitner, General Manager.* Under this was an illegible squiggle, which resembled the wavy line on a cardiogram.

"Thank you, *Khun* Mukda," he said, not sure if he was pronouncing her name correctly, "and thank you, *Khun* Pan." He noticed that Pan's eyebrows had been plucked until they were as thin as two pieces of string.

"Oh, Mister Arm-trong, thank you to remember our name," gleamed Mukda, delighted to receive some guest recognition for a change. Pan decided to do a little curtsey, which Calum found endearing.

As the two padded, quiet as ninjas, to the doorway, Calum scrabbled for some money from his bedside cabinet. They were already through the door and putting their slippers back on when he proffered a brace of one-hundred baht notes.

Mukda's smile was serene. "No need, Mister Arm-trong … good night, *ka*."

"Good night, *kap*," whispered Pan, who had remained silent until this point. They backed away with a synchronised *wai*.

Wow, thought Calum, *Thai people are just wonderful. Such humility!*

****

Crossing seven time zones had left Calum's body ponderous but his mind was becoming annoyingly alert. He brushed his teeth in a bathroom so bright that you could have performed open-heart surgery in it. A switch outside the bathroom door turned on an electronic *Do Not Disturb* notice outside his room.

When it was time for sleep, Calum tried to decode the confusing panel of light switches mounted close to the bed. With each investigative click/click, click/click, illumination flashed on and then off from random corners of the room. Night lights, standard lamps and reading beams cheerily announced themselves before he managed somehow to plunge the room into inky darkness.

The oppressively warm, heavy air meant that it was far too hot to slip under the freshly laundered sheets, so he lay face-upward and naked on top of the bed, with his hands clasped behind his head. He started to pendulum his legs in the manner of a child creating a snow angel, in an attempt to ease his restlessness. He avoided using the aircon, as he definitely didn't want to fall asleep with the room becoming increasingly colder.

The *noir* of the night meant that he literally could not see his hand in front of his face. The only light in the room was from the bedside clock which shimmered cheerlessly in the blackout, its crème de menthe numerals accentuating the fact that it was early morning, and that he was nowhere near sleep. He hadn't noticed the noise of the ceiling fan before he switched off the lights but he could hear it now, croaking annoyingly, like some mechanical bullfrog. To make things worse, an invisible mosquito was orbiting his globe, whining like a distant motorbike.

Calum wasn't known for his patience and jetlag was making him incredibly tetchy; any outside noise became a major irritation. Each distant *ping* of the lift and every clattering footstep on the terracotta-tiled corridor irked him. Ludicrously, he reached the point where he actually sat up in bed and scolded the waves as they crashed noisily onto the invisible beach beyond his balcony.

Resistance was futile and he resigned himself to a night without sleep. Surrounded by his haunted loneliness, he wished it were dawn so he could have breakfast amongst fellow humans or go for a run on the beach. A group of Scandinavians returned from a night out and were chatting uproariously outside their rooms. Calum caught the gist of each unfamiliar word and envied the guests' gaiety, which would undoubtedly be followed by a decent night's sleep.

Out of the blue, as he sweated in the darkness, Hannah Cunningham wafted into his mind. Just thinking of her soothed his mood. All of a sudden, he was remembering Hannah's familiar smile when they'd bumped into each other at the leisure complex. The tiny gap between her two front teeth, which he once found cute, now seemed incredibly sexy. She looked absolutely bloody gorgeous. And how had he not noticed that fit body before? Calum was surprised to discover that he had suddenly become hard.

An unexpectedly exhilarating thought crossed his mind: Calum Armstrong and Hannah Cunningham – maybe more than just good friends? A grin spread across his face in the dark.

****

The clock taunted him. Despite knowing that he shouldn't keep looking at it, he couldn't help himself. The display read 3:28. Calum swung his legs from the bed and blindly felt his way to the minibar. A few cans of Singha beer should anaesthetize him into slumber, he reasoned, as he gathered some against his arm.

Within the hour, he was sound asleep and dreaming of Hannah Cunningham.

CHAPTER THIRTEEN

Jellyfish and Stinkfruit

Hot stripes of sunlight sneaked from behind the curtains and scissored the white walls of Calum's room. In his sleep he had become entangled with the sheet, which was now wrapped around him like an ill-conceived toga. He squinted at the clock: it read 8:02 a.m.

While the rest of the hotel was bursting into life, he felt as if it were still the middle of the night. In fact, his body clock believed it to be only two o'clock in the morning. He was incredibly thirsty and immediately guzzled both of the room's complimentary bottles of water without pausing for breath. After padding over to the glazed patio doors he drew the curtains, exposing himself to a blinding wall of light.

The view was magnificent, like a screensaver image; he visored his forehead with one hand to shield his eyes from the sun's glare. His balcony overlooked verdant gardens whose main focal point was a cobalt-blue swimming pool. Beyond this was the beach and the infinite shimmer of the Andaman Sea. When his eyes were forced into a squint, he could still see the palm trees silhouetted perfectly onto his retina.

Shrugging off his tiredness, he shaved in front of the bathroom mirror and hunted for some clothes in the suitcase. The hotel provided an iron and ironing board and he pressed a polo shirt, so at least he'd have something unwrinkled to wear for breakfast. Slipping on a smart pair of shorts and some stripy espadrilles, he left his room and headed for the lifts.

Breakfast was served in the Papaya Restaurant. He was greeted by two slender girls swathed in tight Thai silk, who stood behind a wooden lectern. "*Sawasdee Ka!*" they said in unison, each girl steepling her fingertips. "May we have your room number, Sir?"

Calum hadn't yet consigned his room number to memory and looking at his key card didn't help him in the slightest.

"It's four hundred and something," he said. "My name is Armstrong."

One of the girls ran an elegant finger down a long list to find his surname. "Your room number is four zero two," she said with an effortless smile. "Would you like to sit inside or outside, sir?"

"Inside please," he replied, feeling that eating breakfast in full sunshine wasn't for him. The other girl guided him through the restaurant and offered him a small table near a window which afforded a view of an elephant-themed fountain.

"Would you like tea or coffee, sir?" she asked in almost flawless English.

"Tea, please," said Calum, resting his phone and sunglasses on the table.

"Breakfast is self-service," she explained, sweeping her arm towards the food stations with a balletic flourish. "I will bring you your tea shortly, *ka.*"

The Redford Hotel offered a bewildering selection of international cuisine: everything from pain-au-chocolat through to dim sum. Like Calum, some of the guests had only recently arrived and were still hopelessly jetlagged; they were easy to spot, as they wore bewildered expressions and moved like confused Daleks.

Calum avoided the egg station, as various nationalities seemed to be engaged in a covetous jostle for position, and instead opted for a plate of fried rice, to which he added some grilled fish that had been doused in a chilli-laden tamarind sauce. This choice didn't seem too unusual; back home he often reheated leftover Chinese takeaway food for breakfast. When he returned to his table, a teapot and a small jug of milk were waiting for him.

After breakfast, Calum began to explore the hotel grounds. Two white butterflies flittered about him, as if they were extracting data. The mature gardens were tended by a team of silent gardeners who wore green uniforms and coolie hats. He watched with interest as one of the gardeners sliced a cluster of coconuts from a tree with a scythe attached to a long pole.

Middle-aged Europeans, who had left their rooms at the crack of dawn to unfurl towels onto their favourite loungers, were already basting their hot, shiny bodies by the hotel's kidney-shaped swimming pool. Incongruously close to this gala of exposed flesh, female staff members walked by in full uniform, shielding their faces from the sun's rays with clipboards.

When Calum stepped onto the beach the sand was so bright he couldn't look at it without squinting, so he put on his sunglasses and marvelled at the view. All of the previous day's adversity was consigned to history and he exhaled the last vestiges of negative energy to welcome a fresh start to his holiday. Although it wasn't much after ten o'clock in the morning, the sun was already vertical in the azure sky. Calum removed his espadrilles to walk barefoot on the sand but it was cinder hot, forcing him to break into a sprint towards the flatter area nearer the shoreline. Tiny crabs scuttled sideways and disappeared into holes, faster than a blink of an eye.

He stopped at the damp, compacted sand near the water's edge and allowed the soles of his feet to cool down. A white bird nearby rattled its wings and took off, executing a weightless landing further down the beach. The sun's savage heat seemed to amplify the volume in his body; he could feel the thump of his heart within his chest and his blood pounded much like a bailiff's fist on a door.

The sea was colder than he thought it would be and even though he was only standing in shallow water, he could feel it tugging at his ankles as if it wanted to drag him out into the ocean. Small fish darted about his feet and there were a few translucent jellyfish nearby that had been washed up on the beach. Calum had never seen one before; they reminded him of large, undercooked eggs. Aware that he hadn't yet applied any sunscreen, he started to troop back up the beach, mindful of the fact that he would need to sprint the final few metres, where the softer sand had burnt his feet.

There were several beach vendors milling around. Most stood near to the hotel, trying to entice female tourists to look at sarongs and silk scarves. One of the vendors, a guy of a similar age to Calum, strolled over to him with a blue coolbox hanging from one shoulder.

"*Sawasdee kap*, my frien'!" he shouted, pressing his fingers into a *wai*. His smile was as wide as the beach itself.

"*Sawasdee kap*, yourself," Calum replied, liking the guy already.

The vendor wore a bashed-to-buggery straw hat, which would have suited Huckleberry Finn, and a pair of board shorts that had faded in the sun. The hat shadowed the top half of his face, enabling that sunshine smile to take centre stage. Stretching from one corner of his mouth was a prominent scar resembling a large wishbone. Around his neck he wore a beaded necklace from which hung a small golden Buddha enshrined in a rectangular capsule.

"My frien' … have cold beer, have cold Pep-see," he said, lifting the plastic lid to display his wares.

Calum fancied a drink, but didn't have any cash with him. "I don't have any money on me," he said, patting his pockets, in the way that people do when they say they don't have any money.

"No problem, can pay me tomorrow … maybe later?"

"OK, in that case I'll have a Sprite," said Calum, sifting through the cans, which were chilled by half-melted ice cubes. He noticed that he was doing that thing that nearly all tourists do when in a foreign land, speaking far slower than he needed to. He resolved instantly to nip this idiosyncrasy in the bud.

"What is your name?" asked Calum, popping the ring pull of the can, which felt wonderfully cold in his hand.

"My name is Sawat, nickname *Mot* … and you?"

"Calum."

"What country you from, *Khun* Calum?"

"England," Calum replied, guessing what would come next.

"England! What football team?"

"Norwich City," said Calum, fully expecting a blank facial expression in return.

"Yeah, baby! No'wik City … yellow and green! Delia Smith!" Sawat exclaimed.

Calum was impressed that not only had Sawat heard of his home team, he knew of Delia, also. "And which is your team *Khun* Sawat? Oh, let me guess … Manchester United?"

"Manches-ter!" Sawat exalted, delighted that Calum had predicted his preference. His dark eyes shone like beetle shells.

Calum was aware that his unprotected skin was already starting to burn and decided he ought to return to the hotel. "*Khun* Sawat, It was great to meet you, but I need to go … don't have sunblock. I owe you money, will you be on the beach later?" He was talking in that artificially slow way again, he just couldn't help himself.

"Maybe you can see me later at hotel? On Tue'day I teach *Muay Thai* kickboxing class at hotel. Three o'clock." Sawat's teeth were spectacularly white against his darkened skin.

"Definitely, I'll be there," said Calum, shaking the guy's hand before padding up the beach in the direction of the Redford.

Holding his ribs, Sawat soon erupted into laughter because the Englishman walked slowly at first, and was forced to scamper like a monkey on a hot tin roof when he got to the blistering stretch of loose sand.

****

Sawat led a two-hour Thai-boxing coaching session in the Redford's grounds every Tuesday afternoon, an event commissioned by the hotel itself. When Calum arrived at three o'clock, his new friend had already attracted a keen audience of adults and children who wanted to learn some *Muay Thai*.

Spread out on a groomed expanse of lawn was an array of striking pads, boxing gloves and focus mitts. Some of the younger boys were kicking their little legs in all directions, thoroughly excited by the whole affair.

Sawat was bare-chested, wearing shiny shorts with a vibrant scribble of Thai writing across them. Calum hung back, preferring to keep his own martial arts prowess to himself.

Sawat's Bruce Lee physique and the way he moved

impressed upon Calum that the guy must be a serious kickboxer. He had a whippet-thin torso knotted with washboard abs and his sturdy legs were disproportionate to his upper body, formed through years of kicking obdurate gym bags. Sawat sheathed his shins, which looked hard as iron, with leg pads - more for the student's protection than his own. Calum noticed that his new friend had a large, stylised wave tattooed across his back and wondered if it was in memory of the Boxing Day *tsunami* in 2004.

Sawat was teaching one of the hotel guests some basic techniques. The tourist, who Calum took to be Italian, found it all a bit much and diffidently rejoined the others who were seated in a semi-circle on the grass.

Just then, the very thing that Calum didn't want to happen, happened: Sawat spotted him trying to distance himself from the group and beckoned him over. He tried to excuse himself but the other tourists waved him on and encouraged him to give it a try. He slipped out of his espadrilles and stood in front of Sawat, who was enjoying the Englishman's palpable air of discomfort.

"OK, I teach you roundhouse kick," he said, adjusting Calum's standing position as if he were a mannequin in a shop window.

Sawat performed his own version of the kick slowly several times to demonstrate the mechanics of the movement and then he moved faster, whipping his foot in a cobra-like strike that flicked against Calum's ribs, returning it to the ground in the blink of an eye. This drew appreciative gasps from the audience, and had the children in raptures of excitement.

"Your turn," he said to Calum, trying to coax the apparent beginner into a posture that resembled a fighting stance. Calum was not sure how to approach this quandary, so he dutifully performed some clumsy-looking kicks, hoping that this would swiftly relegate him to the seated ranks of onlookers.

"No, no!" fussed Sawat, who could not believe that such a fit-looking *farang* could be so ungainly. "You must use hip!" Sawat began to gyrate his hips as if he were spinning an imaginary hula hoop. This drew a ripple of laughter from everyone in the group.

"*Khun* Calum, you can do better, I am sure of this … try again … use hip."

Sawat stood in a ready position and nodded at Calum, hoping that this likeable Englishman wouldn't continue to embarrass himself. So Calum, with exquisite control, chambered his leg to chest height and effortlessly extended it, resting his foot against Sawat's ear, leaving it there for a full two seconds, before returning it, gracefully, to the floor.

His new Thai friend was wide-eyed with amazement and the small crowd was suddenly galvanised into mild hysteria; they whooped and clapped with uncontrolled delight as if they had just witnessed a modern-day miracle.

"Wow, I am so surprise, *Khun* Calum," Sawat beamed, impressed as much by the Englishman's earlier modesty, as by his camouflaged proficiency.

****

After a two-hour, late-afternoon nap, Calum had begun to shake off some of his jetlag. He'd eaten the remainder of Imogen's birthday cake, which he had earlier squeezed into the small fridge, and had taken a lengthy shower. After wiping steam from the bathroom mirror, he noticed a poncho of sunburn had spread about his shoulders, caused by playing water volleyball in the hotel pool earlier in the day.

He paired tapered chinos with some Converse baseball boots and a navy-blue polo shirt. Leaving the room, he walked to the lifts, sending geckos skittering behind lights on the white stucco walls. Soon he was strolling out of the hotel entrance and into the leaden sweatiness of the night.

A vast curtain of darkness had descended on Phuket. The sky was blackboard dark in this part of the world and a chorus of noisy frogs by the side of the hotel's driveway added to the tropical atmosphere.

Once he was past the hotel's security barrier, the driveway narrowed into a dark *soi*, lined with the toothless taxi drivers and massage parlours he'd noticed on his arrival from the airport. "Taxi! Taxi!" the cabbies shouted, each hoping that Calum might change his initial response.

Some of the massage parlours innocently offered reflexology and foot massage, whilst others seemed decidedly sleazy. Sulky-looking women sprang from their chairs and attempted to entice him in by snaking themselves around doorframes and blowing kisses. Behind one of the parlours he saw a mother washing her baby in a tin bath whilst an old man lay fast asleep in a hammock.

The hotel's oasis of calm seemed a world away from the diesel fumes and wall of noise that assaulted his nostrils and ears once he was beside the main road. There was an amalgam of urban sound; the constant drone of motorbikes, buzzing like chainsaws, and the boom-boom pulse of loud music from the go-go bars. Near to him, a blonde gaggle of exuberant Scandi-girls squeezed into a *tuk-tuk* that seemed incapable of accommodating them. At first the vehicle belched and shuddered in protest, before moving through a succession of whining gear changes as it took off.

Attracted by its bright lights, Calum reached a lively street but found that it was an area abundantly favoured by the gay community: He'd never before seen such a proliferation of holiday cowboy hats and indecently tight shorts. After only a few metres, he was swooped upon by bar touts who ran their eager hands over his body as if they were washing him in a shower.

He escaped to a sweaty night market that seemed to sell only flip-flops, T-shirts, belts and baseball hats. The stallholders all repeated the same mantra, and wailed like alley cats, "Hey, you can look, I give you good price!"

He ate chicken satay bought from a roadside stall, where the charcoal smoke stung his eyes, and he tasted some of the spiky *durian* fruit, which stunk to high heaven.

But Calum quickly decided that Patong's *farang-fest* of tawdry bars and touristy hang-outs wasn't for him, so he careered back to the sanctuary of the hotel in a pimped-up rattletrap of a *tuk-tuk*.

Once returned to the serenity of the Redford, equilibrium was restored. Straightaway Calum knew he had made the right choice; the calm restraint of the hotel offered the perfect antidote to the excesses of the world outside. Nuay, the ever-present bellboy, greeted him by name and an in-house band played soothing jazz in a lobby bar, where Bond-girl waitresses served elegant cocktails to guests.

Calum walked through the lobby, down the marble stairs and onto the landscaped lawns, heading for the beach. For the first time that night, his senses were tingling; ambient lighting and cool, sultry music coaxed him into the Sundowner Bar. He returned the *wais* of the friendly staff and sat at a table, where he could hear the sound of waves rumbling against the moonlit beach. He asked for a draught beer which arrived with a complementary bowl of pistachios and because the night air was so hot, the cold glass sweated like a living entity. The black sea was calm as a millpond, its inky darkness only interrupted by the green glow of squid boat lights. The muffled thud-thud of Patong town was but a distant heartbeat.

Calum lifted the glass to his lips and thought of Hannah again, wishing that she was here sharing this moment with him. No sooner had he eaten the pistachios, than a vigilant waiter scuttled over to replenish the bowl.

"Wow, such service," Calum enthused.

"*Mai pen rai, kap,*" the waiter replied, lowering his head obsequiously.

"Excuse me … what does *mai pen rai* mean?"

"Oh, sir, it mean don't worry, everything no problem."

Mai pen rai, thought Calum, loved the sentiment, and immediately consigned the phrase to memory.

CHAPTER FOURTEEN

Friends Reunited

Hannah spent Saturday morning with her friend Sophie, helping her to pick a dress for a family wedding she was attending the following week. Eventually they both agreed that the floral dress from House of Fraser would not only meet Sophie's mother's approval, but also wouldn't make her look like a complete dork. Sophie had to rush off for her 12.15 appointment at the hairdressers', and the two girls exchanged exaggerated kisses.

"Be sure to text me from the wedding, Sophe, I want *all* the gory details."

"Oh, I definitely will. Wish me luck! Love you."

"Love you too, bye!"

Hannah was desperately keen to reunite with Leo again and planned to ambush him at work. She was already in the Chapelfield Shopping Centre, on the exact same level as the Apple store, which was merely a one-minute walk away. Today she had wriggled into some tight dark-denim jeans, over which she'd zipped high-heeled boots. To complete the look, she wore a figure-hugging T-shirt, accessorised with a Kenzo silk scarf. Hannah possessed a natural, athletic grace and strolled through the mall as if on a catwalk, without consciously meaning to.

The Apple store was forensically bright. The floor staff wore a uniform of royal blue T-shirts and had iPod-style name tags strung from their necks. Hannah scanned the area, hoping to spot Leo among their ranks. Even when she looked his way, she didn't immediately recognise him. Instead of the shapeless flop of dark hair and geeky spectacles of his schooldays, Leo was now rocking a hipster look. His sable hair was shorn convict-short at the sides but was kept much longer on top and slicked back with product. He'd grown an on-trend mariner's beard and sported a pair of funky, white-rimmed specs.

She waited for him to finish chatting with a customer, then walked over and stood squarely in front of him, grinning like a Cheshire cat. As much as she barely recognised him, the same could be said for Leo: When he first clamped eyes on Hannah, it took a full second for identification to kick in.

"Oh-my-God! Hannah freaking Cunningham! You look *amazing*!"

"You too, Leo … you too," she smiled.

They became lost in a tight hug that made them forget where they were, then Leo stepped back to regard her at arms-length. "Calum phoned to say you were back in town and he *did* say you looked bootylicious." He studied Hannah as if she were some rare exotic creature.

"Oh come on, Leo, you and I both know that Calum Armstrong would *not* use a word like *bootylicious*."

"Yeah, you're right, it's just me voicing the word for him. Hey, you must meet Tilly, my wife. She's around here somewhere…"

"Well, how about we all meet for lunch?" Hannah suggested.

"Awesome! We break at one o'clock. Where shall we go?"

"YO! Sushi?"

"Euw, I'm not actually a big fan of sushi. How about Giraffe?"

"Giraffe it is, one o'clock. I'll bag a table."

"Awesome!"

"Oh, and Leo…"

"Yeah?"

"Stop saying *awesome*."

"OK."

****

Hannah created quite a stir amongst the waiters in Giraffe. She'd asked for a large table and two of the guys had one cleared and ready for her in double-quick time.

Leo arrived with Tilly just a couple of minutes after one o'clock. From the moment she breezed through the door, Hannah knew that she would like Leo's wife. Even from a distance Tilly exuded happiness and positivity and greeted the restaurant staff as if she were the one serving them. Hannah rose from her seat to hail them both.

"Wow, look at your gazelle legs," Tilly gushed. "Puts my little dumpy ones to shame."

"You look *so* beautiful," reassured Hannah, planting a kiss on each of her rosy cheeks.

Tilly had crinkly blonde hair, cut just below her jawline: she'd held some of it back with brightly coloured clips, leaving one section to curtain the left side of her face. She was blessed with dancing blue eyes and her arms, which were the colour of cooked spaghetti, waved wildly whenever she spoke. Hannah imagined that Tilly's pale complexion and impassioned personality would make her perfect for the casting of 'plucky young governess' in a Brontë adaptation.

"I've got to say, Hannah, you look absolutely stunning," confirmed Leo, picking up the menu.

"So what am I, chopped liver?" Tilly quipped, her eyes sparkling.

After their drinks were served Tilly ordered feta salad, Leo asked for a cheeseburger and Hannah requested a chilli beef enchilada, with a bowl of sweet potato fries on the side.

"Hannah, how on earth do you eat like that and still manage to keep so slim? You've got a figure like a Victoria's Secret model," Tilly pouted, before pushing her own little belly out for public inspection.

"Oh, but I love to rub your tum … it brings me good luck," Leo cooed, before kneading Tilly's stomach as if it were a lump of dough.

It was clear that the pair adored each other. They couldn't keep their hands off each other, even while they were ordering food.

"You guys are so much in love," Hannah remarked. "It's great to see."

"Oh, thank you," said Tilly. "Everyone said that we were too young to get married but we are truly happy, aren't we, fuzzster?"

With that, she planted a wet kiss onto Leo's smiling lips.

"Yuck! Get a room, you two!" Hannah sputtered, with a mock grimace.

"So how did you manage to get your hair so straight, Hannah?" Leo asked. "You've got this whole Rhianna thing going on."

"With the help of my hairdresser and some straightening irons. It's a pain in the butt, to be perfectly honest."

"But you had such lovely hair at school, Han. I seem to remember that all the girls were dead jealous of your curls."

"Yeah, I suppose it might be worth letting it go back

to natural one day."

During lunch, the three got on famously. Of the trio, Tilly talked the most, and occasionally pinched fries from Hannah's bowl. Leo only used the word *awesome* once. In fact, he was so at ease in Hannah's company, it was as if the previous seven years had never elapsed.

"I bet you two finish each other's sentences," Hannah suggested.

"We do!" they chimed, in unison.

Inevitably, the conversation gravitated towards Calum. Leo, who always spoke in awe of his best friend, described the time he was invited to hit him in the stomach. "Honest to God, it was like punching the backrest of one of those leather chesterfields. I think I actually sprained my wrist."

Hannah, who had intentionally held back, not wishing to appear too keen, waited for Leo to mention Calum's name first. "So, what on *earth* is he doing with skanky Gibson?" she grumbled.

"Oh, you obviously haven't heard?" Leo said, his eyes widening.

"Heard *what*, exactly?" pressed Hannah, arching her eyebrows in anticipation of some heaven-sent news.

"Well, he caught Imogen, at her apartment, playing hide the sausage with some guy she knew, and promptly ditched her. In fact, he is currently living it up in sunny Thailand as we speak."

This was the best news that Hannah had heard in an awful long time. "Who's he gone to Thailand with?" she asked.

"He's gone on his own, couldn't get anyone to join him last minute. He even asked me if I'd like to go with him."

"God, I wish he'd asked me!" Hannah blustered, forcing a lustful facial expression, that made everyone chuckle.

"You go get him, girl!" shouted Leo, initiating a high-five.

"Oh, believe me, I will."

"Awesome!"

CHAPTER FIFTEEN

The Consequence of Revenge

Twenty centuries ago, long before the Kingdom of Siam came into being, the Kinnaree, or Swan People, co-existed peacefully with humans:

The Kinnaree, now mythical, were emphatically evident in that era. Their torso and head was similar to that of a human, while their lower half bore the tail and legs of a huge bird. Extending from their shoulder blades were broad wings that could hoist them high above clouds.

At that time the humans lived in tribal territories, ruled by an imperious emperor, whose power was supreme and whose word was law.

The male Kinnaree were known as Kinnara and the females were called Kinnari. They had their own principality, a sacred area of land surrounded by mystical forests that were untouched by harmful demons.

Because the Swan People were favoured by the humans, who were grateful for their healing powers, the emperor decreed that they should be allowed to live in peace. And live in harmony they did: the Kinnaree led an untroubled existence in heavenly surroundings. The warm air was infused with the smell of flowers; fruit grew from almost every tree and birds, their distant cousins, sang jubilantly with no concept of predators.

Klahan Kinnara was a prince amongst his people; he was strong and handsome, with the smooth, chiselled features of a Greek statue. The main characteristic that distinguished himself from a human – apart from his lower half – was that his eyes were yellow, similar to those of a tiger. His name meant 'brave' although with a complete absence of enemies, there was no way of knowing if this title suited him.

His life partner was Anong Kinnari. Her name, which signified beauty, could not have been more appropriate. She possessed an allure no human could hope to rival. Her trusting eyes glittered like sapphires and her lithe body made lustful humans wish that they too could become Kinnaree. As with all of her kind, her top half was naked, displaying skin as soft as an orchid petal, and her slim waist tapered elegantly into the purest white feathers.

Like swans, the Kinnaree coupled for life. Klahan and Anong shared an unequivocal love, which was perfect in every way.

Whenever distressed humans called out from their sickbeds, or from the scenes of terrible accidents, the Kinnaree would always come. They readily took flight over their forest, rushing to the aid of ill or injured mortals. Usually – though not always – they could restore people to good health. It was because of the people's reverence for the Swan People's charitable nature that they were afforded an Arcadian life without persecution. Their only enemies were the deceitful Crow People, who had become bitterly envious of the favouritism shown to the Kinnaree by humans. They shared none of the Swan People's advantages and were liked by no-one.

The emperor, however, had a feckless son, Prince Thuanthong, whose life of privilege had rendered him vindictive and avaricious. The prince, who by the age of eighteen had sampled every rapacious delight that his courtiers could summon, one day decided that he would like to eat the flesh of the Kinnaree. He'd heard from the gossiping Crow People that the meat of the female Kinnari was the most delicious protein in the whole of his father's empire.

The prince dispatched the most celebrated hunter in the territory to bring him the fresh carcass of a Swan Woman. Without his father's permission, he employed the martial skills of Dang Mookjai, who was famous throughout the land. From an early age Dang was trained by his father, a feral warrior responsible for the death of countless men. His father not only taught him weaponry, but imbued him with the life force and characteristics of a wolf.

Eighteen years earlier, aged just fourteen, Dang was conscripted into the emperor's imperial guard. He had recently killed and then beheaded six soldiers, thereby avenging the murder of his parents at their hands. Eyewitness accounts, detailing the savagery of the boy's attacks, soon filtered back to the palace: it pleased the emperor to have such a formidable combatant by his side.

****

As dawn broke one day, Klahan sat in one of the tall mango trees that bordered a wide clearing in the forest. While enjoying the flesh of his favourite fruit, he gazed down from his vantage point to where his love was bathing. Anong had removed her wings so she could wash her body in the shallows of the sacred lake and had draped them over a rock by the water's edge.

His citrine eyes noticed a man camouflaged by some lakeside trees. This confused him. The Kinnaree would normally only see humans outside the forest boundary.

Still, he wasn't unduly alarmed – why would he be?

Dang Mookjai had been watching the swan woman for quite some time. By removing her wings, she had given him the opportunity he needed. All of the Kinnaree had disappeared into the trees to forage and there seemed to be no other creatures around; without her wings, his quarry wouldn't be able to fly away.

Leaning forward on his branch to monitor this human interloper, Klahan was horrified to watch the man surge from the cover of the trees. Before he could react, the human had impaled Anong's ribcage with one swift thrust of his poisoned spear. Klahan swooped from the mango tree, his widening shadow bearing down on the hunter, and crushed the man's skull against a large rock.

In shock, Anong dragged herself from the reddening water and lay grievously wounded on the grassy bank. Klahan removed the spear and pressed his hand against the deep laceration. Blood poured from her body at an alarming rate. He possessed the power to heal her deep wound but not the ability to stem the surge of poison that was coursing through her veins. Anong was in severe pain for the first time in her life; her distress call a haunting lament which was heard throughout the forest.

Anong's three sisters were the first to arrive. Their restorative instincts quickly overcame their initial shock and they immediately flew back into the forest in search of medicinal herbs that might release her from death's grip.

Nang Takian, the tree spirit, heard of their plight and guided them to Suan Arun, the garden that only appeared at dawn. She assured the Kinnari sisters that the magical herbs there would draw out the poison from Anong's body.

Klahan had healed the wound easily and protectively held Anong, who was now limp in his arms. He intoned a gentle lullaby to calm her, whilst an excruciating pain began to paralyse her limp body. He offered silent prayers to the Universe, pleading for the gods to save her life. His vigil was mercifully short. Anong's sisters soon returned from the forest, flying low over the lake, rippling chevrons on its glassy surface.

By nightfall, Anong was returned to full health and rewarded the Kinnaree with a song so hypnotic that even the gods were beguiled.

Phi Pop, the night spirit, didn't care much for such levity. She was busily feeding on Dang's brain directly from his skull cavity. Delicacies, such as this, were usually extremely hard to find.

The Crow People, never ones to pass up an opportunity to ingratiate themselves with the emperor, informed him of the death of his favourite hunter. They took pleasure in describing how Klahan Kinnara had murdered him before callously leaving him to rot in the sun, his head cracked open as if it were a hatched egg.

The emperor was infuriated; he'd expressly forbidden violence by any creature towards humans. He swiftly issued an ultimatum to Prarachar Kinnara, the king of the Swan People, that unless something was done he would have his soldiers burn down the forest and every Kinnaree in it.

Prarachar, for the preservation of his people, was left with no choice. He was reluctantly forced to issue a grievous penalty against Klahan, to set an example that would appease the human emperor. With a heavy heart, he decreed that Klahan be cast into the sea, spellbound and alone for eternity. And he could return to their world only if a human sought him to offer his forgiveness.

CHAPTER SIXTEEN

The Ghost Story

Pim, one of the massage therapists at the hotel's Nirvana spa had just presented Calum with a delicately-strung thong, which was laughably supposed to preserve his modesty. He wasn't sure at first what its purpose was, he imagined that perhaps a small monkey might be able to use it as a hairnet. It was wholly ineffective as a G-string for an adult male.

The therapist turned her back to him, allowing him to remove his bathrobe before embarking on a heroic attempt to jiggle his genitalia into the woefully-deficient netting. Thankfully, when he signalled that he was finally ready, she shielded him with a towel and asked him to lie face-down on the treatment bed.

The spa's treatment room was womb-like and softly lit. As soon as his eyes were closed and his face was buried into a towelled cradle, his other senses came to the fore. A lullaby of pan pipes and birdsong serenaded his ears and his nostrils were treated to a *potpourri* of wonderful smells: sweet basil, ylang-ylang, lavender, and lemongrass.

Although Pim was tiny she possessed a Herculean strength. So now, on the third day of Calum's holiday, the negativity of that first night was finally being consigned to history as Pim's forceful thumbs and slippery fingers kneaded the muscles of his back. With each movement he was succumbing to blissful inertia, so much so that he fell asleep for a full twenty minutes under her determined dexterity.

"E'cuse me … e'cuse me…" she whispered, smiling serenely as he slowly came to. Her voice seemed other-worldly. "Please, sir, to turn over."

Pim deftly safeguarded his decency, screening him again with the towel. As he rolled onto his back she continued with the next phase of her massage whereupon he drifted into another sensory-induced sleep.

Later, he didn't even notice that the massage had finished and that Pim had left the room. When he awoke, upon her return, she helped him into his bathrobe and offered him a tiny drinking bowl of jasmine tea.

"You sleep very good, sir. Massage help you lee-lax," she said with a joyful smile.

As Calum sipped from the bowl he wholeheartedly agreed. He couldn't ever remember being this relaxed in his entire life. Sadly, after today, he only had one more day left. Despite his initial reservations, he had begun to love Thailand and its wonderful people. In the short time that he'd been here, he'd become acquainted with a high number of the hotel staff and was on first-name terms with both of his pocket-sized room maids.

The prickle of his sunburn had honeyed into a golden tan; he spent his days either at the pool, or visiting Sawat on the beach. The previous night, the two of them strolled through the gaudy streets of Patong, while Sawat showed Calum some of his favourite parts of town. They visited a local food market, where they ate sticky rice and coconut cream served with slices of fresh yellow mango. Calum had seen this dessert presented on a square glass plate in the hotel; the rice was shaped like an ice hockey puck and the coconut cream was merely a brushstroke on the plate. However, in the market version a cellophane-gloved lady scooped a large pat of glutinous rice into a Styrofoam container and chopped mango from the palm of her hand. The coconut cream was served separately in a small plastic pot. Based on taste alone, the street food beat its more refined counterpart hands down.

Calum had begun to understand why the Thai royal family was so widely revered across the entire nation. For a start, the Thai king was the world's longest-reigning monarch, ruling over his people for more than sixty five years. He had achieved a god-like status and his regal image was portrayed on huge billboards all over town.

Whilst surfing Thai TV channels in his hotel room, Calum watched some old black and white footage which showed the queen meeting crowds of her adoring subjects. The queen, a person who materially has everything one could desire, received a modest gift from an old lady dressed in rags. The elderly woman had probably walked for miles, and stood for several hours, hoping for this once-in-a-lifetime opportunity. It touched Calum's heart to see Her Majesty take the gift and cup it in both hands, like someone might hold a delicate bird. Then she admired it, as if it were the most precious thing she had ever seen. She thanked the old lady and handed the gift to a courtier who also took great care of it. After watching this touching display, Calum decided that he loved the Thai royal family too.

The queen's selflessness and humility was also ingrained in the psyche of most of the Thai people that he'd encountered. He hoped that he could incorporate some of this *mai pen rai* attitude into his own life when he returned home to England. Considering how calm he was now, he couldn't believe how tetchy he had been on his first night at the hotel:

You actually shouted at the sound of the waves, you idiot, he thought to himself, smiling at the memory of this ludicrous rant.

****

Sawat was on the beach, trying to explain to a Russian man that he wasn't prepared to sell any of his cold beers at a lower price. The Russian wouldn't take no for an answer, acting as if cut-price lager in foreign lands was his God-given right. He clutched a handful of Thai banknotes in his gold-ringed fingers, which he waved about as if he were at a horse auction. The man was huge, his belly alone weighed nearly as much as Sawat's entirety. Despite this, he sported the tightest pair of Speedos ever seen on a human being. In addition, he wore an expensive Breitling watch and yet, although he had the cash equivalent of Sawat's house on his chunky wrist, he still wanted to knock twenty baht off the price of a can of cheap beer. He spoke angrily, talking to Sawat as if he wanted a fight, rather than a can of Singha.

Why were Russian men always so aggressive? Sawat wondered. *Was Russia so awful that it had a terrible effect on the personalities of everyone who lived there?* He made a mental note that if he ever had the money to travel abroad, he would definitely need to avoid the place. He continued to smile at the man, which seemed to enrage him even further.

"You must sell me beer for less money!" the man barked.

Sawat didn't say anything, and continued smiling.

"Can get beer in supermarket cheaper than this!" the Russian added.

"OK, then go to the supermarket," Sawat said, breaking his silence.

"You are little piece of shit! You are fucking crook!" the man bellowed, his pale blue eyes blazing like the Thai sun.

"And you have a stomach like elephant," Sawat countered. His smile spread even wider, especially as he had just seen Calum in his peripheral vision.

At this, the man snorted like a disgruntled buffalo and stormed off, stuffing sweaty banknotes into his snug swim trunks.

****

After changing back into his shorts and T-shirt, Calum left the spa and stepped into the quivering heat of the beach. By now his bare feet had become accustomed to the hot sand and he didn't have to break into a run. It didn't take him long to spot Sawat; his friend wasn't far from the hotel's beach wall, and was being shouted at by a huge European guy, whose shaved head glistened like a dome on a mosque. As he got closer, he could tell by the man's accent that he was Russian, and noticed that his man-boobs drooped like a pair of Salvador Dali clocks.

Jesus, just look at those budgie smugglers, thought Calum, wondering how the guy had managed to squeeze into them.

"You are little piece of shit! You are fucking crook!" the Russian shouted.

Sawat, to his credit, wasn't fazed and easily maintained both his smile and his Siamese composure – something that Calum would have found impossible, given the same circumstance.

Once the quarrelsome tourist had gone, Calum and Sawat stood together in the shade of the beach wall. Sawat removed his T-shirt to cool down and shared a cold bottle of water with his friend. Calum found it funny that when Sawat was bare-chested he looked as if he was wearing a T-shirt, such was the bodily contrast between the darkly bronzed skin of his arms and face and the caramel skin of his torso.

Once more seeing the large wave tattoo across Sawat's back, Calum asked, "*Khun* Sawat, what does the tattoo mean?"

"Ah, I have story, *Khun* Calum. I nearly die in su-namee, eight year ago."

Calum hung on every word, amazed at Sawat's cat-aclysmic story and that he recounted it with nonchalance, as if the *tsunami* had been just an everyday occurrence. This was partly because of Sawat's inherent modesty and also due to his indomitable spirit. Calum, though, wasn't aware of the terrible images that flashed through his friend's mind as he spoke. Sawat had sudden flashbacks of the white, bloated bodies, tight-skinned like human squid. And once again he remembered the death stare of Khomsan, the old security guard.

"So, *Khun* Calum, I think this su-namee day was lucky day for me. Very sad, and many people die, but I am alive … I am very lucky." As he said this, he unconsciously drew one finger across his facial scar.

"Can I take a photo?" Calum asked, removing the iPhone from his shorts. He took a close-up shot of the wave tattoo on Sawat's back, then asked one of the hotel's pool boys to take a photograph of Sawat and himself together.

Now that he trusted the Englishman enough to bare his soul, Sawat decided it was time to go one step further. Speaking to Wuttichai about the spirit under the sea unburdened him in so many ways, and he was suddenly keen to let someone else in on this unlikeliest of secrets. Calum didn't strike him as the kind of *farang* who would ridicule such a far-fetched story; besides, Sawat wouldn't dare to broadcast such an event to anyone in his neighbourhood for fear of becoming a laughing stock. Feeling he had nothing to lose, he allowed his smile to slip as he prepared to tell Calum what happened on that bewildering day, eight years ago. Calum, for his part, sensed a change in Sawat's demeanour and realised his friend was about to broach a subject that was close to his heart.

"*Khun* Calum, I would like to tell you about something that I see out there in the water, many year ago."

Calum, hoping that this was going to be a shark story, was all ears.

"When I was fifteen year old, I go this one time with my uncle in speedboat." As Sawat said this, he pointed towards the dark smudge where the sea shelved into deeper water. "I dive into the water to see if I can touch bottom, but under the sea, I saw *him.*"

Him? thought Calum, thinking that this story was taking a rather unexpected turn.

"He was a *phee sang* ... a gho't!"

"A goat?" Calum asked, frowning.

To make himself understood, Sawat widened his eyes then pawed at the air and went "Whooo-ooo…"

"Ah, a ghost!"

"Yes, a gho't!" Sawat confirmed.

"What sort of ghost?" Calum inquired, puzzled as to why Sawat seemed to be taking this subject more seriously than the *tsunami.*

"The gho't, he sit on the bottom of the sea. His eye are like tiger ... he have feather, like bird ... I think he like a Kinnaree, fifty percen' man, fifty percen' bird."

Calum maintained a straight face because his friend seemed to actually believe in what he was saying. He also had no idea what a Kinnaree was, but managed to conjure up a fleeting image of a creature that was half-man and half-bird.

"So, *Khun* Sawat, why is this ghost living in the sea?"

"Buddhist believe that person, when they die, will come back again. I cannot remember word in English…"

"Reincarnation."

"Yes, that word. I think maybe the man in the sea, he is dead, but to come back, cannot."

"So, is the ghost a good spirit or a bad spirit?"

"Not know for sure. Maybe good, maybe bad. But tomorrow, *Khun* Calum, I have free day. Would you like to go in speedboat, maybe see gho't in the sea?"

"*Khun* Sawat, I would *love* to do that!"

Although this tale of ghosts living in the sea was wonderfully outlandish, Calum found Sawat's candour and his belief in the subject totally endearing.

"And *Khun* Calum, not just me have seen the gho't. Old man, his name Wuttichai, he have seen him also!" Sawat said this as if the mere mention of another eyewitness would somehow validate his bizarre story.

After baring his soul, Sawat felt exposed, and became extremely self-conscious. He inspected the contents of his coolbox so as to detract from his embarrassment. The ice had melted into slivers no bigger than contact lenses, and the remaining cans were now bobbing about in nothing more than water. He pulled his T-shirt back on, then stepped out of the shade and into the sun. "See you tomorrow, *Khun* Calum, at nine o'clock … here on beach, *kap*?"

"Yep, I will definitely be there, see you then, *Khun* Sawat."

Just then, a startling vision caused Sawat to instantly forget about near-death experiences and malevolent ghosts. Walking up the beach with a supermarket bag overstretched with beer cans, and heavily drenched in sweat, was Joseph Stalin. He was accompanied by his spectacularly plump family, each one incrementally smaller than the next, like a set of Russian *babushka* dolls.

"Do the Russia people drink hot beer?" Sawat asked, bemused.

"Only on holiday," Calum chuckled.

CHAPTER SEVENTEEN

His Very First Murder

Kaiserslautern, Germany 1996

Regrettably, the boy he was about to put to death was his best friend.

Even at the age of eleven, long before he became The Mother Killer, he wondered what it would be like to murder someone, to actually take their life away. It was an itch that he was determined to scratch, and that scratch would come today.

When Rudi Schäfer, his best buddy in the whole world, agreed to take the challenge he knew that this would present his first opportunity. The two boys stood on the threshold of the road bridge and Rudi was already enthusiastic about the challenge.

"If you do it, then so will I." he said, rubbing his hands together and grinning with excitement.

"We'll do it together," said the killer-in-waiting.

Rudi was a barrel-chested, optimistic boy, whose heavily-freckled face had earned him the nickname of *Gepard,* or Cheetah. Traffic thundered five metres below the bridge. The bridge, which itself was constructed from reinforced concrete and hemmed by a wrought-iron side rail. The boys' challenge was to walk along the rail's ledge from one end of the bridge to the other. Rudi, with his usual buoyancy, estimated that this would be simple enough given that the rail was considerably wider than his feet.

As soon as the coast was clear, the boys clambered up together, steadying themselves and winging their arms like seagulls to find some balance. The killer walked ahead, confidently placing one foot in front of the other in the manner of a tightrope walker. Rudi followed about three metres behind. Once he was halfway, the killer did an about-turn to face Rudi. He lowered his knees onto the metal and sat with his legs dangling either side of the rail.

"What are you doing?" Rudi huffed, "you're supposed to get to the other side."

The killer was smiling now, all the neurons in his central nervous system firing. He looked to see if any pedestrians were coming then shuffled towards Rudi, gripping the rail tightly in both hands. Leaning back like a rodeo rider, he kicked his friend's legs from under him. The boy's skull clanged against hard iron on the way down, causing the rail to vibrate like a tuning fork.

Exactly as he had imagined, the startled look on Rudi's face thrilled him. His euphoria was further heightened when he saw his friend's slack body smash violently into the windscreen of an oncoming car. He swung his legs from the rail and dropped onto the bridge's walkway. A wonderful commotion was building below his feet.

The killer held a hatred in his young heart that someone so trusting as Rudi could never have imagined. It made him feel good to know that he was the architect of someone's extinction. Simply speaking, Rudi would never exist again.

He removed a comb from the pocket of his jeans and

combed back his lustrous black hair. In his mind, he had already prepared what he was going to say to Rudi's parents and what he would tell the police: *I tried to persuade him not to do it ... that it was far too dangerous...*

But, although he was savouring the exhilaration of his first kill, he was already annoyed with himself for choosing Rudi as his inaugural victim. On reflection, he reasoned, it didn't make sense; loyal friends such as Rudi were few and far between. He could have snuffed out the lives of any number of boys, but – for some stupid reason – he'd chosen *him*.

"I blame *you*, dear mother," he muttered to himself.

CHAPTER EIGHTEEN

The Unlikely Truth

Under the dark cloak of night, Sawat felt a tug at the bottom of his bed sheet but because he was half-asleep, he didn't take much notice.

Then he felt the weight of something on his abdomen – something not much heavier than a cat – and he heard a series of low grunts. All too soon this weight was pressing down on his chest and he could hear the rasp of animalistic breathing. A tiny hand clamped his mouth, compelling him to open his eyes in terror. There, illuminated in the white-silver glow of moonlight, was Phi Am, the night demon.

Sawat struggled to break free, but was paralysed and unable to move. He saw the translucent white of Phi Am's porcelain face and a hissing mouth as cinder-black as the night itself. While he fought for breath, she stared directly into his soul, her scalding eyes blazing with an intense fury.

He choked.

He gasped.

And then he foamed at the mouth.

Sawat woke with a jolt, his fists punching out at the

nothingness that surrounded him. Wild-eyed and frantic, it took him quite some time to realise that the room was completely empty, apart from his sister, Sarai, who was fast asleep nearby. The room returned to normality, reassuringly safe from demons. A search beam of light from a car outside swept the ceiling before disappearing. Somewhere in the distance a dog barked.

It struck Sawat that talking about the sea ghost with Calum yesterday had stirred a repressed apprehension that he needed to confront. He reasoned that, after enduring the destructive force of a *tsunami* and somehow surviving to tell the tale, he surely could muster the fortitude to tackle this further test of his courage.

In just a few hours' time, after taking his English friend out to sea in his uncle's speedboat, he might know once and for all whether or not the sea ghost existed.

Sawat washed himself with some cold water, scooped from a tub in the bathroom, and deodorised his skin with a fragrant body spray. Once dressed, he lifted a loose floor tile concealed by a rug under his bed and retrieved a small handful of cash. After shushing Sarai, who had momentarily stirred from her sleep, he tiptoed out onto the concrete porch.

As he straddled his motorcycle, the first blush of dawn was starting to break over Phuket and after riding his bike for fifteen minutes, he stopped at a street stall to eat a steaming bowl of *Jok*. This was another of his breakfast favourites: rice porridge embellished with shreds of fresh ginger and finely-chopped scallions. The vendor cracked a raw egg into its centre, enabling it to poach slightly. As a final flourish, Sawat added the obligatory dash of fiery *prik nam pla* to spice it up a bit. Before he left the stall, he bought some *Pad Thai*, which he'd already promised to share with his uncle and his family. The vendor heaped the steaming hot noodles into Styrofoam containers which he slid into a polythene bag. Sawat stored this in the compartment under his seat.

Under a flamingo pink sky, he rode his motorcycle to a nearby shrine where he solemnly lit three incense sticks. Sitting on his haunches with knees pressed to the floor, he paid his daily respects to Lord Buddha pressing gold leaf onto his effigy. Then, after phoning his uncle to say he was on his way, he headed for the southern end of Patong bay.

Uncle Jao had already agreed to Sawat borrowing his speedboat for the day, provided his nephew covered the cost of the petrol. Naturally, Sawat didn't dare to tell his uncle the true nature of his venture.

Jao's ramshackle house was raised on grubby stilts above the muddy banks of a river set some way off the beach and sheltered by a coconut grove. The large shack was a modest affair: Inside, bare wood floors were covered with rush matting and flimsy curtains were all that were used for privacy and room separation. Jao shared the house with his wife and daughter, one mud-spattered bicycle and a million mosquitoes.

The sun flashed sporadically through each flickering gap in the coconut palms and gleamed from Sawat's motorcycle mirrors as he rattled along the scrappy dirt track that bisected the coconut grove. When he arrived at the house, his uncle was sitting outside, spotlit by a column of sunshine, repairing a large fishing net that splayed about him like an extravagant dress.

Jao's eyes had in recent years become as cloudy as oysters, his cataracts caused by endless days squinting into the horizon from the slippery decks of fishing boats.

"*Sawasdee kap, sabai dee mai kap*?" Sawat shouted, having to greet his uncle with a one-handed *wai*, because of the large bag of food he was carrying.

Once inside the house he was received by the clang of woks and the heady aroma of lemongrass and coconut.

Sudarat, his timorous auntie, stood in her makeshift kitchen, greeting him with a shy smile and a polite *wai*. She was shrouded in a mist of fragrant steam as she prepared coconut milk soup to accompany the *Pad Thai* he'd brought. Sudarat was so slight that Sawat imagined she could walk on soft sand without leaving a footprint. Her nineteen-year-old daughter, Mook, was much less constrained and rushed from the kitchen to wrap her favourite cousin in a warm hug.

They ate together, sitting cross-legged on the matting while an unseen squirrel scrabbled on the tin roof above their heads. Sawat polished off two plates of soup and, having eaten earlier, he excused himself from the *Pad Thai*, which the others ate with relish.

Uncle Jao's modest speedboat was moored in the malodorous brown water of the river. The boat could barely accommodate two people but Jao had bought it for a song and regularly put it to good use.

Sawat handed his uncle more than enough money to meet the cost of fuel and then, under a chorus of birdsong, idled the boat out towards the open sea.

****

The temperature had already reached ninety degrees when Sawat neared the stretch of shoreline in front of the Redford. Calum was waiting, sitting on the sand with forearms resting on his knees. He immediately waded out to the speedboat, holding his arms aloft as if surrendering to an unseen enemy.

"*Sawasdee kap, Khun* Sawat!" he yelled, intense sunlight bouncing off his sunglasses.

"*Sawasdee kap, Khun* Calum, how are you?" Sawat replied, grinning.

Each time they met, Sawat admired the bright red G-Shock watch that was strapped around Calum's wrist, particularly as the red of Manchester United was his favourite colour.

"*Khun* Calum, how much your watch to buy?"

"Oh, in England, about one hundred pounds. In Thailand that would be – let me see – five thousand baht."

"*Paaang*! So expensive!" Sawat grimaced, deciding that a cheap knock-off that might only last ten seconds under water would suit his budget better. Sawat's interest in the watch immediately gave Calum the idea of gifting it to him at the end of his holiday.

As the Englishman clambered on board, the momentous nature of the day's jaunt began to weigh heavily on Sawat's mind. He'd already steeled himself for eventualities: if he was proved right and the sea spirit *was* still there, sitting like an emperor on the sea floor, then his unease would worsen; however, if Calum failed to see *anything*, he would feel a fool for recounting such a laughable story. It dawned on him that neither of these outcomes would suit. He probably should have sensibly left things just as they were.

Calum, on the other hand, didn't expect anything more from the day other than the opportunity to go out in a speedboat in glorious sunshine and spend some quality time with his friend.

It was easy for Sawat to pinpoint the area where he'd seen the ghost. Whenever the sun shone, a diamond-shaped area of dark water appeared, like an enduring shadow. Here the topography and vegetation of the seabed were at odds with their surroundings, thus causing the loss of reflected light.

As the speedboat skimmed the waves heading for that inky lozenge of mysterious water, Calum looked back towards land. When viewed from the sea the white walls of the hotel, with its colonial-style columns and its cherry red parasols, looked magnificent. He could clearly see the sculpted hedges and the tall coconut trees, some of which had been planted to replace those destroyed by the Boxing Day *tsunami* in 2004.

Pretty soon the hotel diminished in size and the shoreline stretched out into a narrow strip of gold, beyond which were the dark hills that loomed over the town. The sea, when viewed towards landfall, was a swathe of changing blues: azure, cobalt through to a velvety turquoise. When Calum switched his position to squint in the direction of the sun, the water morphed into a blinding sheet of glimmering zinc.

It took no time at all for Sawat to reach the designated spot where he lulled the engine.

Calum pointed at the shimmering water. "Is this the area that you saw the sea ghost, *Khun* Sawat?"

Sawat nodded his head, but a forced smile betrayed his trepidation. He studied the water as if it were an alien substance and peered distrustfully over the rim of the boat as if on the edge of a canyon.

In an attempt to deflect his own reluctance, Sawat offered a counter-proposal. "*Khun* Calum, if you are scare', you do not have to go into sea…"

The Englishman smiled and placed a reassuring hand on Sawat's shoulder, realising that his friend was experiencing a mini-crisis. "Sawat, I *want* to go into the water, I would *love* to see the ghost."

Sawat couldn't even begin to understand why someone would want to see a ghost but was grateful that Calum was prepared to investigate this possibility on his behalf. He helped his friend into his uncle's wetsuit and provided him with a pistol-grip diving torch. "You take deep breath then you dive down to bottom. Not to worry if you cannot see gho't."

At that moment, a pod of dolphins undulated in and out of the sea, no more than five metres away. "Look!"

Calum yelled, excited by their unexpected proximity.

A broad smile returned to Sawat's face. He instantly felt like a child again for these were the fanciful dolphins once promised to him by his uncle; he had never seen them up close before and almost as soon as they appeared, they disappeared as swiftly as mermaids.

Their appearance lightened Sawat's mood. "I think today, *Khun* Calum, is very lucky day," he beamed, his emotions changing like the wind.

Calum slipped into the waves then, treading water, he sluiced his scuba goggles and strapped them tightly against his face. Sweeping all around them was a glorious expanse of blue sky which seemed far removed from the watercolour stain of dark clouds that brooded in the distance.

After filling his lungs with air, Calum flipped into the water. All external noises ceased to exist and the inside of his head became a sound box for the groans and sonar clicks of submerged noise. His eardrums strained under the increased pressure and the temperature dropped dramatically, gnawing at his bones. Sculling the water and streamlining his body to reduce drag, he was soon within sight of the sea floor. He carved semi-circles in the dark water as he illuminated the area in every direction, but saw nothing unusual. The depths had a macabre, Gothic aura and were landscaped by unfamiliar, shadowy objects. He began to understand how easily this could have spooked a fifteen-year-old boy. Then, just as he prepared to return to the surface for oxygen, he he saw *something*.

Calum's burning lungs didn't allow him enough time to investigate this sighting, so he pushed upwards and broke through the surface. Once his head was bobbing above the waves, he siphoned air into his lungs and disappeared underwater again. As he drew deeper, he again caught sight of an opaque outline on the sea floor. It definitely had a human shape. Surely an unusually-shaped rock? he thought. Perhaps this was the object responsible for Sawat's teenage confusion?

Pushing nearer, he was shocked to see an illuminated face in the halo of torchlight, then two arms, one of which moved, as if to acknowledge him. He could actually see Klahan Kinnara in all his glory but was intrigued, rather than scared. Klahan, for his part, looked just as surprised as his human visitor.

With pressure rapidly building in his chest, Calum studied this creature. As Sawat had suggested, he had eyes like a tiger. Surely this is just some local scam? he reasoned, either that or a lavish local joke for the benefit of gullible tourists. Calum was astounded at the effort they must have put into this masquerade, the prosthetics and costume alone would have eaten up a considerable amount of time and money. And how was this guy able to breathe for so long underwater?

His best guess was that Sawat and his pals had gone to great lengths to present this elaborate hoax. The guy's startled expression was hilarious, his face kind of human but his legs and lower torso were made to appear bird-like. The man certainly played his part well, thought Calum, as he swam within touching distance to get a better look. The prankster then looked forlornly at Calum, as if to convey some kind of message – and at that point he put his hand to Calum's head.

Bless him, thought Calum, finding it hard not to laugh. The more he studied this thing that the locals had created, the more it looked back at him with imploring eyes. He admired the man's acting skills. Calum had to hand it to them, these guys had really done a fantastic job. He smiled at the man one last time and gave him a thumbs-up gesture, just to let him know that he got the joke. His lungs were almost depleted of air, so he kicked at the water to thrust himself skywards again.

Up, up he pushed towards the sun, relieved to see the dark silhouette of the speedboat guiding his return. The groan of the ocean became ever louder. His lungs were screaming for oxygen and his head felt as if it was about to haemorrhage. He broke through the surface, spat salt water and gulped at the air as if it were water in a desert.

"Very good!" he said to Sawat, catching his breath, after being hauled into the boat.

Sawat looked back at him, perplexed.

"The man in the sea, absolutely brilliant," he continued, with a knowing grin. The goggles had imprinted a red figure of eight onto his face.

"You saw man in water?" Sawat asked, recoiling rather too theatrically for Calum to take him seriously.

"Of course I saw the man in the water!" Calum chuckled, thinking that any moment Sawat would also break into a smile.

But Sawat didn't smile, he just looked truly terrified which Calum instantly found disconcerting.

The sky rapidly shifted from cornflower blue to a sullen zirconium grey and distant thunder rumbled like an ogre's stomach. The wind picked up dramatically, a sinister, almost portentous, storm was crawling towards them, forcing splenetic waves to slap against the hull of the craft, rocking it from side to side. Sawat, thinking that they must have incurred the wrath of sleeping ghosts, quickly decided that it was time to leave. After pushing the throttle, the speedboat erupted into life, spinning one hundred and eighty degrees in an arc of churning water.

He was uncharacteristically quiet as the boat bounced back to the beach. Calum was perturbed by the tension in his friend's face and became acutely aware that the smile which normally lit up Sawat's face was noticeable by its absent.

So, if this wasn't a prank, Calum pondered, then what the hell had just happened?

By now, Calum's own smile had dropped and he looked back to the area of dark sea they had just vacated. Beyond the speedboat's wake there was nothing but clear water for as far as the eye could see with the incoming storm beginning to blur the horizon. His eyebrows furrowed: nobody, but *nobody*, could be seen bobbing to the surface. Now Calum was beginning to doubt his own flippant evaluation of this weird scenario. He never imagined, in his wildest dreams, that such a thing could be possible, but he was starting to actually believe that he may have seen a ghost. Struggling to come to terms with such an outlandish notion, he also understood why Sawat had harboured this secret for so long: it was hardly the sort of thing you would want to run around town bragging about.

By the time they neared the beach, the heavens were well and truly open and heavy rain came down in grey sheets, hammering dents into the sand. A Thai woman further along the shoreline fought with her black umbrella which unfurled inside out, like a bat wing.

After securing the speedboat, they scrambled to the sanctuary of an abandoned water-sports shelter beneath a cluster of palm trees at the rear of the beach. By the time they reached the shelter, torrents of water were cascading from its roof, and a silty estuary of fast-flowing rainwater had formed in a ditch that bisected the sand. As white flashes of lightning X-rayed the coconut trees, a lame beach dog, also seeking shelter, looked at them through doleful eyes, as if seeking reassurance.

Calum hadn't thought that he could ever feel cold in Thailand but he was shivering now and hoped that the sun would soon reappear to warm his bones. The rain was incessant; it caned the palm fronds above them as they bounced around like the hands of a marionette. The strength of the downpour prompted Calum to think of Geoffrey, his paternal grandfather. *"God's got his watering can out today, boy,"* was his customary proclamation each time it rained.

As thunder boomed overhead, Calum tried to broach the subject of the sea ghost but Sawat seemed to think that mentioning it would only invite danger. Calum was already thinking ahead; if he couldn't talk to Sawat about this incredible event, then who on earth *could* he discuss it with?

When the rain stopped, it halted abruptly as if someone had turned off a great tap in the sky. The dog stretched and then limped back onto the wet beach, its gammy leg hovering in mid-air, as if it were dancing the conga. The sky was suddenly blue again and the sun reappeared, bathing Calum's cold skin with its warmth. Sawat, meanwhile, had regained his composure, his mood transformed, like the weather. A rainbow appeared in the sky, which reminded him of Wuttichai, and his immortal finger.

"*Khun* Calum, for your last night, you would like to go to local-style bar, not tourist bar?"

"Yeah, sounds great!" Calum replied, acutely aware that they were still dodging a most obvious issue.

"Really? You sure?"

"Sawat, I am positive."

"OK," smiled Sawat. "Will pick you up at hotel security, five thirty."

"It's a date," grinned Calum.

****

When Calum tramped up the beach steps leading into the hotel grounds, white frangipani flowers, thrashed by the storm, were strewn everywhere and platoons of green-uniformed gardeners were beginning to scoop their petals from sodden lawns, depositing them into rattan baskets.

At the top of the steps, the hotel provided a large tub of water wherein floated a ladle fashioned from a coconut shell and a length of bamboo. Its purpose was to enable guests to rinse granules of sand from their bare feet. As Calum poured the cool water onto his gritty toes, he was still trying to digest what he had experienced less than an hour earlier. He was more than certain that he had seen some kind of amphibious ghost while the logical side of his brain told him that this was clearly preposterous. And yet the fact had clearly presented itself. On this day, with his own eyes, he had undoubtedly seen a ghost.

CHAPTER NINETEEN

The Lost Opportunity

Klahan Kinnara, alone as always in his watery abyss, looked skyward through the murkiness of the sea. He grimaced at a shoal of brainless fish that paused to pout at him as if they expected to be entertained. The silhouette of a boat appeared above him, ordinarily an inconsequential diversion.

Shortly after, he saw a man. Why the man was in the water Klahan neither knew nor cared. The human weaved an awkward dance before him, swimming like a fish that had been tied to a rock. Inevitably, the man was quick to depart, returning to his splendid world of trees and radiance. But then he returned, only this time he actually entered Klahan's personal space.

He raised one hand wearily in his latest futile attempt to attract attention. Most extraordinarily, this human actually saw him! He was certain of that.

Because Klahan could not speak, words being of no use to him underwater, he silently pleaded with the human to remain, his eyes and his hands were his only useful means of communication. Thunderbolts of desperation began to shoot through his chest.

'Oh, please, human, acknowledge me! Know me, *help me!*' he implored, using every fibre in his body to convey his message. And at that moment he even dared to believe that he might soon be able to hold Anong in his arms once again. But the mortal just continued to return his beseeching gaze. Oddly, this human wasn't at all scared; he was even smiling at him, mocking him!

Klahan reached out to grip the human's head, downloading everything that this mortal had ever seen, read and heard. He now had a full comprehension of the English language for the very first time and, in that same instance, was astonished to learn of mankind's ability to journey beyond the sky. But then the human smiled one last time and turned his back to leave.

At that moment, Klahan wished he could have sucked the ocean back himself and guided this, the rarest of men, to be his saviour, but the mortal was as predictably spiteful as all humans. Without the slightest trace of compassion he consigned Klahan, once more, to his wretched eternity.

In the soul-crushing anguish of this moment, Klahan referenced a poignant section of poetry from the vast new database that he'd stolen from the Englishman's mind:

I pass through the pores of the ocean and shores;
I change, but I cannot die.

CHAPTER TWENTY

The Consequence of Violence

While most of the Redford's guests gathered at the rear of the hotel to marvel at a lava-lamp sunset over Patong bay, Calum headed in the opposite direction, passing through the landscaped gardens en-route to the lobby.

As usual, he was hailed with a succession of polite *wais* and friendly *sawasdees* by each member of staff that he encountered and each time Banyat, the effete concierge, floated past in a waft of male cologne, he dropped compliments as if scattering seeds. Without looking directly at Calum, he purred adjectives such as "handsome", or "gorgeous" under his breath, whilst simultaneously fanning himself with his fingers. The first time this happened Calum assumed he must have misheard him but now, because it occurred with such a flattering predictability, he'd become accustomed to it.

Nuay, the bellboy was also pleased to see Calum strolling across the marbled floor of the lobby and stepped out from behind his lectern near the hotel entrance.

"*Sawasdee kap*," he chirped, approaching Calum with his lopsided walk, his palms already pressed together in front of his chest.

"*Sawasdee kap*," Calum replied, offering his own *wai*. For him, Thai greetings were now a reflex action rather than an etiquette that required conscious thought.

"Would you like me to call you taxi, *Khun* Calum?"

"Uh, no thanks, *Khun* Nuay. I'm meeting a friend at the security gate."

Nuay was pleasantly surprised that one of the hotel guests took the trouble to remember his name. "Are you meeting a lady, sir?" he probed, thinking that such a handsome *farang* must have pretty girls falling at his feet like frangipani flowers.

"No, Nuay, my friend is a Thai guy."

This disclosure instantly threw Nuay, who immediately jumped to the conclusion that *Khun* Calum was one of those westerners who preferred the company of Thai men – a *rice queen*. Calum chuckled, sensing that his statement had created some confusion. He reassured Nuay that, in this instance, *friend* actually did mean friend.

"Oh, hope you have good time tonight, sir," Nuay said, relieved that he hadn't caused offence. Then he moved a step closer to whisper some sage advice that he only offered to his favourite male guests. "*Khun* Calum, be careful for chick with dick."

These words of caution tickled Calum, for they were spoken in such a serious tone. Nuay had genuinely intended it as an important piece of inside information for the benefit of an unwary tourist.

"Thank you, I shall definitely bear it in mind," laughed Calum, stepping from the cool of the lobby into the early evening heat.

The driveway was striped by the lengthening shadows of coconut palms and the area was bathed in a flattering pink glow signalling the last dusky blush of daylight. As soon as he reached the beginning of the driveway, the hotel security staff jumped to attention and saluted Calum as if he were an army officer on an impromptu inspection. Calum, although tempted to salute back, offered an all-encompassing *wai* instead.

Beyond the security stop he caught the dazzling smile of Sawat who, while loitering near his parked motorcycle, was talking to a taxi driver whose trousers were rolled up past his knees. He noticed that Sawat was dressed casually in flip-flops, a T-shirt and surfer shorts, every inch the cool beach dude. Calum instantly regretted wearing jeans, trainers and a smart short-sleeved shirt that now made him feel overdressed.

Although he was bursting to talk about the ghost that lived in the sea, he thought that he would respect Sawat's wishes and try to avoid the prickly subject altogether.

After the usual pleasantries were exchanged, Sawat wanted to check that Calum was ready for an urban safari into the hinterland beyond the tourist sights of Patong. "*Khun* Calum – so you want to see local-style bar, for real?"

"Of course!" reaffirmed Calum, wondering why Sawat would have any doubts. "I'd love to get away from all the touristy stuff."

"OK," shrugged Sawat, climbing onto his motorcycle. "Sit here on back of bike."

"No helmet?" Calum asked.

Sawat's grin widened at this question as if such an enquiry was so daft it didn't merit any kind of response.

Calum was thrilled at the idea of riding pillion without a helmet, but was worried about the local police. "So what happens if a policeman stops you?"

"If that happen, then we say 'so sorry, so sorry' … and we pay him two hundred baht."

"OK, let's do it," Calum decided, straddling the rear seat.

Calum found this new experience exhilarating. The motorcycle careered down the road, slaloming between cars, the speed creating a pleasant breeze which cooled his face. Framed in each passing gap between buildings was the fiery sun, which glowed like a blacksmith's forge, searing the sky with an orange blaze. A celestial dimmer switch was beginning to darken the backdrop and Patong's light bulbs twinkled in the distance. No sooner had the sun's orb sunk into the bosom of the ocean than the heavens darkened to a midnight blue. The only hot colour remaining was a crimson flourish that stroked the vanishing sky, the day's parting gift to the canopy of night.

Sawat threaded his motorcycle through a rabbit warren of dimly-lit streets. The Day-Glo hustle of Patong's touristy epicentre suddenly seeming a distant memory. Here, some of the ramshackle houses looked as though they'd been hit by cannonballs such was the size of the open wounds in their concrete walls, and Sawat skewed around potholes the depth of shallow graves.

Each time Sawat slowed his bike, a fetid stench invaded Calum's nostrils. This wasn't the Phuket of funky bars beautified by mood lighting; the tatty streets, with their scribbled walls, were underworld dark. There were no sea breezes in this part of town; the hot, sticky air a miasma of bonfire smoke, rotten fruit and open sewers.

An air of incurable abandonment hung over the neighbourhood. Work on some buildings had started but was never finished, their footprint of low walls, barely two breeze blocks high, now heavily overrun with weeds.

Sawat stopped to allow Calum to dismount, then parked his motorcycle in a line with several others as a pineapple truck thundered past, churning warm clouds of dust from the parched road beneath them. The sky was now blackboard dark and silhouetted mosquitoes dotted every light and a rancid stench seemed as pervasive as moisture in the hot night air.

"The bar, it not far from here," Sawat said, making a

vague gesture. "Better to leave the bike here, much safer."

A welcoming committee of four children, excited by the appearance of a blue-eyed *farang* in their stomping ground, started to follow Calum as if he were the Pied Piper of Hamelin.

"Hello! Hello!" they yelled, becoming ever-bolder. One of them ran ahead, turned his back to Calum and wiggled his backside, thereafter chuckling delightedly.

When they reached the bar, Calum thought that the average tourist would never have imagined that this was even a drinking establishment. There was a conspicuous absence of illuminated beer signs, music, or indeed drinkers. Instead, this open-air venue incorporated a large concrete floor, strewn with metal chairs and tables that looked as if they'd been salvaged from a skip. Dominating the space was a floodlit tamarind tree, the only natural organism to survive the onslaught of quick-setting aggregate. Such was the hermetic stillness of the night, not one of its feathery leaves quivered and the whole setting seemed as inanimate as a stage set.

At one end of the colossal slab was a long, laminated counter, serviced by three glass-fronted refrigerators and a large charcoal griddle. They'd tried to coat the floor with fern-green paint at some stage but the surface had mostly chafed away, leaving an atlas of imaginary continents emerging from an ocean of grey concrete. The area was partly lit by a fluorescent strip that hung at a jaunty angle under a mildewed canopy, the awning was torn to shreds and crudely held together by duct tape. A long swag of light bulbs represented the bar's only decorative touch.

The only other people unfortunate enough to be in the bar were a middle-aged couple at a table near the counter: Calum assumed they must be the owners of this sorry establishment. There were also three drunken Thai men and a pretty teenage waitress who interrupted her sweeping of tamarind pods to receive Sawat and his guest. Apart from this modest number of humans, Calum spotted a brindle-coloured dog fast asleep under one of the tables.

Naturally, Calum had anticipated that a local bar would be pretty basic but this was beyond primitive: *Why would you want to leave your house to drink here?* he wondered. Despite this, he hid his disappointment, not wanting to offend his buoyant host. Then, almost as if to rubber stamp the venue's squalid credentials, a large rat scuttled past, hugging the shadowed fringes of the bar.

As they entered the joint, the pretty waitress skipped forward and greeted them both with a *wai*. "*Sawasdee ka!*" she enthused, her lovely beam could have won a smiling competition in the Land of Smiles.

"My girlfrien'," Sawat preened, searching Calum's face for signs of approval. "Her name is Nok. This mean *bird* in Thai language."

"*Sawasdee kap, Khun* Nok, it's a pleasure to meet you," Calum said offering his hand.

Nok feebly gripped his fingertips and glanced worriedly towards Sawat for guidance, unaccustomed as she was to western-style handshakes.

"She cannot speak English … maybe only a little bit,"

"Not a problem," Calum breezed, hoping to reassure Nok that she needn't be so nervous of foreigners.

Sawat asked his girlfriend for two Chang beers.

"Ka!" Nok confirmed, her smile restored. It was a huge relief that she wasn't expected to converse with Sawat's foreign friend.

"Nok, she is eighteen-year-old. When she older, I would like to marry her."

"Well, she certainly is beautiful," Calum encouraged. "I would say that you are a very lucky guy."

"Oh, thank you *Khun* Calum," Sawat replied, smiling

proudly. "Do you have a girlfrien' in England?"

"No, I don't…" Calum hesitated, suddenly realising he was about to discuss a deliberation that had been occupying his mind of late. "There *is* this girl I like. I've known her since we were eleven years old. I've always liked her but now I do think that I love her."

"Have you told this girl that you love her?"

"No … no, I haven't."

"Then you must, *Khun* Calum. Love can fall through your finger, like sand on the beach. What is her name?"

"Hannah."

"Nek' time you come to Phuket, please bring *Khun* Hannah also … you promise?"

"I promise."

While waiting for the beers, Sawat shed his exuberance momentarily and fidgeted nervously. Calum allowed his friend a moment of reflection, guessing the subject matter that he was about to broach. Sawat lowered his voice, as if he believed that all of the other patrons were somehow embued with superhuman hearing. "*Khun* Calum, we both see gho't in the sea but now I am afraid, think maybe we make him very angry."

Normally Calum would have thought such a superstitious fear totally irrational but the day's events had also made him question the foolishness of disturbing of a real-life spirit. No sooner had Sawat said his piece than the drinks arrived. The bottles felt refrigerator-cold and were beaded with condensation. Sawat clinked his beer bottle against Calum's, heralding the start of an enjoyable evening.

****

Recognising the potential for confrontation, Calum wished they had sat further away from the three Thai men, who were all conspicuously drunk. These guys were wild-haired and nasty-looking. Sawat knew them by reputation and profession; fishermen, he said. Their watery eyes, reddened by cheap booze, glistened like wet pebbles under the glow of festooned bulbs above their heads. Each sported a wispy moustache, the bristles as sparse as those fallen from an overwroked paintbrush.

They sat, not in a westernised way, but cross-legged with accustomed suppleness. Beneath a cirrus of cigarette smoke, their table was a clinking wind chime of bottles and glasses. One of them accidentally knocked a beer bottle over, causing its froth to spill across their table. This simple occurrence was enough to make them all cough and splutter with coarse, unrestrained laughter. The men talked loudly, their earthy voices strangulated by booze. Two were bare-chested, displaying large intricate tattoos inked in a Prussian blue almost lost in the darkness of their skin. Calum found it amusing that one of the guys was still wearing sunglasses, even though the sun had set nearly an hour ago. The third man bore a puckered scar where an eye used to be. He was the most vocal of the group and stared at Calum with territorial suspicion, his scowl all the more fearsome with one inescapable eye.

As the evening progressed, Calum and Sawat covered a multitude of topics, starting with the Manchester United football team right through to the core beliefs of Buddhism. Sawat asked if there was a castle in the city of Norwich to which Calum said yes, but then had the complicated task of trying to explain to Sawat why no-one lived there.

A combination of cold Chang beer and Sawat's agreeable personality relaxed the Englishman; he was pleasantly surprised to find an aura of tranquillity in such cheerless surroundings. In fact, the only thing putting a dampener on the evening, was the open hostility from One-eye, who clearly didn't like the idea of a *farang* drinking on his home turf. The fisherman took every sly opportunity to dart Calum a shit-eating grin.

Bats squeaked overhead, dark, jagged shadows that, in fleeting moments, were captured in a light's austere glare. Though it was nearly ten o'clock at night, the humidity was still oppressive. Calum could feel a stream of sweat puddled in the ravine of his back. Sawat, in contrast, displayed only a few microscopic beads of perspiration on his joyful face.

"Sawat, I'm going for a Jimmy Riddle," Calum announced, getting to his feet.

"Who is Jimmy Liddle?" Sawat asked, wondering if Calum was expecting another friend to turn up.

"Jimmy *Riddle* ... this means to go for a pee."

"Oh," Sawat replied, looking none the wiser, but nodding his head anyway.

"How do I say 'where is the toilet?' in Thai?"

"Hong nam yoo tee nai kap?" Sawat instructed, slowly enunciating each word.

"Yep, got it," Calum affirmed, repeating the line over and over in his head, until he reached Sawat's girlfriend.

"Hong nam yoo tee nai kap?" he asked.

Nok, initially alarmed that the foreigner was going to talk to her in an alien language, burst into a broad smile. She directed him to a small toilet block partly obscured by trellis. Tamarind pods trampled underfoot left their sticky thumbprint, as he threaded between tables.

Sawat watched Calum with keen interest and felt a flutter of pride at the foreigner's readiness to embrace his culture. Many of the *farang* ex-pats he came into contact had barely mastered the simplest of phrases, despite being married to Thai women.

On his walk back from the toilet, Calum deliberately ignored the fishermen's table, aware that they were following his every step; alley cats watching a mouse.

As he returned to his seat, Wuttichai, the local drunk, shuffled to the entrance of the bar, dragging a trolley containing sacks of flattened plastic bottles. As well as coming into the premises to collect surplus plastic items, he would beg for food and whiskey. The owner of the bar, although not innately philanthropic, was happy to send him off with a few recyclables and a small polythene bag filled with soupy rice noodles.

Wuttichai's arrival was met with a chorus of salty derision from the fishermen, something he had learnt to ignore. Sadly, there had been so much ridicule in his life he was impervious to it.

Quietly concerned, Calum and Sawat put their conversation on hold to monitor the situation. Despite the fishermen's self-satisfied grins, Calum couldn't believe the spite in their shiny faces. *Leave the poor guy alone, he's just a harmless old man*, he thought. The irony of this little melodrama wasn't lost on him. These guys, numbed by a nightly consumption of rotgut whiskey, were unable to see their own wretched destiny in this crumpled, broken old man.

Sawat watched with quiet vigilance, thinking he might soon be required to calm things down. "I know this old man," he said, pointing a finger in Wuttichai's direction. "This guy, his name Wuttichai, he is the other guy who see that gho't."

Not content with hurling verbal abuse, the one-eyed drunk lurched from his seat to shoo the older man off with some vicious kicks. He removed one of his flip-flops and used it to strike Wuttichai, slapping him hard across the back of his cowed head. The other two drinkers cackled like mad witches; cigarette smoke caught in their throats and billowed in fits and starts from their nostrils. The cruel rattle of their laughter filled the air. The bar owner looked across in consternation.

Calum skidded his chair backwards and sauntered towards the scene. He grabbed One-eye by the sleeve of his T-shirt, stretching it completely over one shoulder to expose a backstreet inking of a tiger. He instinctively thought to hit him in the throat but showed restraint. The man wheeled towards Calum with a savage hostility blazing from his one furious eye. He spat out his cigarette and threw a wild punch that thudded against the side of Calum's head. The momentum of his attack caused the man to overbalance, and he crashed head first into the Englishman's chest. Calum found himself momentarily entangled in the sweaty heat of the man's struggling body, close enough to taste the sour stench of his whisky breath.

They wrestled for a brief moment. *Christ, he's strong for a skinny guy*, thought Calum, surprised by the fisherman's sinewy muscle power. One-eye made every attempt to fight with the foreigner. Extreme exertion had caused a jolt of pearly mucus to thread one of his cheeks and his eye blazed with rabid fury. He renewed his attack, flailing at the *farang* with gnarled fists.

Calum, after blocking each wild swing on his arms, decided that enough was enough and broke his assailant's nose with one punch, sending him crashing to the concrete. Behind him, all hell had broken loose. He heard one of the other fishermen's feet clattering across the table tops while the drinker with the sunglasses picked up a metal chair, to use as a weapon.

Sawat slipped out of his flip-flops and intercepted the guy with the chair. He absorbed the man's swing, paying scant attention as two of its metal legs battered his ribcage. He let rip with a succession of arcing kicks and elbow strikes, smashing his assailant's sunglasses and rendering him senseless. Each blow amplified a slapping crack of noise that echoed through the emptiness of the night. Nok screamed at the top of her lungs for him to stop, but he was in the zone, unaware of her frightened pleas.

Sawat coiled himself, ready for the next attack, but was surprised to see Calum presiding over the other two drinkers, both of whom sat bewildered and bleeding on the concrete pad. Their sudden proximity to the sleeping dog had forced it to seek a quieter floor space.

"That was fun," Calum grinned, displaying a cockiness that Sawat certainly didn't approve of.

"Not fun, *Khun* Calum ... not fun, one bit," Sawat snapped, glancing around to check if anyone else was about to surge forward.

Because Calum could see his friend's uncommon display of anger, he instantly felt a great deal of remorse. Sawat continued his rebuke, while at the same time offering the indignant bar owner a conciliatory hand gesture to calm him down.

"I live here, *Khun* Calum. Tomorrow, you can leave. This is OK for you but this is my home. These men, bad men ... maybe make problem for me ... maybe make problem for family." Sawat shook his head and cast a sad look to the floor. "*Jai rawn*, Calum. You have a hot heart."

He left Calum and walked over to the three men, who were being helped to their feet by the bar-owner's wife. One-eye was using his T-shirt to wipe blood from his busted nose. Every heartfelt attempt that Sawat made to apologise to them fell on deaf ears. Sunglasses stumbled to the roadside and began vomiting into the gutter while the other two men stabbed bony fingers at Sawat and left the bar issuing threats. A tearful Nok tried to distance herself from the fracas, worried that she might lose her job as a result of her boyfriend's incautious behaviour.

Calum righted fallen chairs and straightened tables in an attempt to mollify the proprietor who couldn't bear to look at the foreigner and just wanted him gone. It was a struggle even to get him to accept any payment. As they left, Sawat continued to offer apologetic *wais* to the owner and his wife. Calum followed suit, duplicating his actions.

When they stepped down onto the street, Sawat surveyed the road to see where Wuttichai had disappeared to. He spotted the old man a few hundred meters away, illuminated by the glow of moonlight and still trying to escape from his own shadow. He had wisely decided to trundle his cart and its precarious load to a position of safety.

Sawat retained a dignified air, his demeanour sad, rather than angry. By the time they reached his motorbike, Calum couldn't have felt guiltier. This was a wake-up call and he was beginning to question his own character. He cursed his own hotheadedness, especially as he'd embarrassed his kind host. Several people in the past had joked about Calum's short fuse, and it was finally dawning on him that their banter camouflaged a serious point. He needed to re-evaluate his response to conflict. In short it was about time he grew up.

Just as the silence between them had become oppressively awkward, a large moth fluttered into Calum's mouth, causing him to puff and spit like a man who had fallen into a cesspit. Sawat's mood lightened immediately. A smile spread across his face and he laughed delightedly as Calum brushed a residue of moth powder from his lips.

"Taste good?" Sawat joked before throwing Calum a forgiving look with only a nuance of reproach. He really needed his new friend to understand his deep disappointment about what had just happened.

Magnanimously putting his feelings to one side, he beckoned Calum nearer, lifting his motorcycle seat to reveal the storage compartment underneath. Inside was a red paisley bandana which Sawat carefully unknotted. From the folds of the bandana he withdrew a Buddhist amulet that was attached to a wood bead necklace.

"*Khun* Calum, I buy this for you. Bring you good luck. Bring you good luck for rest of life. *Chok dee Kap.*" He offered it to Calum almost ceremonially.

Calum was touched, not knowing quite what to say. "*Kap Khun kap*, *Khun* Sawat. I will *never* forget this." He trailed off, feeling choked and studied the amulet as it lay in his hand. It was a small gilt rectangle, in which sat an effigy of a cross-legged man whose hands covered his eyes.

"Who is this man?" Calum asked, looping the necklace over his head.

"This man, very famous monk in Thailand; his name, Phra Pid Ta. He protect you from bad spirit, can help make you money, even."

"Wow, protection from bad spirits *and* extra money, that can't be bad. When I wear this, I will always think of you. Thank you, *Khun* Sawat, thank you very much." He held it away from his chest as if it were a pocket watch, to admire it again.

"*Mai pen rai kap*, no problem, *Khun* Calum, I hope we can be good frien', long time."

****

After clearing security, Sawat dropped Calum off at the hotel entrance. A frail *tuk-tuk*, which had stopped by the lobby, rocked like a hammock when its occupants – two hefty German guys – clambered out. Calum and Sawat smiled fraternally as the sunburnt tourists haggled noisily over their measly fare.

"Tomorrow, *Khun* Calum, you fly to England. You can meet me at beach? Come to say goodbye?"

Calum placed his hand on his friend's shoulder. "Of course! I'll be there, for sure."

They hugged before starting to go their separate ways. Calum thought to apologise, one more time, but instinctively felt that Sawat wanted to draw a line under tonight's unsavoury incident.

"I must go home for Jimmy Liddle," Sawat announced, deciding that such an enigmatic phrase should be a valuable part of his linguistic repertoire from this day forward.

Peeling away from his friend, Calum strolled up to the driver's side of the *tuk-tuk*. "How many baht?" he enquired, while circling an attributing finger in the direction of the two sullen German passengers.

"One hundr' fifty baht," the driver responded, relieved that someone else appeared to be intervening.

"There you go," breezed Calum, pressing two hundred baht into the guy's hand.

He walked around the vehicle en-route to the lobby, and paused to have a gentle dig at the two stunned tourists. "I just felt sorry for you as I could see that you couldn't afford it." He breezed past the delighted bell-boys, who were cupping hands over giggling mouths.

Sawat admired his friend's performance as he watched him from the driveway. His grin widened into a chuckle, causing a sharp pain to jab his bruised ribs. *I like you, Khun Calum*, he thought, *I like you a lot.*

****

The lift doors swished shut and Calum turned to face the full-length mirror as he surged upwards. A shiny lump, which wasn't too noticeable, had formed along the ridge of his cheekbone. His initial euphoria at winning the bar fight seemed immature and pretty pathetic now.

I didn't have to engage with that guy, he thought. *If I hadn't, the fight wouldn't have started in the first place and poor Sawat wouldn't have been dragged in.* Calum decided that, at the age of twenty-two, he sorely needed to change his ways. Plus, this definitely wasn't the kind of example he would want to set his students. *Valuable lesson learnt,* he thought, as the lift doors gasped open.

Even now, he looked forward to establishing a lifelong relationship with Sawat. In particular hoping that some of his friend's cool-headedness might brush onto him as easily as lily pollen to a passing sleeve.

Outside his room someone had trodden a beetle into the walkway floor. Calum slid his key card in the door slot and paused to recognise the 'never say die' instinct of the insect. Despite its exoskeleton being split like a pistachio and its squished abdomen being overrun by a troop of red ants, the beetle's antennae still continued to purposefully scribble at the air.

****

Sawat rode back to his neighbourhood. After dismounting from his motorcycle, he wheeled it onto the concrete pad outside the entrance to his home. It was then that he became aware of a dark presence.

Pacing towards him like spectres were the three drunks from the bar. Sawat steeled himself. Having already survived a *tsunami,* he wasn't anywhere near as scared as he perhaps ought to be. Each man carried a different weapon: one held a length of wood with nails hammered through it, another flourished a baseball bat and used it to scribe a figure of eight pattern in mid-air. One-eye took the lead, brandishing a long chain, which he slapped against the dusty road for pernicious effect.

Long after he'd writhed on the road like a trampled lizard, Sawat's motionless body was discovered by a neighbour, bloodied and caked in dirt. He was battered beyond recognition and very close to death; two of his vertebrae were crushed like peppercorns, leaving him paralysed from the waist down.

CHAPTER TWENTY-ONE

The Fox in the Woods

A doe rabbit was quenching her thirst in the water of a stream, whilst her buck stood guard:

The hungry fox, who had crept upon them, weighed up his options: the buck rabbit was so much bigger, would be easier to catch and would provide a more satisfying meal.

But instead he cornered the doe who, with the stream behind her, had no means of escape.

"Why do you take my mate?" asked the buck. "She has a litter of kittens, who will be lost without their mother. Why not take me instead? As you can see, I would make a far grander dinner."

But the fox killed the doe anyway and, before setting about the business of eating her, he said to the buck, coldly: "This is my nature. You may leave, or you may stay to watch."

****

Frankfurt, Germany 2012

This murder, he decided, was going to be fun.

An execution.

A message.

He knew that Detective Lieutenant Otto Netzer was hung up on the fact that the so-called Mother Killer only murdered pregnant women. But this wasn't always true; sometimes he killed simply because he enjoyed doing so.

It was easy to find out where Netzer lived. Because of his high-profile TV appearances, and the numerous articles written about him in glossy magazines, Herr Netzer had exposed both himself and his family to public scrutiny. And why go after the senior detective, when he could damage him so much more by murdering his wife?

Kirsten Netzer was a presence in Frankfurt's privileged class: a successful defence lawyer who also organised high-profile charitable events for the *haut monde* of the city.

The killer tracked Kirsten down and noted her daily routine. *Almost everyone has a routine*, he believed. Hers was to go for a run every morning at six a.m. through the woods near to her home. The killer was suspicious of the true motive for her philanthropy but was nevertheless impressed at how well she looked after herself. At the age of forty-four she was undeniably beautiful and retained a body that much younger women would undoubtedly envy.

Even though she was nearly twenty years older than he, the killer imagined meeting her for secret assignations in swanky hotel rooms. His penchant for killing women definitely didn't preclude him from also desiring them. Such a pity that she had married the wrong man.

He needed to be much more judicious with the preparation for this hunt. The Netzers' splendid house was heavily protected by security cameras and Kirsten herself was seldom alone. So, the fact that she jogged solo early every morning in the woods was an unexpected gift that fell right into his lap.

****

When Kirsten Netzer left her house for her daily run that bitter morning, she couldn't have possibly imagined that she wouldn't make lunch later with representatives from the Frankfurter Kultur Foundation, or that this would be the last day of her life. She jogged along a frost-crisped track, her blonde ponytail bouncing rhythmically from side to side. Chalky plumes of breath curled around her moisturised lips.

She was listening to *The Drinking Song* from *La Traviata* when she was stopped by an incredibly handsome young man with black glossy hair and a charming smile. Despite being in the middle of the woods, and it being so early in the morning, she wasn't alarmed. The man was in uniform and looked as if he had approached her in some official capacity. She removed her headphones to hear what he had to say.

"Frau Netzer, I am so sorry to trouble you but your husband has asked me to find you. It's a matter of extreme urgency regarding a terrorist threat, not only to him but also to yourself."

"Oh? But Otto hasn't phoned me. Could you please allow me to call him?"

No sooner had she entered the passcode into her mobile than he plunged his knife blade deep into her neck. At first she recoiled in wide-eyed horror and searched his face as if to find some motive for his brutality. As arterial blood spurted through her elegant fingers, Placido Domingo's dramatic voice could still be heard seranading through the headphones that looped around her savaged neck.

"This is my nature," he said matter of factly, as if gifting Kirsten an explanation. He watched her crumple to the ground, her life force ebbing away.

The killer retrieved her mobile phone from the ground and was irritated to notice that blood spatters had marked the sleeve of his uniform. Standing above Kirsten, like a phantom, he took a photograph of her blanched face, now frozen in a terrified rictus.

****

Otto Netzer was drinking black coffee in the kitchen of their home when his wife sent him a text while out on her early morning run. Smiling to himself in anticipation of something amusing, he tapped the screen to access the image attachment.

CHAPTER TWENTY-TWO

Returning Home

Calum's hand hurt like hell. He hadn't noticed until he returned to his room the previous night. It didn't concern him particularly; it was the sort of thing you should expect from slamming your fist against hard bone. He wondered if Sawat had any similar injuries but thought it best to avoid the prickly subject when they were due to meet later that morning.

And uppermost in his mind, no matter how many times he tried to invalidate his recollection of the ghost on the sea bed, it seemed undeniable. He had clearly encountered something so questionable, and so unlikely, that he really ought to keep it to himself. His suppressed comprehension of such a strange discovery was already causing him talk to himself, occasionally blurting out unanswered questions to an empty room.

On the way to breakfast, he couldn't walk more than twenty paces without receiving a cheerful greeting, or a dignified *wai*. He needed to be at Phuket International Airport by late morning, so rushed breakfast and strode purposefully back to his room, allowing himself enough time to pack and to also meet with Sawat on the beach.

His effervescent room maids were frantically cleaning a neighbouring room when he called on them to offer a farewell tip. Receiving their money, they circled him in a tight hug, both of their heads only just coming up to his chest.

When he walked into his own room, a fly was repeatedly beating itself against the glass of the patio door. Calum slid open the door, hoping to allow it out but it lay on its back with its legs in the air, buzzing. Once it remembered how to fly, it launched itself off the doorsill and darted out into the breezy freedom of the world beyond.

Now that his mind was focused on the journey back to the UK, Calum again thought about Hannah, and the possibility of them becoming more than just good friends. She had inhabited his dreams, slipping naked under his sheets each night as a willing bedmate. His pants tightened. Without question, she had become his favourite nocturnal fantasy.

He recalled a few instances, during his stay at the hotel, where he could have easily enjoyed a passionate fling. There was Paige, the flirtatious Australian surfer-chick who swam up to him at the pool bar; Natasha, the Scottish businesswoman, who grabbed his butt each time he passed, and Astrid, the Viking girl from Stockholm, who insisted that he should come back to her room one booze-fuelled afternoon.

But, despite being sorely tempted, Calum declined each seductive invitation; he had developed a hunger for Hannah's body and soul, a biological urge that compelled him to channel his desire exclusively towards her.

During the course of the holiday he had nearly texted her on more than a few occasions but instead of doing so, he just stared at his phone, unable to make that quantum leap from friend to boyfriend. If the two of them didn't have a history and they had only just met, then it would be ridiculously easy to ask her out on a date.

But here, on the last day of his holiday, prompted by Sawat's words and sitting on a bed covered in crumpled clothes, he decided to bite the bullet and go for it:

> *hey hannah, last day of a holiday in thailand. have been thinking of u since our meet last week. no longer with imogen. was thinking, would u like to go on a date? love, cal xxx p.s. u did look gorgeous!*

He looked at the time on the screen of his iPhone; it read 8:06 which meant it was just after two o'clock in the morning in the UK. He imagined that Hannah would read his message when she woke up. Then, to his surprise, the phone pinged back. As he read the incoming message, a wide smile spread across his face.

> *in a cab after night out with the girls. would LOVE to go on a date. & u didn't look too bad yourself! ;) love n hugs, hannah xxx*

At that precise moment, six thousand miles away, Hannah squealed with delight in the back of a taxi while at the same time sharing the text message with friends, Sophie and Rachel.

Calum reread her message three times. Hannah was already writhing naked in the boudoir of his mind. He grinned like a Cheshire cat, brought the phone to his lips and gave it a loud celebratory kiss.

****

After more or less completing his packing, save for what he was going to be wearing, Calum walked down to the beach expecting to see Sawat waiting for him with his trademark smile lighting up the morning. But he was nowhere to be seen. Calum strode over to Viset, one of the other vendors with whom Sawat was very good friends.

"*Khun* Viset, have you seen *Khun* Sawat?" he asked.

Viset surveyed the beach, expecting to see Sawat somewhere, then shrugged his shoulders. "Maybe Sawat come *proong nee, kap?*" he suggested. "Maybe tomorrow, *kap?*"

Greatly disappointed, Calum scuffed the sand as he strolled back to the hotel grounds, where he stood under a sunshade keeoing a watchful eye on the beach. Frustratingly, both he and Sawat hadn't thought to exchange phone numbers. He stood for nearly an hour, constantly checking his watch. By now he had reached the point where he should have been back in his room. Despite conceding that Sawat just wasn't going to come, he continued to look up the beach, more in hope than in expectation.

Calum had planned to give Sawat the red G-Shock watch, which he knew he liked, as a parting gift. He padded back to Viset and handed him the watch. He spoke slowly and deliberately, not wanting Viset to jump to the conclusion that it was for him.

"*Khun* Viset, this watch it is for Sawat. OK? Can you give it to him?"

Viset nodded his head, fully understanding who it was meant for.

"*Kap Khun kap*, *Khun* Viset."

"*Kap.*"

Calum was crestfallen that his friend hadn't made good on his promise to meet up on the beach. Only last night Sawat stated that they should remain friends for a long time, yet he hadn't bothered to say goodbye. It was confusing, to say the least. He speculated that Sawat might have been angrier than he had let on.

He sprinted back to his room, where he quickly

removed the shorts and the T-shirt that he was wearing. After stuffing them into the suitcase, he called for the bellboys and slipped into his travelling clothes. Shaking his head with incredulity, he stood on his balcony for one last time and gazed in wonder at the small stain of dark water that marred the bright turquoise blanket of the sea.

A little later he heard the suitcase trolley trundling along the corridor. Beyond the threshold of his door stood two bellboys in Star Trek uniforms, one being Nuay, whose head was still dipped to one side, listening to that invisible parrot.

"*Sawasdee kap, Khun* Cal-um!" Nuay greeted, his singsong voice slightly louder in honour of the Englishman's last day.

As Nuay checked the minibar, continuing to talk ten to the dozen, the other guy loaded the suitcase and bags onto the trolley. Nuay's colleague had the disgruntled look of someone accustomed to doing all the work while his chatty cohort received all the recognition. Calum tipped each guy and took one last look at the room to ensure that he'd left nothing behind.

After settling the bill at reception, he walked to the lobby entrance where Nuay's co-worker was already cramming his luggage into a taxi. Banyat, the effeminate concierge, minced over to offer a coquettish goodbye. "Hope to see you again, handsome man," he purred, raising one tweezered eyebrow and clasping Calum's hand.

"Likewise, *Khun* Banyat, thank you for all your help," Calum beamed.

Nuay held the heavy plate glass door open for Calum. The fierce heat of the day immediately violated the cool of the lobby. "Goodbye, *Khun* Calum, we hope to see you at Redfor' Patong Beach Resort again nek' year."

"Thank you, *Khun* Nuay. I hope so too." Calum concurred as he slid into the cab. "Oh, and Nuay?"

"Yes, sir?"

"Watch out for those chicks with dicks!"

CHAPTER TWENTY-THREE

The Shattering of Dreams

An imprecise perception of light bulbs and unfamiliar sounds was all that Sawat could understand of his journey from the dusty road surface to the hospital. He was vaguely aware of forceful voices and an agonised inhuman scream which seemed to come from his own throat. He dimly heard the slam of heavy metal doors and saw a succession of bright ceiling lights streaking overhead, like lane markings on a motorway.

He was in a confused state of consciousness, as yet unaware that the severe neuropathic pain which was coursing through his body was in sharp contrast to the loss of all feeling in his lower torso and legs.

The gurney that transported him rattled into a dimly-lit treatment bay which smelt strongly of disinfectant. Curtains were pulled noisily along a rail and a trauma team crowded his mutilated body. Amid a frenzy of frantic voices an orderly cut at his blood-stained clothes with scissors while nurses swabbed dirt from his puncture wounds and abrasions. At one point, a catheter was inserted into his urethra and a blood bag, hung from a stainless steel stand, slowly filtered its contents into his left arm.

Supanee arrived at the scene to find her broken son attached to various tubes, being attended to by five people, all of whom shared the same concerned expression. The trauma team included a general surgeon, who was later joined by a neurosurgeon and an anaesthesiologist. Sawat's face and lips were grotesquely distended and the swollen skin about his closed right eye was dark as a bruised mangosteen. Sawat's mother was accompanied by daughter Sarai, and Uncle Jao, who had driven them both to the hospital in his pickup.

The attending doctor ushered them to one side. He mentioned the loss of function in Sawat's legs and the probability of paraplegia.

****

The sound of his mother's anguished cries was the first thing that Sawat could remember properly; this, and the repugnant smell of excrement emanating from his bed. He wasn't able to comprehend that his own body was the source of the smell. At that moment, he simply wanted to slide from the bed and walk to his mother and his sister to console them. He also intended to extricate himself from the foul stench of shit, which girdled him on the bed sheet.

He found that he was unable to accomplish either of these straightforward tasks.

CHAPTER TWENTY-FOUR

The Hot Date

On his second day home, Calum discovered that his jetlag wasn't anywhere near as bad travelling west as it had been flying east. Today, he had arranged to meet Hannah for Saturday lunch in Bill's Restaurant at the Back of the Inns, right in the heart of Norwich city centre.

Calum arrived first and selected a table on the first floor, which afforded him a view of the street below. Because he'd never visited the venue before – it was suggested by Hannah – he paid its décor more attention than he would have done otherwise. The restaurant was much more interesting than its lacklustre name suggested. The joint had a New York loft, shabby chic, industrial vibe, with exposed aircon ducts and distressed floorboards.

On the way in, Calum noticed that they had made clever use of some catering-sized tins of Italian olive oil, which had been flattened to create a decorative flourish on the service counter's façade. The place had an easy charm, housing a selection of junk shop leather chairs, and some kitschy candelabras. From his vantage point he could see Hannah approaching and quickly texted her phone, so that she would know he was sitting upstairs.

Despite it being a cold November day, Hannah arrived without a jacket, wearing a crisp white shirt that accentuated her cappuccino skin. Calum enjoyed watching her stride across the floor, causing a dozen interested heads to turn. He rose from his seat to kiss her on both cheeks.

"Wow, you look so tanned," she beamed, holding her forearm against his for comparison. "Nearly as dark as me."

"You look great," he said, waiting for her to park her handbag and sit down. "I like what they've done with the place. I used to buy T-shirts here when it was a beachwear shop."

"Me too," she said, sliding an orange silk scarf from her neck. "I sometimes pop in here with a couple of girls from work during my lunch hour."

In Calum's company, Hannah was already experiencing the same excitement that she once felt as a schoolgirl. He was wearing a sky-blue shirt that not only complemented his tan, but also intensified the impact of his cerulean eyes. Around his neck was a Buddhist necklace which Hannah guessed he'd bought from an exotic market stall in Thailand. She spotted a shiny bruise on his cheekbone and assumed it was sustained while sparring at the karate class.

Calum, meanwhile, was enjoying every detail of Hannah's alluring physicality: the seductive Eden-green eyes, the imperfect gap at the front of her perfect teeth, and the discreet show of lustrous, brown cleavage in the V of her white shirt. Being together like this seemed so natural. There was never a moment of awkward silence and Hannah took every opportunity to touch Calum's hand when she wanted to emphasise specific parts of an anecdote.

They shared a chilled bottle of Pinot Grigio and when Hannah ordered an avocado salad, Calum assumed that she must have become some kind of health food freak during her absence. That was until she ordered apple crumble and custard for dessert.

"So what actually happened with slutty Gibson?" Hannah sassed, shooting him a told-you-so smile, whilst tucking a section of hair behind one ear.

"Well, it will come as no surprise to you that I walked in on her shagging some smarmy bloke from her office. But I'm fairly certain you've already heard all the juicy details from Leo."

"So what made you want to go out with her in the first place?" asked Hannah bristling slightly but trying to hide it.

"I don't know really. She sort of lured me in, like a drive-thru McDonalds. On reflection, we were never really suited."

"Well *something* must have kept you together."

Calum drummed his fingers against his lips and suppressed a naughty boy smile.

"Oh, you dog!" Hannah blurted. "Well, it's not as if she hadn't had much practice."

"Ooohh, saucer of cream for Miss Cunningham," Calum chuckled, draining the last of the wine into their glasses.

At that moment, a familiar face from both their pasts swanned onto their floor: Lucas Saunders, who seemed to be even camper now than when he was at school, had arrived with another guy. They clutched matching Louis Vuitton man bags and walked like marionettes. Lucas's hair had changed dramatically; it had gone from high-school ginger to bleached blond, and was styled into an extravagant quiff that seemed to invalidate Newton's Law of Gravity.

Calum stood up to catch their attention, prompting Lucas to slalom round diners like an airport sniffer dog.

"I seriously *do not* believe it! Calum-flaming-Armstrong and *gorgeous* Hannah Cunningham. Haven't seen you two in years!" his voice was sing-song, his hugs theatrical. "This is Edison, he's from Brazil, and he is my current boyfriend."

"What do you mean *current* boyfriend?" Edison countered, sulkily.

"Well, you'll do for the time being," Lucas teased before turning his attention back to Calum and Hannah. "I always knew that you two would end up being an item. *God knows* what you Olympians get up to in the sack! I imagine you're at it every spare second, like a pair of wild animals!"

Hannah burst into laughter, narrowly managing not to spray the table with wine. Calum followed suit.

"We're not even an item," Hannah explained. "This is kind of like a first date."

"Well, if you're not rutting like wild beasts, then you definitely should!" advised Lucas, while gaining a wider audience, such was the volume of his foppish voice.

"Oh, and you do know that this one is my hero?" he piped, directing a bony finger towards Calum.

"No, how come?" Hannah asked.

"Well, *obviously* because of that time at school when those vile Adcock twins attacked me in the science block."

"Why, what happened?"

"You *don't know?*"

Calum interjected. "I think that Hannah had left for Peterborough by then."

"Oh, my God, Han … They had me pinned to the floor, writing unpleasant things on my back with a frigging marker pen, then in walks Tarzan here, to save the day. He even managed to draw Hitler moustaches on their ugly kissers!"

Picturing the scene, Hannah had a fit of giggles.

"Oh, and guess what Hannah? Dumb and twatting Dumber turn up at school the next day and, hilariously, they *still* had dark smudges under their snotty nostrils!"

At this, Edison burst into enthusiastic applause, clapping his hands in front of his chest, without moving his arms. "And then, just so my day wasn't *totally* ruined, he-man Calum here takes me off to buy me a new shirt. I'd much rather it had been jewellery, mind."

"Aww, Cal, you're *so* sweet!" Hannah teased, pinching his cheeks.

"And d'you know what?" Lucas continued, "I *so-o* had a crush on this one…"

"Yeah, you and just about everyone else," Hannah chuckled.

"You *are* hot," Edison confirmed, looking straight at Calum, secretly wishing he could spend a passionate afternoon with him.

"Anyway," Lucas sighed, "we're going to leave you two lovebirds in peace." He presented Calum with a shiny business card that read *Lucas Saunders, Clinical support worker.* "Don't be a stranger, guys. Those are my contact details. We really should get together sometime. Must fly. Lovely to see you again, mwah, and mwah!"

Lucas and Edison peeled away after a round of hugs and were about to head for a table at the far end of the restaurant, when Calum stopped them in their tracks. "Hey, Lucas!"

"Yeah?"

"You've got something nasty stuck under your left foot…"

"Omigod … where?" Lucas panicked, pirouetting on one leg like a flamingo to examine the sole of his shoe.

"Oooh, get you!" Calum chuckled, wafting his hands in Lucas's direction, delighted that he'd made him strike such a camp pose.

"Oh, you bleeding tosser!" Lucas cursed, before slapping Edison on the arm for joining in the chorus of giggles.

"Hannah, I take back all the nice things I said about him earlier," Lucas harrumphed. "You're *far* too good for him. Must fly, *ciao!*"

"Aww, this is precisely the kind of thing that I missed after I left Norwich," Hannah cooed. "In Peterborough I felt so disconnected. There just wasn't anyone with whom I could really have fun with. And of course I loved hanging around with you."

"Well, if it's any consolation, me and Leo missed you like crazy, too."

"Hey, Cal, can you remember that time when you tricked Gollum into eating those joke shop sweets?"

Calum grinned at the memory. "Yeah, yeah, and his mouth went blue."

"Well, I've recently found the school photo from that year and noticed that Gollum had to keep his hand over his mouth for the duration of the shoot."

"Oh, excellent," Calum cheered. "I'd love to see that photo."

"And here's another thing that I always liked about you, Cal – you hardly ever swore. All of the other boys were total potty-mouths."

"Well, it's great that you have this virtuous view of me, Hannah, but I *do* swear when the situation requires it."

"Oh yeah? Like when?"

"Like, you are *so* fuckable, that if we weren't in a restaurant in broad daylight, I would love to take you right now."

"And I'd let you," she said, without flinching. A mischievous smile played across her face. An electric moment of silence passed between them; sexual chemistry and eye contact became their conversation.

"We really need to get our freak on," Hannah purred, stroking his collar.

"Fuck, yeah," agreed Calum.

****

They decided to meet for dinner that evening, at Calum's. His house on Dover Street was handily situated for shops, bars and restaurants. In fact, if you stood at his front gate and spat out an olive stone, you could almost hit the Mad Moose gastro pub. In common with most terraced streets, there were long lines of vehicles parked on each side, allowing barely enough space for a fire engine to pass through.

When Hannah's taxi pulled up, Calum opened the front door sporting a pair of tapered chinos and a smart navy blue shirt, which he wore with the sleeves rolled up to his biceps. Earlier, he'd sprayed Vera Wang eau de toilette about himself and a waft of it reached his nostrils as the cool night air breezed into his face. Before Hannah had the chance to pay the fare, he scurried to the driver's window clutching his wallet.

"Very gentlemanly," she said, approvingly.

Hannah stepped from the cab, in a floaty maxi dress that brought some summer colour to the cold November night. A firework fizzed and burst across the night sky, adding to the excitement of her arrival. "I've been thinking about you all afternoon," she declared, moving into his personal space.

Calum's intention was to greet her with a chaste peck on each cheek, but this somehow developed into an impassioned kiss whilst they stood on the pathway to his front door. Hannah instinctively pushed her hips into him. She felt him grow and continued the kiss, ruffling his short hair with her fingernails.

"Mmm, you smell nice," she whispered, when they

finally paused for air. Her voice was low and husky, betraying the urgency of her desire.

"And so do you," replied Calum, acutely aware of the burgeoning tension in his tight briefs. His pants constricted some more when she bit her lower lip and cast a passing glance at his promising bulge.

"So, are you actually going to invite me in or are you going to leave me panting on the doorstep?" she teased, coquettishly raising her eyebrows.

Hanging from the crook of her arm was a large, flowery holdall. "What on earth is that?" he asked.

"It's my overnight bag," she breezed.

"Bit presumptuous," he grinned, letting Hannah coast into the hallway ahead of him.

Not sure where to go, she allowed Calum to guide her through to the dining room where he'd carefully assembled a colourful platter of sushi on top of a tempered glass table.

"I collected these from Shiki, the Japanese restaurant on Tombland," he explained, absent-mindedly drumming chopsticks on the rim of a plate.

Hannah barely acknowledged the food. Instead, she took Calum's hand and led him up the staircase, acting almost as if he had walked into her domain. On the landing, she saw that the main bedroom was lit by a trio of scented candles that softened the darkness with a dreamy glow. On top of the bedside cabinet was an aluminium ice bucket which held an opened bottle of Veuve Clicquot in its frigid grip.

"Also presumptuous," she chuckled, pulling him towards her by his trouser belt.

They undressed each other in the half-light of the room. She helpfully unclasped her Agent Provocateur bra and let it fall to the floor. Naked now, except for a diamante necklace, she exhibited her body, allowing him to feast his eyes on her firm breasts and slender body. Calum stood in his white briefs, undeniably aroused. His physique was as buff as she had imagined – he could have easily graced the front cover of *Men's Fitness* magazine.

The time for flirtation had passed. She gazed into his eyes with a sudden serious intent and peeled away his pants to release his eager cock, which felt agreeably hard in the palm of her hand. Hannah guided him to the bed and continued to work him with her fingers. Calum flipped her onto the mattress, where she flung her arms behind her head in wanton abandonment. He smothered her velvety skin with soft kisses whilst she ground her pubis against his thigh. Her fingers traced the corrugation of his hard abs and he cupped her breasts and sucked at the firmness of her dark nipples.

Calum recognised the hunger in her eyes and felt the urgency in her hips.

"Look what you're doing to me," she whispered, guiding his fingers to her pussy. She dug her nails into his buttocks and drew him closer. His aching shaft discovered her inner wetness.

"What about...?" he started to ask, wondering if he needed to retrieve a condom from the bedside drawer.

"Relax, I've got it covered," she hushed, touching his lips.

With no further need for words, he placed one palm against her taut stomach and then, after lifting one of her legs, thrust himself deep inside her. Hannah gasped, whispered his name, and wrapped one leg around his hip, orchestrating his rhythm with a metronomic dig of her heel. She flopped one arm across her forehead, as if it were suddenly boneless. Whilst they moved together, he enjoyed the low sound of her groans and the slick intimacy of her athletic body.

When her orgasm came, she arched her back and

clamped her hand against her own mouth to muffle the noise of her groans. Then, when Calum was done, she opened her green eyes languidly and smiled up at him, sharing his heartbeat. He exhaled a satisfied puff of breath, before offering her an 'I'm all yours' smile.

"God, I love you," she gasped, without any self-consciousness. Tears of happiness had formed in the rims of her eyes.

"I love you too," he grinned, surprised that the words arrived at his lips so readily.

Hannah stretched, cat-like, underneath him; her sleepy smile showcased her perfect teeth, with that tiny gap which Calum found so incredibly sexy.

"You *bad* boy," she said, elongating herself to reach for some tissues.

"I can be badder," he confirmed, fishing the Champagne bottle from the ice bucket and pouring her a glass.

"Go for it," she urged.

CHAPTER TWENTY-FIVE

Bad Karma

For some reason, police crime reconstructions in Thailand often descend into a carnival atmosphere that is totally at odds with the gravity of the situation.

On the day of the Loy Krathong Festival of Light, when all bad luck is carried away by river and sea, Sawat's three assailants were paraded in front of the local media while their uniformed captors smiled and posed for jaunty photographs. With the sun reflecting off the shiny black batons and holstered handguns that hung from their belts, the policemen were snapped pointing towards the attackers, almost as if the audience needed reminding that the men sitting on the floor in handcuffs were indeed the accused. The whole event was a macabre slapstick sitcom, with the rueful fishermen being forced to re-enact the way in which they attacked Sawat as the police ridiculed them.

Despite having the stomach of a pot-bellied pig, causing his tight laurel-green uniform to resemble overstuffed vine leaves, Police Chief Colonel Pongrit Somwan happily got in on the act. After tyrannically stomping about the crime scene like Napoleon Bonaparte for at least two hours, he put in a modelling stint for the cameras as if he had suddenly morphed into a catwalk queen.

The bedraggled fishermen displayed varying degrees of facial damage and looked so sheepish and repentant that it was extremely difficult to imagine any of them being capable of such horrific cruelty. Their blood-stained weapons were splayed out on the ground before them at the same location where the assault had taken place. It was reported that the victim had sustained thirty-six puncture wounds, multiple broken bones and was now paralysed from the waist down.

****

Uncle Jao dipped into the savings he had diligently set aside for his own cataract operation to help Supanee with the sudden shortfall caused by Sawat's inability to work. Supanee, Sarai and Nok took turns to be by Sawat's bedside twenty-four hours a day.

Despite Sawat's exhaustion, he brightened dramatically when Viset brought him the red G-Shock watch which Calum had gifted. Nok would have preferred him to have refused the present, feeling nothing but hot anger towards the Englishman for initiating the sequence of events that led to her boyfriend becoming crippled.

Each day, Sawat felt no external sensation from the doctor's pinprick tests to his legs, yet internally it felt as if someone was raking barbed wire down his thighs and shinbones. His legs might just as well have been banana leaves for all the use they afforded him, oh but when he slept he was transported to a parallel universe, where his limbs regained their purpose. In his dreams he cycled to the *Muay Thai* gymnasium after school, where he was once again able to thud his bare shins into leather punch bags; he gleefully jogged on soft sand beaches, and even climbed the steps of a glittering temple that was so high it rose like a mountain into the clouds.

In one dream, he found himself back at *Khun* Mae's food stall in the dawn light, eating delicious steamed rice with squid. He wasn't sure why he'd never thought to do it before, but he was beginning to tell Mae how much he loved her. Then, without warning and before he could finish his heartfelt declaration, the *tsunami* thundered in like a passing express train, and swept her away again.

Supanee studied her son whilst he slept, seeing her own features in the serenity of his still face. It was plain to see that he'd inherited her almond-shaped eyes and his father's squashed nose. Apart from the pink scar that branched out from one corner of his mouth, his smooth skin was youthfully unblemished. It broke her heart that upon waking, and despite the awfulness of his situation, he flashed the same optimistic smile that used to grace Boonrit's face when he was alive. She missed her husband terribly; even now, more than a decade after his watery death, Supanee still couldn't pass by his photograph without touching it and telling him all about her day.

Forever etched in her memory was that stormy night when Boonrit's brother appeared at her door in the middle of a typhoon. As a savage wind whipped at the loose hood of Jao's rain mac, the tremble of his lips was enough to convey the terrible news he had to deliver. Although Sawat had since become the man of the house, with all the noble attributes of his brave father, Supanee was now obliged to regard him once more as her vulnerable little boy.

Sawat, for his part, was consumed with guilt. It seemed too much of a coincidence that on the same day he revisited the sea ghost, he also became a cripple. It was common knowledge among Buddhists that bad deeds led to bad karma, thereby provoking future suffering. He felt that by foolishly antagonising the sea ghost he had returned despair and poverty to his mother's world.

With so little else to offer her, his only hope was that his encouraging smile might mitigate some of her sadness.

Supanee was at a loss about what to do in such a desperate situation. It didn't seem enough just to plump up the pillows behind her son's head, to offer words of encouragement, or to fetch him food and water.

The Thai government's welfare program ensured that his family didn't have to bear the burden of paying for Sawat's current – and future – hospital care. Then, when he was strong enough to return home, he would have to adapt to life in a wheelchair.

On one occasion - when he was alone with his girlfriend - Sawat, in a moment of selflessness, suggested to Nok that her life would be better without him. She was incredulous that he should entertain such an idea and scrunched her face up in astonishment:

She plucked tissues from a box and wiped the tears from his distraught face, then dabbed at her own wet cheeks. With all the strength he could muster, and racked with pain, Sawat hoisted his shoulders off the bed.

"I hope that one day, Nok, I can make you proud of me."

Nok sat by his side, gently held his broken fingers and slid her other hand through his hair. "Can't you see, Sawat, I am already so proud of you."

CHAPTER TWENTY-SIX

Hungry Hippo

Hannah's mother, Sinéad, and her father, Marvin, were getting on each other's nerves in their kitchen. Marvin was attempting to eat spicy chicken drumsticks that Sinéad had only just dragged from the oven. Despite being too hot to even hold, he tried to gnaw at their steaming flesh, foolishly imagining that a short puff of breath was enough to cool them down.

Sinéad, who had so far managed to bite her lip, folded her arms disapprovingly, hoping to God that he would blister his tongue. Marvin pretended to be unaware of her Medusa stare and continued to juggle hot chicken in his mouth. His wife couldn't hold back any longer: "Sweet Jesus, just look at yourself. Those drumsticks are as hot as coals, you prize idiot. Can you not wait until they're properly served on the table?"

"I'm hungry," he grumbled, his face like that of a sorrowful bear. "But, man, these are truly delicious."

"You're getting far too fat," she taunted, before seeking some back-up from her daughter who, enticed by the smell of food, had just entered the kitchen.

"Hannah, isn't your father getting fat?"

"Well he *has* put on a little bit of weight…" She winced, not wanting to hurt his feelings.

"See! Even your daughter thinks you're fat!"

"Mum, that's not entirely fair. He's *not* fat, he's a big guy, it suits him."

It was true that Marvin was an imposing man; the sort of guy you would see in the role of black police station chief in a gritty New York cop drama. Because his pretty wife was as willowy as a catwalk model, she could eat like a sumo wrestler and never gain an ounce, whereas her once-gladiatorial husband had periodically throttled his armchair into submission just by sitting on it.

Sinéad continued her tirade with a fervour usually only seen at an evangelical rally. "Your father will eat a sandwich that's as fat as a telephone directory and then shortly afterwards he'll moan that he's starving."

Hannah felt that she should still fight his corner. "So, Mum, if you don't want him to put on weight, why do you keep cooking him so much food?"

"Well, he used to have a dreamy body like an Olympian when we first met. Now he looks like the Hungry Hippo."

"Oh Mum, that's *way* too harsh."

Marvin, as always, remained impervious to his wife's barbs and blithely grabbed another hot drumstick from the tray. "Well, you know what my Mom always says to me? Better your belly bust, than good food go to waste."

At this, Sinéad's frown quickly disappeared, replaced by a sparkling Irish smile. "Ahh, but just look at him," she said with adoring eyes. "Now, who in the world wouldn't love him?"

Marvin held the ravaged chicken bone in his hand and stood like a guilty schoolboy. A slick of red grease glistening his lips. "I've burnt my damn tongue," he said, sorrowfully.

CHAPTER TWENTY-SEVEN

Nest building

Calum couldn't understand why his chest was straining, or how he had somehow returned to the Andaman seabed and was staring once more at the illuminated face of a mythical creature.

Five fathoms underwater and desperate for oxygen, he kicked for the surface. The creature implored Calum to stay, although its words could not be heard. Its mouth moved in speech, but it was as silent as a fish. The creature's eyes bulged with a frantic desperation and it grabbed hold of one of Calum's legs to stop him leaving. As his lungs filled with seawater, Calum's last thought was that he would never see Hannah again...

****

Calum erupted, bolt upright, from the duvet and gulped noisily at the night air in his bedroom.

"Hey babe, it's just a nightmare," Hannah whispered, stroking his arm.

"Wha'? Yeah ... God I'm fine ... please honey, get back to sleep."

Hannah rolled over into a foetal position, momentarily

wishing Calum would share his anxieties with her, before sinking into a deep slumber again.

****

By mid-December, when only the most stubborn of leaves were still clinging to bare twigs, Hannah had stealthily soft-furnished Calum's terraced house and de bachelorised it. Initially, she'd only stayed over at weekends, returning from pubs and restaurants eager to enjoy each other's bodies. But pretty soon she had all but moved in, introducing dramatic cushions and scented candles to his austere house. Not that Calum minded. He secretly enjoyed opening his bathroom cabinet to suddenly find magenta bottles of perfume, pouches of wet wipes, and sachets of Frizz Ease. He loved the fact that his house was starting to feel like a home.

Until she lived with him, Hannah had no idea how much time and effort Calum devoted to his karate training. Every day, without fail, he set the alarm for 5.30 a.m. so he could take his early morning run. Then, whenever he wasn't teaching or training at the sports centre, he stretched his legs for more than an hour, like a ballet dancer, to improve flexibility.

It didn't take long for Hannah to discover some of his bad habits. In addition to using the laundry basket as a podium for his dirty washing, rather than bothering to lift the lid to drop the clothes inside, she didn't enjoy seeing him demonstrate the canine instincts of a bulldog by chewing on pens and pencils. He even gnawed at the TV remote control.

Calum, for his part, found his house suddenly exhausted of power outlets, such were the number of Hannah's leads and electrical devices. In addition, he became accustomed to fishing out mucilaginous sods of black hair from plugholes that had suddenly ceased to function.

"Look, Han, a bird could build a nest out of that," he teased, holding the soggy mess against his chin to form a beard. But trifling bad habits aside, they grew closer and more in love each day, both managing to find a work/life balance that suited their busy schedules.

Because of the burden of parking permits and the scarcity of vehicle spaces on Calum's street Hannah left her shiny Mini Cooper at home, preferring to be chauffeured to work, and step classes, in Calum's utilitarian Land Rover, replete with its scabs of rusted metal. Although the car somehow suited Calum's heroic personality, she didn't instantly warm to it; when he first introduced her to his pride and joy, she placed her hands on her hips and said, "Are we going on a safari?"

To supplement his income as a martial arts instructor, Calum helped his father install boilers and radiators in people's homes. Working part-time allowed him the freedom to continue his training with the England karate squad. Hannah was impressed that nothing ever seemed to faze him. Even his famously short temper appeared to be a thing of the past. But despite his air of calm assuredness, Hannah's sleep was interrupted from time to time by his recurring nightmares, the subject of which remained a tight-lipped mystery.

Weeks earlier, on his first day back in England, Calum scoured the internet for mention of creatures that were half-man, half-bird. Under the heading 'Avian humanoids' he learnt about mythical creatures such as the Valkyrie and the Garuda. But the one fabled hybrid that jumped out at him from his iPad screen were the Kinnaree of Thailand. He recalled Sawat using the same word to describe the sea ghost. All the descriptions bore some resemblance to the creature he'd witnessed in Patong. The Kinnaree were described as having the upper body of a human, plus the legs and wings of a swan. The male of the species – which the one in Patong bay most definitely was – were called Kinnara.

Calum discovered that descriptions of the Swan People's nature had been translated from ancient Sanskrit religious texts:

We are everlasting lover and beloved.
We never separate.
We are eternally husband and wife; never do we become mother and father.
No offspring is seen in our lap.
We are lover and beloved, ever-embracing.
Our life is a life of perpetual pleasure.

He was bursting to tell Hannah about his holiday dalliance with a submerged mythical creature but, after rehearsing the improbable story in his head, he realised that this would be a most ridiculous idea.

****

When he arrived to pick Hannah up from the Aviva offices on Surrey Street, Calum waited with the window down, allowing a cold blast of December air to chill his face. She approached while listening to music through headphones, dancing towards his Land Rover like someone in an R & B video. She poked her head into his car for a quick kiss and then pranced energetically round to the passenger side:

"Party rock is in the house to-nighhht, everybody just have a good time!"

Calum couldn't help but grin, her one-woman dance party continued inside the car, and each time he tried to speak, she'd press a theatrical finger to his lips.

"Every day I'm shufferlin'...!"

Hannah bounced about in her seat and pumped her elbows like there was no tomorrow, undeterred that she was getting some of the words wrong and that amused passers-by were beginning to point into the vehicle. Then, when the music stopped, she made a face like Popeye to puff out some air and sedately fastened her seatbelt.

"Finished?" chuckled Calum, as he turned the key in the ignition.

"Yeah, I'm good thanks," she said, a little breathlessly.

"Guess what?" said Calum. "You know your parents asked if my dad could come round to replace the faulty ball valve in their loft?"

"Ye-es?"

"Well, he's going round there tonight – free of charge, obviously."

"Wow, that's great. But I can't see my dad letting him get away without paying him something…"

"Seriously, he won't mind, and he lives on Dussindale anyway. Besides, it's a simple job, even I could do it."

"Oh God, Cal, I've just thought … your father hasn't met my parents. Your dad is outspoken, my mum's really gobby – it's a recipe for disaster!"

"Relax, it'll be fine. My dad loves a bit of verbal sparring."

"My money's on my mum."

"Yeah, same."

****

Calum's father, Gary, arrived at the Cunninghams' front door and ignored the doorbell, preferring the sharp rat-a-tat-tat of the knocker. When Marvin appeared at the door, Gary waved a ball valve above his head, as if he was bidding at an auction.

"I'm Gary, Calum's dad, come to fit you a new ball valve."

"Gary, come in! I'm Marvin, pleasure to meet you," effused Mr Cunningham, pumping Gary's hand with great gusto.

Hannah's mother joined them in the hallway, "Hello, Gary, it's grand of you to come round. I'm Sinéad, wife of this great lump. I must warn you now, I'm Irish so I can talk the hind legs off a donkey."

"When we were in Jamaica last year, I swear she even got sunburn on her tongue," Marvin said, laughing at his own joke.

"The thing I love about the Irish," Gary chirped, "is that they ignore anything they can't drink or punch."

"I'll punch *you* if you keep talking drivel like that," beamed Mrs Cunningham, waving a friendly fist in Gary's direction.

"Tea, white, one sugar, please," instructed Gary, pushing his luck.

"You'll get it over your head," she quipped, heading for the kitchen with a smile on her face.

"You and me are going to get on fine," Marvin chuckled, as they climbed the staircase after Gary had found the stopcock. "Do you want me to get the ladder down?"

"Ha! I think I can manage, Marv. I've encountered more loft ladders than you've had hot dinners," Gary said with an overconfidence in his voice, inviting hubris with each word.

He unlatched the trapdoor. Then, as he unhooked the ladder, it shot down like a toboggan and hit him squarely on the forehead. The blow poleaxed him, leaving him sprawled, semi-conscious, on the landing carpet.

As Gary came to, Marvin was looming over him like a Caribbean grim reaper. "Are you OK, man?" he asked, worried that a shiny bump the size of a quail's egg had already appeared above Gary's eyebrows, "I really need to get that ladder fixed."

"No shit," croaked Gary.

CHAPTER TWENTY-EIGHT

Christmas Moonwalk

Because both Hannah and Calum's fathers had immediately hit it off, Sinéad invited the Armstrongs round on the twenty-third of December for pre-Christmas drinks and nibbles. Word of this harmonious development was music to the ears of Hannah and Calum, who were also due at the Cunningham family home.

Stopping off at Sainsbury's, they headed to the wine aisle to buy two bottles of Champagne, which were advertised as half price during the festive period.

"This is the one," Hannah said, scrutinising the label. "Oh, my God!" She hissed, nudging Calum to alert him to two guys who were sliding bottles of Absolut vodka into concealed pouches within their coats. "It's the Adcock twins!"

"Han, just ignore them."

"What do you mean ignore them? This is my dad's supermarket! How can I ignore them?"

Hannah's whisper had become a raised voice, which attracted the attention of Dumb and Dumber. They glared over with a familiar feral intensity. Each boy had bulked up since school and heavily-tattooed hands emerged from their coat sleeves. Sudden recognition appeared on their cheerless faces:

"Whatchu looking at, Armstrong?" Dumber growled.

"Nothing much," Calum replied, placing himself between Hannah and the twins.

"You thought you were something special at school, dintcha?"

"Not particularly."

"Don't mean nothing now, you fucking prick."

"I'm sure it doesn't."

"He's fucking scared," Dumb snorted, with a gratified smirk on his rodent face.

"You're dead right, I'm scared, terrified in fact, so how about we all pretend we haven't seen each other and go our separate ways?"

The twins fell silent for a while, but continued to look at Calum as if his very being repulsed them. "Next time we see you, Armstrong, we won't be so charitable, but as it's Christmas, you've dodged a beating, you fucking ponce!"

"I'm extremely grateful."

With a triumphant spring in their step, Dumb and Dumber peeled away and clanked like a bottle bank towards the front of the store.

"God, you *have* changed," marvelled Hannah, proudly rubbing the small of Calum's back.

"Glad you were impressed."

"Admit it, though, you probably *were* scared, really," she winked.

After paying for the Champagne at the self-service checkout, Hannah suddenly jabbed Calum with the gold foil end of the bottle that she was carrying "Look! Look!" she shouted. She could see Dumb and Dumber outside the exit doors, wrestling on the frozen tarmac with three security guards, who were trying to detain them for shoplifting.

Hannah quickened her step to get nearer to the action; Calum duly followed.

"Merry Christmas boys," she chimed, offering the twins a cheery wave as she passed by in the frosty air.

****

On the short drive to Hannah's home, Calum confessed to having had a schoolboy crush on her mother.

"And there was I thinking that you came round just to see me," Hannah chuckled.

Once inside the warmth of the Cunningham's house, kisses were exchanged and Calum felt the bone-crushing grip of Mr Cunningham's handshake.

"Oooh, Champagne," Hannah's mother clucked. "Mind you, I've never heard of this brand, is it from Albania?"

"Mum, guess what? Calum had a schoolboy crush on you."

"Oh, thanks, Hannah!" Calum groaned, his face suddenly flushed with embarrassment.

"And who could blame the poor boy?" Sinéad beamed, before shovelling ice cubes into a stainless steel bucket.

Marvin had yet to form an educated opinion of Calum, only remembering him as the boy who couldn't be bothered to turn up on the day they left for Peterborough, thereby leaving his daughter in tears. As a teenager, Calum had only ever seen Hannah's father on a few brief occasions; he always found him a big, playful man, who seemed inordinately pleased with life. So, when Marvin suggested that he and Calum should 'have a little chat' while Hannah and her mother were preparing food in the kitchen, he wasn't overly concerned, despite Marvin's heavy arm bearing down on his shoulders like a fallen tree trunk.

"So Calum, I wanted to touch base with you. I can see

that Hannah thinks the world of you and as far as I can tell, you are her first serious boyfriend."

Calum noticed a distinct change in Mr Cunningham's accent; there was a sudden Jamaican Rude Boy edge to his normally jovial voice:

"Now I am a simple guy, Calum, a simple, simple guy. If Hannah is happy, then I am happy too. My family means *everything* to me … you get me?"

"Yeah, yeah, of course," Calum stuttered, not quite sure where this was leading.

"So, Calum, if you treat my little Hannah right, I will love you like my own son."

"I'd like that," Calum brightened, hoping that this awkward chat might be nearing its conclusion.

"I have good instincts, Calum, and I've got faith in you. Please don't let me down."

"Mr Cunningham, I want you to know that Hannah is in my heart. I think she's amazing."

Marvin slapped his big hand into Calum's palm and shoulder-bumped him, before swamping him in a bear hug. "Come on, let's get you a beer," he smiled, turning once more into Mr Cunningham, the middle-aged supermarket manager.

****

When the doorbell rang, heralding the arrival of Calum's parents, Sinéad scurried to the door, patting her hair and casting off her apron like a stage actress during costume change. She ushered in the Armstrongs as if they were old friends, interspersing greetings with loud, theatrical kisses.

When she sashayed into the kitchen to fetch Champagne, Victoria's instinct was to follow her.

"Marv, 'cause you're from Jamaica, I've brought you some bottles of Red Stripe." Gary explained.

"Hey, that'll do for starters. I'm more of a Guinness

man myself. Come, let's get drinking before they find us something to do."

"Where are the two lovebirds?"

"Oh, they're out in the garden, kicking a ball about."

"Outside? But it's bloody freezing!"

Victoria, who had been privately-educated at an exclusive boarding school in Hampshire, felt slightly intimidated by the streetwise, combustible personality of Sinéad. The woman was vivacious and terrifying in equal measures. Victoria hoped that by helping her out with the food, she could get onto her good side. Sinéad delighted in listening to Victoria's cut-glass accent, thinking that the woman reminded her of someone from a 1970s' sitcom.

The kitchen window overlooked the halogen-lit back garden, where Hannah and Calum scampered about the frosty lawn, punting a party-deflated football which belonged to Marcus.

"Ahh, now would you just look at my daughter?" Sinéad cooed. "Fabulous legs right up to her armpits."

"Well, yes, she does have a great set of pins," Victoria affirmed, not quite knowing how to respond to such a statement.

"Of course she was very much the same when she was born. Jesus, it was like giving birth to a stork!"

"How lovely for you," Victoria chuckled. Sinéad's effervescent company and the half-price Champagne were swiftly dissolving her guardedness.

Gary and Marvin cemented their bromance by discovering they were both into hip-hop and breakdancing, back in the day, so when food was spread across the dining table, they insisted on sitting next to each other so they could muck about like overgrown schoolboys.

Marcus, who had already eaten, introduced himself to Calum's parents before announcing that he was retiring to his bedroom. Tucked into the back of his tracksuit bottoms was an illicit packet of chocolate digestive biscuits.

"So, Gary, how did you two meet?" Sinéad enquired, curious to understand how this Jack-the-lad had bagged a princess.

"Well, as you can see, Victoria is quite posh, and I'm her bit of rough."

"Posh! I *hate* that word," Victoria harrumphed.

"Vicky was doing an ecology degree at the University of East Anglia, which is where I first saw her at a Pet Shop Boys gig, in the mid-eighties."

"Was she your *West End Girl?*" Marvin chuckled, digging Gary in the ribs.

"Well, from the word go, I could tell she was classy. When I asked her what she wanted to drink, she said 'a glass of Chablis please' - and there was me expecting something along the lines of a Bacardi and Coke. In fact, Vicky is *so* posh, she actually gets out of the bath if she needs to have a wee."

"And Sinéad, how did you and Marvin meet?" Victoria interjected, knowing that if she didn't quickly change the subject, Gary would describe every explicit detail of their first night of passion.

"Hell, you wouldn't think it to look at him now, but my darling husband used to be an aerobics instructor…"

"Get away!" Gary roared, almost leaping out of his chair.

"It's true! I was one of the girls in his class. He had tidy dreadlocks and buns of steel back then. All of the women lusted after him."

"Good on you, Marvy boy!" Gary shouted, slapping him on the back. "Bet you had your fair share of hot totty."

Marvin barely stifled a grin. "Well, I can't really…"

"Oh, sweet Mother of God, didn't he just?" Sinéad interjected. "I'm only surprised he didn't catch anything."

Hannah and Calum were superfluous to the social

activity that surrounded them, and sat back to enjoy the show.

"So, Shin, can you tell us anything embarrassing about Mister Motivator here?" Gary asked.

"Oh, I have plenty, don't you worry," Sinéad purred, opening the second bottle of Champagne. Marvin rolled his eyes, in resigned anticipation. "OK, so here's a typical example of how my wonderful husband stampedes through life like a bull in a haystack…"

"I think you'll find that's a mixed metaphor," Marvin interrupted.

"I'll mixed-metaphor you, if you keep butting in!" she barked. "So, before we were married we lived together in a tiny house in London. I'd invited my mother and father to come over from Dublin, so they could meet this little charmer. Well, on that day, he gets himself into a rare old flap, fussing over this and that. Then, the doorbell rings and there's my mammy and daddy, ready to greet him with open arms. But, oh no, *that* would be too normal, wouldn't it? *This* is what *actually* happened…"

"Oooh, this is gonna be good," said Gary, excitedly.

"He rushes to the door, all-of-a-fluster, and says to them, 'Look, I'm really sorry, but I haven't got time for this. I'm sure you're both very nice people, but I've got family coming over from Ireland.' And then he shuts the sodding door in their faces!"

"Oh, classic!" Gary yelled.

"I thought they were Jehovah's Witnesses," Marvin explained, chuckling at the memory.

"And to think that Sainsbury's trust him to run one of their stores," Sinéad, concluded, with a resigned shake of her head.

Whilst his wife went off to get more drinks, Marvin disappeared upstairs and fumbled about in the spare room, returning with some 1980s' baseball caps so that both he and Gary could wear them back-to-front in an act of middle-aged defiance.

"Euw, cringe!" Hannah groaned, secretly loving the fact that they were both having such boisterous fun together.

"Hey, Victoria, there must be some equally embarrassing tales about Gary," Marvin prompted.

"Oh, my God, yes," declared Victoria, keen to turn the tables on her husband, "Hapless Harry, here, can definitely trump your own experience."

"Go on, Mum!" Calum urged.

"So, right from the outset, my parents didn't like the sound of Gary. They would have much preferred that I dated someone more suitable … an architect, or a doctor perhaps. In truth, they are consummate snobs but that's by the by. So, on their very first meeting with him, I was hoping he might put his best foot forward and succeed in charming them."

Marvin started to bubble with excitement at this point, while Gary clamped both hands over his face.

"OK, so they have literally just met, Gary has introduced himself and has shaken my father's hand, so far, so good. But then he somehow imagined he could endear himself to my prissy mother by removing a stray eyelash that had fallen onto her chin…"

Hannah and Sinéad were on the edge of their seats, both pre-empting what happened next. Marvin, who was also rapt with attention, took a distracted swig of Guinness.

"Of course, the eyelash *wasn't* an eyelash at all – and it remained stubbornly attached, even after he tugged at it a few times!"

At this, Hannah and her mother collapsed into a fit of throat-choking laughter. Marvin sprayed stout as a fire-eater spurts flames; his ribs threatened to break asunder and tears cascaded down his well-fed cheeks.

"Well, if I knew I'd be marrying into a family of bearded ladies, I might have thought twice about buying her that first Chablis," Gary grinned, delighted to be the source of such amusement.

"I love you man," Marvin spluttered, initiating a hi-five.

"I love you too," Gary gulped, feigning choked emotion. The two men hugged each other like long-lost brothers.

"Dear God, we've married a couple of idiots!" Sinéad wailed.

"Man, these girls really drew the short straw with us," Marvin said, saluting Gary with his beer bottle.

"The sad thing is they stayed with us, how stupid is that?" Gary crowed, clinking Marvin's bottle in triumph. Sinéad looked as annoyed as an owl.

Once the table was cleared, and crockery stacked into the dishwasher, the evening's entertainment revolved around the two fathers trying to recapture their youth, by busting some best-forgotten dance moves.

Hannah and her mother checked in on Marcus, who was sound asleep with the TV on in a bed sprinkled with a thousand biscuit crumbs.

Sinéad and Victoria found further common ground by sharing a whole raft of anecdotes, wherein their respective spouses lumbered from one disaster to another. This included Victoria's retelling of how Gary stubbornly trusted his Satnav to get them to Stratford-upon-Avon, but had accidentally selected *Stratford*, in London. "Hannibal's crossing of the Alps took less time," she chuckled.

Hannah and Calum were asked to judge their fathers' moonwalk dance-off. "So, what d'you think, Hannah? Your old man might have a little bit of junk in the trunk, but he still got the moves."

"Oh, for sure. I'd be amazed if Simon Cowell doesn't sign you two up for *Britain's Got Talent*."

Hannah and Calum agreed that there was enough sarcasm, arguments and laughter for them to class the get-together a resounding success. The true accomplishment of the night, though, remained unseen:

Marvin Cunningham, without anyone noticing, kept a close eye on his precious daughter's interaction with this, the finest of young men. By the end of the evening his brown eyes were twinkling with unadulterated pride.

CHAPTER TWENTY-NINE

Thumbnails and Influenza

Christmas Day morning in Norwich wasn't exactly the winter wonderland depicted in the movies. Outside Calum's French windows the clear sky presided over a lifeless garden with its dark skeletons of denuded trees. The pale sun glimmered like a faded torchlight and the lawn, instead of yielding to a luxurious blanket of snow, was the same dirty green colour it had been throughout autumn.

Calum had succumbed to a fever and spent the previous night tossing and turning, simultaneously sweating and shivering under their shared duvet. Then, because Hannah kept moaning at him to keep still, he found a spare quilt, wrapped it around himself and dragged it downstairs like a ceremonial robe.

Upon waking, Hannah pranced into the living room full of Christmas spirit, to find Calum sprawled across the sofa, swaddled like a baby and surrounded by a scattering of crumpled tissues.

"I'm really not well, Hannah. I've got the flu," he said, dolefully, his nose full of snot. "I need looking after." His bottom lip drooped as if anaesthetised.

"Oh, you poor thing. So you're not going for your five mile run then?" Hannah teased, suppressing a smile.

"You're smiling!"

"I'm not! So, what can I get you?"

"A Lemsip and some soup perhaps?" His voice was quavering; he sounded very near to death.

As the radio blared out the Pogues' *Fairytale of New York*, Hannah found a sachet of Lemsip Max in the bathroom cabinet. "You've got the choice of chicken noodle soup or oxtail soup."

"Chicken soup would be nice." He brightened, his voice that of an old lady.

"God, you are such a baby. If only your karate students could see you now."

They had planned to spend Christmas day with their respective families, Hannah at her parents' and Calum at his. Instead, Hannah phoned her mother and father to inform them that she would be staying on to look after her patient. There was a sudden pause in the conversation as she smothered the phone against her shoulder.

"Mum's gone to get Marcus. Those kung fu pyjamas that you bought him, he's already wearing them. Ooh, here he is… Hi, Marcus, I'm just passing the phone to Calum, and then we'll have a chat afterwards, OK?"

"Hiya, buddy," Calum croaked, his blotchy head resting on a cushion.

"Thank you for my present, Calum."

"You like it?"

"Yeah! Can I show you my karate kicks later?"

"Maybe when I'm better … I'm afraid I've got a bad cold, Marcus."

"Make sure you keep warm."

"Oh, I will Marcus; I've got the heating on and the fire on, too."

"Can I speak to Hannah now?"

"Of course you can. Merry Christmas, Marcus."

"Thank you."

Calum passed the phone back to Hannah. "I think he got bored with me," he sniffled.

A little later Calum called his own parents to deliver news of his terrible affliction. This elicited opposing responses: tremulous concern from his mother, and jubilant derision from his father, who subsequently passed the phone to Calum's Norwich-based grandparents. Calum's paternal grandfather, Geoffrey, was as Norfolk as Colman's mustard, and spoke with a broad accent. Even his road name, Cucumber Lane, sounded as if it had jumped straight out of a Beatrix Potter story:

"What, you got the lurgy, boy? Thass what you get for going out without a vest, in't it?" he bleated, whilst Calum's father could be heard egging him on from the sidelines.

After further enlightenment about the merits of thermal underwear, Calum made the courtesy call to his other grandparents in Surrey, who disingenuously wished him a speedy recovery. Meanwhile, Hannah wasted no time in rummaging under the Christmas tree to search for whichever wrapped present was sure to contain some Maltesers. Her tambourine-style shake of the likeliest box confirmed its contents. Then she settled into an armchair to phone both sets of grandparents in Ireland and Jamaica. As usual, all were joyously ebullient, making her hoot with laughter whilst Calum looked on from the sofa, his mopey eyes barely peeking out from above the duvet.

Once these overseas phone calls were made and Calum had been served another Lemsip, Hannah planted herself in front of the TV to watch a Christmas movie. The clichéd storyline followed a basic premise: super-busy career woman, working in a big American city, with no time for dating, has to return to her provincial hometown to endure Christmas with her diffident family.

Straightaway, the viewer knows that the laid-back guy, dressed in a lumberjack shirt – who the businesswoman finds annoying – will later become the love of her life, and that she will eventually be imbued with a Yuletide spirit.

"Why is it that suitcases in movies are always so obviously empty? Seriously, what would it take just to fill them with stuff?" Hannah moaned, as the actress pretended to struggle with luggage that swung like paper lanterns.

One and a half hours later, to amuse herself, Hannah pulled her Nordic woollen hat over Calum's head, then she dangled thick wads of tissue from his nostrils and placed a thermometer in his downcast mouth. After this, she photographed him with his own phone.

"You won't show that to anyone, will you?" he croaked.

"Of course I won't," she fibbed, before secretly texting the image to Leo and some of Calum's karate buddies.

****

While fiddling with Calum's iPhone, Hannah noticed five thumbnails in the photo gallery of pictures he'd taken in Thailand. "Crikey, you're not one for taking photos, are you? Surely these aren't the only pics you have from your holiday?"

"Probably," he mumbled, draping a flaccid arm over his weary forehead.

"As I've got nothing better to do, would you like me to upload them onto your laptop?"

"Do what you feel is best, babe. I probably shan't make it through the day, anyhow. Please tell my family that I always loved them…"

After lighting some pine and eucalyptus candles that Calum wasn't able to smell, Hannah set about the simple task of uploading the few photographs onto his Adobe Photoshop catalogue. In the process, his preexisting photo files sprung into view on the screen, like a kaleidoscopic photo journal of his bachelor life:

"Whoa! There are some good ones here of slutty Gibson."

"Aw, no! Please don't look at those," Calum grumbled, miraculously finding the energy to cast off his duvet, like a man revived.

"Yay! She seems to be wearing a nurse uniform that's two sizes too small!"

"Just delete any you don't like," Calum surrendered, flopping back onto the sofa of death.

"No, I think you should keep them. These photos might comfort you in your later years."

His holiday pictures consisted of three aerial shots from his hotel room balcony, one close-up of a wave tattoo on someone's bare back and a photograph of Calum and a cheerful Thai guy, against the backdrop of a glorious beach.

"Who's this chap?" she asked, holding the laptop in front of Calum.

"He's the guy I told you about, the one who gave me this amulet," Calum looped the necklace over the folds of his duvet. "We really hit it off."

"So have you kept in contact?"

"Well, no … we arranged to meet at the beach on my last morning, but for some reason he didn't turn up. Because of that I never managed to swap phone or email details."

"Why do you think he never turned up?"

"I don't know, it was a huge surprise to me, especially as we'd got on so well together."

"Well, there's probably a perfectly reasonable explanation. Maybe he contracted deadly man flu or maybe he just turned up late … rather like you and Leo did, seven years ago."

"Possibly." Calum cringed, then exaggerated a cough and held out his empty mug to Hannah as if it were a begging bowl.

"Well, there's only one way to find out what happened. I've always wanted to visit Thailand, you want to see your friend. It's simple! Let's go!"

"Yeah, but you probably won't like that particular part of Thailand. Patong is a bit like Great Yarmouth on Viagra."

"If the view from your hotel balcony is anything to go by, it looks wonderful, and I would love to walk on that beach. Plus, your friend lives there … what's his name, anyway?"

"Sawat, his name is Sawat."

CHAPTER THIRTY

A New Life

For the six months that Sawat was confined to Patong Hospital, Nok never once gave up on her promise to support her boyfriend. Despite being young and painfully timid, she unearthed a hidden maturity which galvanised her into speaking with doctors, social workers and occupational therapists – something which would have proved far too daunting at the outset.

Unfortunately for Sawat, waking up to the grim reality of morning after running around, miraculously cured, in his dreams all night, was a bitter pill that he could never get used to. In spite of this, he never complained, nor did he feel sorry for himself, and a beaming smile was never far from his face. In fact, he considered himself incredibly lucky to merit a girlfriend who loved him so deeply. This, he felt, was reason enough to be happy with his life.

Por, the chief physiotherapist, had never previously encountered a patient with so much determination. Her role usually was to coax patients to the limits of their physical capabilities. Not only did Sawat meet every target that she'd set him, he always surpassed them. Nok, too, approached the programme with zeal, keen to learn as many physiotherapy techniques as possible, so she could help Sawat with his recuperation when he was fit enough to leave the hospital.

Sawat adapted to manoeuvring a wheelchair with his usual positivity. Although his legs would always remain as flaccid as bath towels, his arms and back grew stronger each day. He even helped other paralysis sufferers, who weren't as physically or mentally capable as he was. In addition, he taught English to one of the nurses who hoped to live in America one day. His sunny disposition and his natural mentoring abilities made the rehabilitation team wish they could keep him on as a full-time employee.

Some of Sawat's favourite moments were spent watching Manchester United football matches on a hospital television with some of the other fanatical patients. One particular day, late in December, he watched with great interest as Manchester United played at Norwich City's football ground. He scanned each shot of the crowd, hoping that he might spot his friend Calum among the home supporters. It intrigued him to see the team managers in their thick winter coats, the air cold enough to turn their noses red, and he could actually *see* their breath. It made him shiver just to witness such a phenomenon.

Despite Sawat's family finding some comfort in his ever-cheerful demeanour, Por confided that he must be masking an excruciating amount of pain.

On the day that he left the hospital, he propelled his wheelchair under his own steam, foregoing assistance from his family. He received a heroic send-off from the health-care professionals and fellow patients, many of whom wept unfeigned tears of happiness and loss.

Once outside, Uncle Jao, fighting back tears of his own, unceremoniously hauled Sawat onto the back of his pick-up truck, helping to slide his nephew's useless legs across its metal floor so that he could lift the dropped tailgate back into position.

Sawat smiled at the bright blue sky, which today was feathered by the faintest of wispy clouds. "Uncle Jao...?"

"Yes, Sawat?"

"Before you take me home, can we visit the beach?"

CHAPTER THIRTY-ONE

The Concealed Letter

In mid-June, almost six months after its inception, Hannah's idea to visit Thailand had almost reached fruition. On Calum's recommendation, they opted for two weeks at the Redford Hotel in Phuket.

The day before they were due to fly, Hannah was selecting her holiday garments from the temporary clothes rails that she'd assembled in the spare bedroom. Over the preceding weeks, Calum was astounded by the steady accumulation of beachwear and boho floaty kaftans which entered the house either by parcel courier, or in glossy shopping bags. Hannah also committed herself to a shoe-shopping spree that would have given Imelda Marcos a run for her money.

"It looks like *TK Maxx* in here," Calum quipped as he passed Hannah a mug of tea.

"I think I've bought too many things," she announced, stating the obvious.

"You *do* know that we're not emigrating to Thailand, Han?" he teased. "This is just a two-week holiday. I've seen fewer shoes outside a mosque!"

"Oh, but they all look so-o nice. I can't decide which

ones to leave behind."

"It's easy, just pick the ones you absolutely can't do without and stick the rest in a wardrobe."

Galvanised into action, Hannah started separating the wheat from the chaff, reducing the footwear count by two-thirds and arranging a sensible number of colourful clothes into orderly piles on the bed.

****

Unknown to Hannah, Calum had sought counsel from her best friend, Sophie, as to whether Hannah's response to a wedding proposal would be favourable.

"Oh, come on, Calum, you already know the answer," Sophie replied. Enthusiastically happy, but sworn to secrecy, she promised not to breathe a word. Calum also tipped off Leo and Tilly about his secret assignment. Both were as excited as puppies and couldn't wait to congratulate the engaged couple on their eventual return from Thailand.

"And naturally I'd love for you to be my best man, Leo," Calum said.

"Aww, dude! It's a total honour. That's awesome!"

"Leo, you *do* realise that you are actually English, right?"

****

Calum had surreptitiously purchased a deliberately garish proposal ring from Claire's Accessories in the Castle Mall shopping centre: this was for symbolic purpose, an ironic precursor to a more fitting engagement ring of Hannah's own choosing.

So, while Hannah brooded over her burgeoning summer collection in the next room, Calum packed his own suitcase in the main bedroom. He hid the lurid ring in a side pouch of his Samsonite, along with a schoolgirl letter that Hannah had once sent to his family home address.

Hannah had forgotten about the letter long ago but at the time that she wrote it, it touched Calum's fifteen-year-old heart, and was therefore worth holding onto. He had never shown it to anyone. Now, nearly eight years later, he wanted to share it with its author, a girl whom he loved with every fibre of his being, someone he had probably loved from the day they first met, aged eleven.

He had already devised a plan for revealing Hannah's letter, which also involved the proposal ring, and their destination hotel. On his previous visit to the Redford he had watched with interest as the staff prepared a pre-sunset dinner table for two people. This was set up alongside the beach. The table was draped in white linen and the scene was embellished further with flower garlands and candlelit pathways. His plan was to organise this same romantic meal for Hannah. At first he would surprise her with the letter, possibly before dessert and then, after it had been read, he would produce the ring and propose.

Before tucking it into the side pouch of the suitcase, he unfolded the note and read it for the hundredth time:

Dear Calum,

I know you probably don't want to hear this, but if I don't tell you how I really feel, you might carry on through life without ever knowing just how much I love you and care for you.

Every time I see you I can't help smiling. My feelings for you grow stronger each day.

When you look at me with your sexy blue eyes I go weak at the knees, which should tell you that I would like us to be more than just good friends.

We think the same way, we laugh at the same things. So maybe we could be compatible in other ways?

Yehh, I know you love your football and your karate, but perhaps you could grow to love me just as much?
You don't know it yet, Calum, but I WILL marry you one day !!!!
Luv you forever,
Hannah xxx

****

At Heathrow's terminal five, Hannah shopped at WH Smith for a magazine and an extra paperback while Calum phoned his ever-anxious mother to let her know that they hadn't been involved in a mass pile-up on the M25.

"Don't forget to call me just as soon as you arrive in Thailand," she urged, as he pushed a finger in his other ear to block out the noise of the announcements: *"Please keep your baggage with you at all times. Unattended baggage will be removed and may be destroyed."*

"Yep, of course I'll phone you, Mum. Love you … speak soon … bye."

Calum had opted for a flight with British Airways this time, paying extra for a premium economy service so they could sit comfortably in a row just two seats wide and so wouldn't be forced to sit next to a passenger from hell for twelve soul-destroying hours.

Once seated by the window, Hannah enthusiastically started to tap the personal entertainment screen, as if it might yield all the hidden secrets of the universe. Then she liberated a toothbrush, flight socks and other items from the airline's amenity kit.

"Are you going to settle down anytime soon?" grinned Calum, as she eventually stopped ferreting about in the storage pouch, only to switch the overhead reading light on and off for no apparent reason.

"Look, I need to know where everything is," she giggled, before draping a flight blanket over his head.

Hannah turned her attention to the other passengers. Through the gap between the seats in front of them, she spotted a man's right ear from which grew a forest of incredibly long, hairs.

"Calum! Calum!" she hissed, pulling her boyfriend's headphones away from his head.

"What now?"

"Calum, you've got to check out this guy's hairy ears, they are unbelievable."

Intrigued, Calum peered discreetly around the edge of the seat and started chuckling quietly with Hannah, as if they were kids at school again. Almost as if he sensed his shaggy ears were the subject of conversation, the man started to twiddle with the whiskers.

"His ears must be burning," whimpered Hannah, through suppressed laughter.

"I hope not, we'll all go up in flames," bubbled Calum, trying to muzzle his own chuckles.

"Are you two OK?" asked a stewardess who had appeared alongside with a tray of orange juice.

"Yes, we're fine thanks," Calum squealed, as he took two tumblers from her tray. By now his voice was at a pitch that could only be heard by dogs, and his eyes were filled with tears of laughter.

Because the attendant looked so bemused, Hannah pointed to the gentleman in front and performed a lively mime in which she fluttered fingers next to her own ears. Perplexed, the stewardess watched this charade with interest, but after looking at the target passenger's lugs, she soon got the message and stifled a giggle of her own.

"I can see I'm going to have my hands full with you two," she said, bending her head below headrest height and dropping her voice to a conspiratorial whisper. "Gosh, he's got enough there to stuff a cushion, hasn't he?"

This statement pushed them deeper into juvenile

regression; both squirmed in their seats as if exposed to laughing gas.

"I shall catch you two crazies later," the attendant breezed as Calum smothered his gurgling face with the flight blamket.

****

Several hours into the flight, Hannah made her way to the toilet in the dimmed light of the cabin. As she waited outside, the cubicle remained steadfastly engaged for an inordinate amount of time. More worryingly, whoever was in there kept grunting "Oh God!" repeatedly. Eventually, the door clicked open, revealing the occupier to be the gentleman with the handlebar ear hairs. He shot Hannah an apologetic look before squeezing by in a haze of body odour. After opening the door, she gasped in horror as a large puddle of urine and a splatter of misdirected diarrhoea greeted her startled eyes.

So Hannah, because she didn't want any incoming toilet users to imagine that *she* was the guilty party, set about the unpleasant task of scrubbing and deodorising the entire capsule. Retching from the faecal stench, and using only what was available to her from the toiletry shelf – a bergamot and grapefruit spritzer – plus wads of airline tissue. She removed every trace of bodily fluid and doggedly saw the job through to the bitter end.

Finally unlocking the toilet door, her face was like thunder as she allowed a waiting flight attendant to enter the newly-sanitised cubicle.

"Are you OK, Han?" Calum asked, noticing she seemed none too pleased after her prolonged trip to the washroom.

Hannah didn't answer and stood, quietly smouldering in the aisle. Her conscience was weighing up two options: on her left shoulder was an Irish devil who urged her to confront the antisocial defecator, while the Jamaican angel on her right shoulder suggested she should just let things be.

Unfortunately for hairy ears, the toilet vandal, she chose the first option.

"Excuse me!" she shouted, tearing off the man's headphones. "I have just spent the last twenty minutes clearing up your shit and your piss! Farmyard animals behave better. You should be ashamed of yourself!"

The man gaped at her with astonishment in his eyes. "Uh, actually that mess was already there before I went in. I had a terrible job trying to avoid it and since asked the cabin crew to attend ... I can't believe you cleaned it up yourself.Ugh, how revolting!"

Calum watched the whole sorry episode between splayed fingers, melting into his seat with acute embarrassment. The altercation attracted the attention of several passengers who were roused from their slumber by Hannah's raised voice. Suitably contrite, she returned to her seat after offering a mumbled apology.

"Your mother would be *so* proud," Calum grinned, delighted to have been gifted an anecdote that could be put to good use for years to come.

CHAPTER THIRTY-TWO

The Final Surrender

Otto Netzer removed his Walther semi-automatic pistol from the gun safe installed within his bedroom. He chambered a round, then calmly stepped out onto the landing.

The shocking murder of his wife, nine months previous, had left him with an emptiness in his heart that was too much to bear. He was haunted by the faraway stare on her bloodless face and the savage manner in which she died.

"I let you down, Kirsten," he cried out loud each day, as if she were still with him.

Otto's only children, two adult daughters from his previous marriage, had tried their best to comfort him but the thought of his own death drew him in, like a moth to a flame. Friedrich Nietzsche once wrote that it was sometimes consoling to think of suicide. This was certainly true in Otto's case as he continually endured the desolation of night and the heartbreak of day.

So, on a glorious summer morning in June, while his affluent Frankfurt suburb was alive with the distant hum of lawnmowers, Otto had already posted apologetic letters to loved ones, and was descending the stairs, aware of nothing but the weight of the gun in his hand.

After closing the living-room curtains, he settled into his leather armchair, which he reclined so that the backrest was at a forty five-degree angle to the floor. He had taken the trouble to shave and to iron a shirt, choosing to wear the colourful *Brioni* tie which Kirsten had bought him.

After disengaging the safety mechanism, he raised the pistol to his lips and felt its cold steel against his teeth. Otto slid the gun barrel further into his mouth, angling it so that the bullet would pass behind his eyes and through his brain.

He wasn't usually aware of the metronomic noise of the grandfather clock in the hallway, but now its unstoppable *tick-tock* invaded the room, becoming ever louder. The violence of what he was about to do was completely at odds with the normality of his surroundings; there was to be no orchestral *fortissimo* in the background, just the hollow echo of the clock's rhythmic noise.

His throat resonated to the thunderous drum of his heartbeat. An inner voice begged him to fire the gun. He made a slight adjustment to the positioning of the barrel and, with tears spilling from his eyelashes, he squeezed the trigger, causing the top of his skull to explode against the wall behind him.

While the grandfather clock maintained its enduring *tick-tock* amidst the stillness of death, the Mother Killer had claimed his latest victim.

CHAPTER THIRTY-THREE

Brought Down to Earth

After waking in his family home for the first time in more than six months, Sawat was surprised to discover that he wasn't imbued with a huge feeling of joy. Instead, unusually for him, he was full of self-doubt.

In the safety of the hospital he had the full support and assistance of numerous health care professionals; now, with his mother about to leave for work at her market stall, and Sarai already en-route to the small hotel where she worked as a chambermaid, he felt vulnerable.

Of course he didn't broadcast his nervousness, preferring instead to sit in his wheelchair putting on a brave face. His family had worked incredibly hard to ensure that the transition from hospital to home was as straightforward as possible: Uncle Jao, pre-empting Sawat's mobility needs, constructed two ramps, which afforded him wheelchair access to the entrance of the house. Jao had also built a platform so that Sawat's mattress was at an elevation that enabled him to comfortably shuffle into his wheelchair. Supanee and Sarai had also thoughtfully placed any items that he might need at a height where they could easily be reached.

Supanee delayed her departure for work for as long as possible, trying to convince herself that her son could cope on his own. She left him packets of Tom Yum-flavoured dried noodles that he could boil with water in a saucepan, and a covered bowl of sliced fresh fruit to eat with coconut ice-cream. Though he sought to reassure his mother that he would be absolutely fine, she still continued to fuss until the reins of time pulled her from the house.

It hurt Sawat's pride to know that he could never fulfil his duty, as the eldest child, to look after his family; instead, they had to take care of him. He already knew that the shortfall of money coming into the house was forcing his mother to work longer hours, adding to her distress. Now, all that remained of Supanee was the diminishing noise of her motorcycle engine as it whined into the distance, leaving Sawat to wrestle with sudden solitude.

One of the many things that he had to think about was the disposable drainage bag strapped to his right leg and connected to his bladder via a catheter. As it was three-quarters full, he substituted it for a fresh one before washing his body with a damp sponge. Then he pulled out and replaced the towel, which his mother had earlier placed on his seat. Even though this was something he had accomplished numerous times already, he was buoyed by the ease with which he performed his first task of the day without the reassurance of back-up.

Nok had texted to say that she would come over later; in the meantime, dressed in a T-shirt and a lap blanket which skirted his ankles, he guided his wheelchair across the tiled floor and set about tidying the house. He wasn't yet confident enough to venture out of the front door on his own, imagining that any solo descent of the ramp might cause his wheelchair to tumble over into the street. His only view of the outside world was of the rooftops and trees, seen through the ornate metal window grills which cast swirls of intricate shadows into each room. From the other side of one of the flimsy house walls he could hear his toad-faced neighbour, Somboon, urinating loudly as a horse. It was difficult to maintain any level of domestic secrecy on Soi Hwang; you not only knew what television programmes your neighbours were watching, you could hear every belch, fart and marital mattress creak.

Sawat studied the cluttered walls of his home through fresh eyes, noting that the framed wedding photographs of his parents were given much less prominence than a large, faded picture of the King and Queen, taken when they were much younger. There were also some baby-faced photographs of Sawat with his father and some instructors at the *Muay Thai* gymnasium. His mother made good use of limited space by hanging cooking pans, utensils, and large colanders from the wall, and by using foldaway furniture wherever possible.

An electric fan swept the hot room, its cooling breeze periodically catching Sawat's face as he manoeuvred his wheelchair without difficulty, leading him to wonder why he had been so apprehensive earlier. He was already looking forward to Nok guiding him down the ramp later in the day so that they could enjoy hot banana pancakes together in front of *Khun* Panit's food stall at the end of the *soi*.

At one end of the living room was a small family shrine, consisting of a nest of tables bedecked with statuettes of Buddha. Surrounding these effigies were candles, plastic flower garlands and sepia photographs of deceased grandparents. Sawat lit three incense sticks, which he held in prayer as the electric fan continued to purr like a contented cat. After paying his respects, he spiked the incense sticks into a sand-filled metal bowl, where their fragrant smoke continued to dance in the draught of the fan.

His initial confidence, however, proved to be short-lived. Stretching up from his seat cushion during an attempt to shift a large propane gas cylinder that limited his access around the kitchen, his wheelchair teetered onto two wheels and spilled him onto the tiled floor. He managed to push the chair upright, but each attempt to clamber back into it proved too arduous. A stench of excrement told him that he had also involuntarily soiled himself in the process. At first he contemplated opening the front door to call for help from neighbours but its handle was clearly out of reach. He could only crawl across the floor, using the strength of his arms and back, his lower torso dragging behind him like a seal carcass. A gecko, which had skittered across the wall in front of his eye line, stared at him with a dispassionate curiosity and the fan continued its monotonous drone with a similar indifference.

For some reason in this desperate moment, his thoughts returned to the sea ghost. It occurred to Sawat that, like him, the spirit was trapped and unable to move freely. For the first time, he felt a kindred sympathy for the creature; they were both helpless victims of circumstances beyond their control. He hoped that his friend Calum hadn't been similarly cursed and that one day he would return to Patong to find him.

Now sweating profusely from his exertions, Sawat used a floor brush to drag his phone from the table top and managed to catch it in one hand. He twisted his body and propped himself up so that he could lean against a table leg. His father watched him from the wall with pity in his eyes.

Crushed by the reality of his situation, he regarded the dark, serpentine trail of his own excreta. Desperate for assistance, he texted Nok, just as the first uncontrollable sobs finally burst forth.

CHAPTER THIRTY-FOUR

Sharing a Taxi with David Beckham

Hannah and Calum's connecting flight from Bangkok to Phuket was on its final descent. The fuselage shuddered as the aeroplane passed through saturated clouds and into the glare of tropical sunshine. It banked to the right, offering a bird's-eye view of the island's beaches and its impenetrable jungle.

Hannah pressed her forehead against the window. The sea was pistachio green and a steamy mist rose from dense canopies of trees. Some of the smaller beaches resembled elephant tusks.

"Wow, it looks like paradise," she cooed.

"Well, it's not quite so virginal when you see it at ground level," declared Calum, worried that her expectations might be a touch too high.

****

At the airport there was the usual plenitude of dishevelled holidaymakers, including a contingent of oriental tourists who wore surgical masks as if they were in the midst of a bubonic plague.

Hannah, who travelled in a white summer blazer,

that paired with a silk scarf and dark denim jeans, was surprised to see a middle-aged man standing near the baggage carousel wearing the type of shorts that were intended for bedtime, rather than international travel. In a further crime against fashion, he matched these flimsy shorts with ordinary socks and shoes that were never intended to be seen at the end of bare British legs.

Calum joined the throng of passengers impatiently waiting for their suitcases to appear. Hannah hung back with the trolley, more than happy to people-watch. Her unannounced award for strangest behaviour immediately went to the middle-aged couple who somehow seemed to have forgotten what their luggage looked like. The husband made a grab for every black suitcase that trundled by, giving each one an inquisitive twirl, before tossing it back like an unwanted fish. His wife, who must have also contracted amnesia on the flight over, double-checked the same suitcases which he'd rejected. This double act kindled the interest of the people near to them, who were thankful for a little light relief to ease the torpor of hanging around in a foreign airport.

A diminutive Thai woman, attempting to snatch her enormous suitcase from the carousel, was summarily dragged along behind it. Calum was the first to react and heaved the heavy suitcase from the belt, eliciting a succession of grateful *wais* from the flustered woman.

"My hero," mimed Hannah, as Calum looked towards her with a boyish grin. He accepted her silent applause with a courtly bow.

*****

Even though she had been warned by Calum, stepping from the air-conditioned airport terminal into the pressure-cooker heat of Phuket still came as a complete shock to Hannah, who puffed out her cheeks and removed her jacket.

"Phew, how humid is this?" she gasped, ineffectually fanning herself with her fingers.

"You'll be fine once you're in the cab," Calum said, jogging off to bag a taxi.

What followed was an efficient display of kerbside ingenuity, where an excessive amount of luggage was successfully crammed into a small vehicle by a female taxi driver who channelled the strength of Samson into her pint-sized body. The lid of the car boot was left gaping to accommodate two of the suitcases and was secured with elasticated bungee straps. The other suitcase travelled next to the driver and was buckled into the seat, like a silent passenger. Hannah and Calum both offered to help but were shooed away and ushered into the taxi, which was filled with the smell of fresh jasmine, courtesy of a garland hanging from the rear-view mirror.

"Welcome to Phuket *ka*," said their driver, activating the aircon and blasting out some Thai music with a turn of her ignition.

Once away from the airport, Hannah was beguiled by the sheer foreignness of the island and bounced from one window to the other like an excitable collie. They passed expressionless families huddled together in the back of dusty pick-up trucks, and mothers transporting their babies on motorcycles as if it was the most natural thing in the world. On one side of the highway, tall radio masts rose above coconut trees to spear the skyline; on the other side – beyond the advertising billboards – were dark, bosomy hills, huge golden Buddhas and lush green fields.

"What country you from?" asked the driver, turning the music down.

"England," Calum replied.

"Oh, you handsome, like David Beckham," she said, smiling into the rear-view mirror.

"I wish I had his money," Calum chuckled.

Hannah was fascinated by everything around them. A motorcyclist who was sensible enough to wear a visored helmet but didn't feel the need for footwear sped past with his nylon jacket billowing like a windsock.

As the taxi reached Patong town, Hannah continued to absorb the sights and sounds of the place. Everywhere she looked, there were gigantic gilt-edged photographs of the Thai king and queen, depicted at various stages of their lives, sometimes dressed in brocaded uniforms. The air was alive with vehicular noise and the constant shrill of police whistles. A pack of stray dogs slept in the cool safety of an underpass. Above the convenience stores and the open-sided restaurants were dark lines of overhead cables, which stretched like yarns on a thousand looms.

When Hannah saw other holidaymakers walking on the sun-drenched pavements, wearing T-shirts darkened with sweat and others who gleefully climbed into ornate *tuk tuks*, she was keen to begin her own adventure. She instantly recognised an inner beauty among the raw chaos.

"I love it here!" she yelled, returning the cheery wave of a young boy who rode pillion on his father's motorcycle.

Soon, their taxi approached the turn-off for the Redford Patong Beach Resort where the dissonance of road noise gave way to the gentle rumble of tyres on a block-weave driveway. The hotel's vigilant security guards continued to ensure that Al-Qaeda could never terrorise this small corner of Thailand by casually checking under the vehicle with their grimy mirror.

"They look for bomb," their driver chuckled, covering her mouth with her hand.

"What is your name?" Hannah asked, leaning towards the front seat.

"My name *May*. My parent call me that because I born in month of May."

"Well, thank you, May, you are a great driver."

"Of course, we women the best driver, *na*?"

"Oh, definitely!"

No sooner had May stopped her taxi at the hotel entrance than a cluster of white-uniformed personnel descended on the car, opening doors amidst a multitude of warm greetings. May stood to one side whilst the bellboys unburdened her vehicle of its load.

"Madam, can I give your husban' a hug?" she asked, with a desirous glint in her eye.

"Oh, he's not my husband, but, yeah, you go for it…"

May seized her opportunity and clung onto Calum like a limpet, triggering toothpaste commercial smiles from all of the bellboys. Hannah joined in, just for fun, turning it into a group hug.

"Why not marry to this beautiful girl?" scolded May, slapping Calum hard on the arm as he recoiled in mock fear. Hannah was ushered into the coolness of the hotel before she heard his answer.

As he joined her in the marbled opulence of the lobby, a familiar voice rang out: "*Khun* Calum! Welcome back to the Redfor' Hotel!" exclaimed Nuay, who approached with an exuberant *wai*, still walking with his head leaning to one side.

"*Khun* Nuay, I would like you to meet my girlfriend, Hannah … Hannah, this is Nuay…"

"Great to meet you, Nuay," said Hannah, putting her first *wai* into practice.

Nuay did a heart-stopping double-take at first, thinking that Calum might have said Rihanna, and that Hannah was the world-famous singer in the flesh.

"How long you stay this time, *Khun* Calum?" he asked, realising he was allowing his excitement to get the better of him.

"Two weeks."

"Oh, everybody here will be *so* happy to see you again, *Khun* Calum. Please, we get you check in at reception, and then I will take you to your room, *kap*."

****

Their room was sited on the top floor, a short distance from the one which Calum occupied previously. As a courteous gesture, the hotel had provided a canoe-shaped wooden bowl, filled with exotic fruit and a squat vase of orchids, accompanied by a welcome card from one of the management team.

Hannah opened the balcony door and marvelled at the panoramic view. The sky was a screen print of the brightest blue, and much of the sea was a milky turquoise, with pleats of gentle waves rolling onto the shoreline. While his girlfriend admired the view, Calum's eyes were only fixed on the sinister blemish of dark water that remained within swimming distance of the beach. A sudden chill travelled down his spine and, unseen by Hannah, he shook his head in bewilderment.

Because they had managed to sleep well on the flight from London, neither Hannah nor Calum were jetlagged and they set about emptying their suitcases as efficiently as any customs officials ever could. Hannah regarded the fifteen wooden hangers in the wardrobe with a shake of her head and immediately ordered twenty more from housekeeping.

"Any clothes that we need for today, we can iron ourselves," Calum suggested. "Everything else we could have pressed by the hotel's laundry service."

"Sounds good to me," Hannah agreed, casting her eyes over the colourful jumble of clothes that engulfed their bed.

****

By the time they had tidied everything away, ironed

clothes, phoned home and shared a shower, the sky was crow-black, leaving only moonlight and the emerald green lights of the squid boats to puncture the darkness. Calum, who had already phoned the hotel's Talay Thai seafood restaurant to reserve a table, rolled up the sleeves of his slate-grey shirt, while Hannah shimmied into a purple party dress and spritzed herself with perfume.

"Could you zip me up, Cal?" she asked, offering up her back to him.

"Of course," he said, resisting the urge to remove the dress and forget about dinner altogether. "You smell wonderful."

"It's Alien, by Thierry Mugler."

"Didn't he used to play for Arsenal?" he grinned.

"So, how do I look?" she asked, in her best smoky lisp, slinking back onto the bed to afford him a better view.

"You know already," he replied, grinning from ear to ear.

Before putting on her new pair of Jimmy Choos, Hannah stuck two strategically-placed blister pads onto the soft tissue of each ankle. Then she sprang to her feet and struck a pose: "Ta-dah!"

Calum held her waist and planted a kiss on her cheek, before taking a step back. "You look *amazing*," he gasped.

"So you're not going to run off with May the taxi driver just yet?" she chuckled.

"Could a man not have two women?"

"Come on, Beckham, let's eat. I'm starving."

****

With the noise of rolling waves in the distance, Hannah and Calum enjoyed a mazy walk through the hotel grounds past floodlit coconut trees. As ever, the night was haunted by noisy insects, and the warm air was suffused with the scent of oleander and jasmine. The Talay Thai restaurant was open on all sides, surrounded by koi ponds. Its pathway was flanked by flaming bamboo torches and a lady, dressed in traditional Siamese attire, played music on a curved wooden xylophone. Female restaurant staff, similarly dressed, fanned out from the entrance with their palms pressed together, welcoming them. The centrepiece of the restaurant was an ornamental wooden boat propped up on a stand and loaded with a screed of ice cubes. This was lit from above and laden with fresh lobster, crabs, red snapper and fat tiger prawns as big as croissants. Patrons were encouraged to select their favourite items from this seafood selection and have them cooked to order.

Hannah and Calum were shown to their table, while some of the restaurant's seated guests peered over like inquisitive meerkats. The head waitress explained the food available, while a waiter placed a wooden bowl containing a smoking mosquito coil by their feet. Another waitress stood back, clutching leather-bound menus almost as big as herself.

"Tonight, *ka*, we have seafood barbecue," announced the head waitress, casting her dainty hand in the direction of the ornamental boat, "or you can choose from the à la carte menu."

On cue, the other waitress shuffled forward with the oversized menus. Because they were both famished, Hannah and Calum plumped for the barbecue choice, sensing they might get their food a whole lot quicker.

While the couple feasted, they drank chilled white wine from glasses wet with condensation. Their taste buds rejoiced in a sensory overload of ginger with lemongrass, and also lime juice, chillies and coriander. From their table, they had a partial view of the sea; the moonlit water had a magical, silver tint and, in the distance, Chinese lanterns ascended the night sky almost as if angels were returning to Heaven.

"Oh God, I love it here," Hannah gushed. "And this is only my first day."

Calum beamed. "I can't tell you how happy that makes me."

His girlfriend's face was aglow in the soft candlelight that highlighted the freckles dusting her cheeks. Her eyes sparkled as she held out her palm to caress his face. "Calum, I hope that this doesn't come off as being really cheesy, but us being here together, like this, is the kind of thing I dreamt of when we were younger. I couldn't be any happier."

Hannah was so overcome with love that her eyes glistened with tears. He took her hand and kissed it. He dearly wished he could propose to her right there and then – and would have done – were the ring and letter not still hidden in his suitcase.

CHAPTER THIRTY-FIVE

The Temptation

Shivering beneath a constellation of stars, Sawat clung to a solitary coconut tree, which rose from the tar-dark surface of a moonlit ocean. Just at the point where he felt he could not hold on any longer, a familiar figure swam towards him through the black water.

"Father!" Sawat shouted, a broad smile lighting up his face. "We thought you were dead!"

"Dead? No, Sawat, I lost my boat in a storm but luckily I found you, instead."

"Father, if I let go of this tree, will you swim back to the shore with me?" asked Sawat, imagining how happy his mother would be when they returned home together.

"I would love that with all my heart, Sawat, but how can you swim without the use of your legs?"

While Sawat tried to come to terms with the shock of this statement, Boonrit gently prised his son's fingers away from the trunk of the coconut tree. "Follow me," he whispered, guiding his son downwards into the inky depths of the sea.

With his father by his side again, the deeper that Sawat went, the happier he became.

****

Sawat was saddened to wake from this fateful dream. For the first time, in nearly a decade, he wished that he had not survived the 2004 *tsunami*.

CHAPTER THIRTY-SIX

The Poisoned Chalice

"Hannah, I'm just going for a run on the beach before breakfast," said a bare-chested Calum, as he laced up his running shoes.

"Yeah, you go for it, Tarzan," Hannah exhorted, waving her electric toothbrush in his direction.

While Calum was jogging on the beach, Hannah hunted for nail scissors in the pouches of her toiletry bag. Unable to find them, she decided to search inside the suitcases which were stowed in one corner of the balcony. When she moved the first one, a flurry of hidden mosquitoes took to their wings and scribbled the air, causing Hannah to chase after them, slapping her hands together, as if in the grip of demonic possession.

Neither of her suitcases contained the scissors, so she opened Calum's. Tucked inside an elasticated side-pouch, she discovered a small velveteen box, which contained a garish ring – the kind of thing a girl might wear for fun to a music festival. Hannah's heart soared. *Oh, my God. He's going to propose.* She instantly imagined a fabulous wedding where both sets of grandparents made the overseas journey.

Barely able to contain her delight, she hastily returned the ring to its hiding place and closed the suitcase, only minutes before Calum returned, drenched in sweat and bleeding profusely from one knee.

"What on earth have you done to your leg?" she asked, alarmed at the sight of a nasty looking flesh wound.

"I got bitten by a dog on the beach," he said matter-of-factly, seeming pleased with his early-morning battle scar.

"I don't know why you're smiling, you wally! What if that dog had rabies or something?"

"It was wearing a collar, I'll be fine," he breezed, before slipping out of his shorts and pants and stepping into the shower.

****

After breakfast the couple took a walk on the beach, where the briny smell of the sea hung on the morning breeze. It was too early for the first influx of beach vendors but Calum was hoping to catch sight of Sawat a little later.

Wandering about the hotel grounds, Calum found it endearing that Hannah pointed her camera at every foreign object that caught her eye: lizards that scuttled around tree roots, dragonflies that hovered above lotus pads, and even the birds that visited their balcony. She also photographed a tiny red beetle, on the off chance that she might have made some rare entomological discovery.

Because she seemed to be such a dab hand at photography, honeymooners approached her with their cameras and smartphones, confident that she would take excellent photographs of them. With her usual enthusiasm, Hannah tried to elevate these snapshots to another level and suggested alternative locations, adjusting the subjects' positioning with an attention to detail that surpassed the efforts of their own wedding photographers. She pictorially improved the holiday experience of two sets of Japanese honeymooners, who afterwards smiled and bowed with inexhaustible gratitude, and an elderly American couple in matching shirts who assumed that she would just love to view screenshots of their two bloodhounds. Hannah graciously marvelled at each of these canine photographs as if she were gazing upon the eighth and ninth wonders of the world.

Watching her from a distance, Calum's chest brimmed with pride and each time that he lost his girlfriend to a new legion of fans he fell ever-deeper in love.

By eleven o'clock, the sun was almost vertical in the sky. Hannah chose two sun loungers from a selection that were arranged like dominoes around the large swimming pool. A smiling attendant appeared from nowhere with an armful of thick towels. "Welcome back, *Khun* Calum ... we all so happy to see you again."

"*Sawasdee kap, Khun* Boontham," replied Calum, relieved that he remembered the guy's name. "This is Hannah, my girlfriend."

"My pleasure to meet you, *Khun* Hannah. Mister Calum, he very popular with the staff."

"Pleasure to meet you, too," she said, omitting his name, worried that she might pronounce it incorrectly.

"Oh, you have injure yourself, *Khun* Calum," Boontham said, concerned about the ugly gash on his leg.

"Shark bite," Calum quipped, before realising his irony was lost in translation.

After chatting about the weather, Boontham smoothed the towels onto the loungers and left two courtesy bottles of water on their table. "You want umblella up, or down?"

"Down is fine," assured Calum, pressing a cluster of twenty-baht notes into Boontham's palm.

"*Kap Khun mai kap,*" Boontham thanked, executing an extra-reverential *wai* before departing.

"Crikey, you were only here for five days and yet

everybody knows you," marvelled Hannah.

She peeled off her white, gauzy kaftan to reveal a tangerine-coloured halter-neck bikini and a body that drew envious glances from all the women relaxing nearby. Unaware of the furtive attention, she adjusted her bikini top so that it evenly cupped the firm swell of her breasts. A middle-aged German woman, whose spiky hair was dyed cherry-red, scolded her husband for dropping his paperback in order to ogle her.

Calum stripped down to black shorts and draped his polo shirt over the back of the lounger. A neon-blue butterfly chose that moment to land weightlessly on the crook of Hannah's outstretched arm and then began to pulse its wings in perfect synchronicity with her heartbeat.

"This is truly bliss," she gasped, removing the cap from her water bottle.

"So you think you could handle two weeks of this?" asked Calum, rhetorically.

"God, yeah," Hannah sighed, dropping the tortoiseshell sunglasses over her eyes, allowing her smile to widen even further as she thought about that secret engagement ring.

****

Two virgin mojitos later, and after an hour in the sweltering sun, they both needed to cool down, so Calum suggested going into the sea, which also afforded him his first opportunity to look for Sawat. Hannah couldn't get off her lounger quick enough; she was so looking forward to meeting his Thai friend for the first time. Calum followed her, enjoying the natural grace of her walk. He noticed that her caramel skin was now glistening with perspiration and that, because of the humidity, her hair had started to reclaim some of its natural curl.

Beyond a row of trembling palm trees the sea was sapphire-blue, and Calum was suddenly excited at the thought of reuniting with Sawat. Looking in both directions for a swaying coolbox and a smiling face, he still couldn't spot him. Then Calum remembered a good reason to stop Hannah, just as she was about to step barefoot onto the beach:

"Hannah, you might need to go back for your flip-flops, this first part of the beach can get really hot…"

"Oh, don't be such a wuss," she scoffed, carrying on regardless. Within seconds she was hopping about on the hot sand, as if bullets were being fired at her feet. "Shit! Fuck! Shit! Ouch!" she yelped with each burning step.

"Hey, no need for that, potty mouth!" Calum chuckled as Hannah sprinted to the water's edge to cool the soles of her feet.

"Quick! Look!" she shouted, as a silver arc of flying fish burst from the sea, glinting like coins in the sunlight. Then, after this eye-popping spectacle, they spent some time frolicking in the waves, as if they were teenagers again. But no sooner had they waded out of the sea than Calum's eyes were scouring the foreshore, hoping he might recognise Sawat's outline, even from a distance.

Most of the other beach vendors milled around in one area, their conversation hanging in the breeze like turkey gobble. As he drew nearer, Calum recognised one of the guys whose salt-stained baseball cap perched above mirrored sunglasses. He left Hannah's side to approach him. "*Khun* Viset, *sawasdee kap*, do you remember me?"

"*Yes! Khun* Calum, you frien' of *Khun* Sawat."

"Is *Khun* Sawat on the beach today? I would really like to see him."

"Oh … uh, I think maybe you not know," Viset faltered, suddenly averting his gaze, "*Khun* Sawat, he terrible injure, he cannot work…"

Horrified, Calum immediately assumed that Sawat must have been involved in a motorcycle accident of some sort. "Terrible injury? Please, what terrible injury?"

"*Khun* Sawat, he attack by three men las' year. They break his back, now he in wheelchair."

Cold dread washed over Calum, chilling his bones. He remembered the three fishermen and the fight at the bar. "Viset, can you take me to Sawat? I can pay you. Please."

"Money, no need, *Khun* Calum, we can go on my motorbike right now, *na*?"

Calum turned to Hannah, who had only caught the end of the conversation. "Hannah, something bad has happened to Sawat. I need to go with this guy to see him, right now."

"Of course! Do you want me to come with you?"

"No, it's OK, I'm going on the back of his bike. I'll be back later."

While Viset waited for him, Calum walked back to the lounger with Hannah in silence. He towelled himself dry and slipped on his polo shirt. "Take care, I'll see you later, yeah?" he murmured, giving Hannah a spiritless kiss on the cheek.

"Take as long as you want, Calum," she said, trying to catch his eyes. "I love you…"

He didn't utter a word and turned away. Hannah watched him jog back to the beach, worried about his state of mind. She feared that his friend's condition would be every bit as terrible as it first seemed, and she felt powerless to help.

****

Calum followed Viset from the beach, up a rugged concrete slope and into the shadows of a narrow *soi* where his motorcycle was parked. After wheeling it from its space, he needlessly buffed the leather seat with his forearm and jumped on, waiting for Calum to follow suit.

On the way, Viset confirmed Calum's worst fears,

telling him that Sawat's injuries were indeed a result of a revenge attack by the three fishermen at the bar.

"How far, *Khun* Viset?" Calum asked, placing the soles of his flip-flops on the motorcycle's foot pegs.

"Oh, not far, *kap*, maybe twenty minute."

As they weaved through the shabby streets that diverged from the main drag of the town, Calum thought about the circumstances that led to Sawat being confined to a wheelchair, accepting his own culpability in the build-up to this violent assault.

Viset decelerated his motorcycle near to a street corner where Panit, the pancake vendor, was slicing pineapples at his small street stall in readiness for late-afternoon trade.

"That one," said Viset above the engine noise, pointing to Soi Hwang, the small, dusty street immediately after the pancake stand.

Calum dismounted the motorcycle, leaving Viset to park it in the shade of a weather-beaten tree. The road was parched, burnt by the midday heat. Calum attempted to take a deep breath but the air this far from the beach was dense and suffocating. His nostrils were filled with the smell of charcoal smoke and caramelised fruit. The knot in his chest further-tightened as Viset led him towards Sawat's house. He glimpsed television screens through the open doors of neighbours' homes and a small boy ran onto a porch to point a toy laser gun in his direction.

As Viset pointed to the open door of Sawat's house, Calum regarded the makeshift wheelchair ramp with deep sadness. He was sick with guilt and deeply apprehensive about meeting Sawat again. Viset, who had walked ahead in solemn silence, stood at the threshold and called inside.

Nok was first to appear, scampering barefoot from the shadows, wearing a pair of lime green shorts and a *Hello Kitty* T-shirt. Calum noticed that her radiant smile dropped when she realised who else was there.

Nevertheless, she greeted Calum without any outward signs of animosity and beckoned them both inside. Just as they were slipping off their flip-flops, Sawat appeared in his wheelchair, wearing just a pair of surfer shorts:

"*Khun* Calum! I cannot believe!" he cheered, beaming from ear to ear.

Calum was shocked to see that Sawat's once-powerful legs were now spindly as a foal's. Strikingly atrophied, they hung from the saddle of his wheelchair, flaccid as deck ropes. Sawat propelled his wheelchair forward and, after offering an effusive *wai*, extended his arms upwards, whereupon Calum stooped to share a prolonged hug with him.

"Oh, Sawat, I don't know what to say…" Calum croaked, gripping Sawat's hands as he knelt before him, forcing back tears.

Nok returned from the kitchen holding two glasses of iced water for their guests.

"Please not be so sad, *Khun* Calum. You make me very happy today. So many time I hope that you come back to Thailand." Immediately though, the strain of his substitute life came to the fore; Sawat bowed his head and began to sob quietly.

Calum shook with raw emotion and rested his forehead on Sawat's knees, where he wept unashamedly. Nok placed Calum's water on top of a teak sideboard and was unexpectedly touched by the foreigner's display of humanity. Sawat, in an attempt to lift everyone's spirits, forced a smile and used his thumbs to wipe the tears from Calum's cheeks.

"*Khun* Calum, thank you for my watch," he said, lifting his wrist to show it off, "and look! You still wear the necklace of Phra Pid Ta. Did he bring you good luck?"

"Uh, yes he did," Calum replied, uncomfortable at the mention of *good luck*. "You remember the girl I liked …

Hannah? Well, she is my girlfriend now."

"Yeah baby!" Sawat shouted, slapping his hands together, delighted to hear such wonderful news. "And did you bring *Khun* Hannah to Phuket, also?"

"Sure, she's back at the Redford Hotel," explained Calum, in awe of Sawat's sudden cheerfulness.

"So, tomorrow you can bring *Khun* Hannah here, *kap?*"

"Of course, she would like that," Calum said, finding it impossible to mirror his friend's positivity.

Sawat wheeled round so he could face Viset and Nok. He said something to them in Thai, whereupon they nodded before making themselves scarce, disappearing into another room. Sawat turned towards Calum again and lowered his voice. "Do not worry for me, *Khun* Calum. Everything happen for a reason. The gho't in the sea, he angry with me ... so he like to punish me, *na?*"

"But we both know, *Khun* Sawat, that this is nothing to do with a ghost. If I hadn't started the fight, then those men would not have attacked you."

"*Khun* Calum, you must not think like this. The sea spirit, he very sad, like me. Two time I disturb him ... he think I not learn my lesson the first time, so he show me who the boss."

Calum felt all the more guilty, realising that Sawat was attributing his terrible plight to something supernatural rather than basing it on cold, hard facts.

Sawat looked Calum directly in his eyes; his voice became hushed and deadly serious. "*Khun* Calum, can you do something very important for me?"

"Anything," Calum replied.

"When you go back to the beach today, say sorry to the sea gho't for me. Perhap' he give me a second chance?"

Calum wasn't quite sure how he could achieve this apology but he nodded his head anyway, understanding how much this meant to Sawat.

"Also, please to tell him that I forgive him…"

"OK, *Khun* Sawat, I will do that this afternoon."

"You promise to me?"

"I promise."

Calum drank the water, then wrote down his phone number, hotel room number and email address. In turn, Sawat scribbled his own contact details, and then called out for Viset and Nok to rejoin them.

Calum seized the opportunity to offer support in any way he could. "I am going back to the hotel now, but I am coming back later, with as much money as I can. I know how tough things must be and I am going to help."

Nok understood the gist of this declaration and stepped forward with a fulsome *wai* to show her appreciation. "Thank you, *ka* … Sawat, he too proud to take money."

Calum looked at Sawat, whose bottom lip had started to quiver. He knew what he needed to do. After saying his goodbyes, he stepped out into the fierce heat accompanied by Viset, who was also visibly upset by his friend's distressing circumstances.

"You want to go back to the beach, *kap*?" Viset asked, sliding his mirrored sunglasses back onto his face.

"Yep, back to the beach, please."

****

Viset had left the silk scarves, which he sold, in the safe keeping of the massage ladies, who kept a canopied stand on the beach. He promised Calum that whenever he was ready, he would take him back to see Sawat. Before returning to the room to take money from the safe to pass on to Sawat, Calum wanted to make good on his promise to call out to the sea ghost, as desperate as that idea seemed. So Calum stood on the shoreline, in alignment with the sinister area of dark water that lurked like an oil slick further out to sea. With the sun's rays burning the nape of his neck, he waited for a break when no one else was around. As soon as the opportunity presented itself, he hollered at the top of his lungs towards the sparkling horizon.

"Sea spirit, please reveal yourself to me!" He called out more in hope than expectation, in the same way a confirmed atheist might instinctively pray to God in a desperate moment of need. "Please, I need to speak to you!"

Even as he shouted, Calum realised how ridiculous this was. He was grateful that the nearest beachcombers were some way out of earshot.

"My friend Sawat says he is sorry! He also wants you to know that he forgives you!"

Unbelievably, at that precise moment something broke the surface of the sea no more than five hundred metres from where he was standing. A sleek funnel of water coursed towards him, almost as if a small submarine was moving beneath the surface. And then, astonishingly, just ten metres out, the creature rose majestically from the waves, like King Neptune.

Calum's blood pounded through his body. Despite his initial hope that the Kinnara would show itself, nothing in his young life could have prepared him for such a terrifying reality. Klahan's chiselled face and athletic torso were the first things to appear, as if a sunken statue had come to life. Klahan further announced himself with a triumphant flap of his magnificent wings. This sent a nursery of sleeping fish scattering in every direction from the sanctuary of their feathered dormitory.

Calum staggered backwards and almost tripped. Despite a shockwave of fear and panic passing through his body, he was transfixed by the spectacle. The image of his previous underwater encounter paled into insignificance compared to this jaw-dropping spectacle.

Having reached the shallower water, Klahan waded purposefully towards Calum. From his waist upwards, apart from his wings, he looked human with an epidermis that was completely hairless from navel to cranium, while his lower half was clearly that of an unusually large bird. Hidden under a luxuriant layer of feathers, Klahan's muscular thighs were as sturdy as those of a Samoan rugby player; in stark contrast, his raw-looking shinbones appeared to be as gnarled and as rickety as old tree branches. The Kinnara's feathers extended across his hips in a grubby fringe and thickened into a dense quiff at the tail.

Calum couldn't understand how the creature's brisk paddle through the thigh-deep water didn't create so much as a single splash, and why no droplets of seawater dripped from its feathers. It was almost as if this being were no more solid than the very air which surrounded it.

Klahan stared at the mortal, having already identified him as Calum Armstrong – the same merciless human who had so casually deserted him after their first meeting. The elation that Klahan should have been experiencing now that he was successfully liberated was constrained by his bitter resentment of this unsympathetic wretch who, without even a moment's hesitation, abandoned him to his torment.

Calum took several steps back, intimidated by the creature's presence. Fear and adrenaline made his fingers tremble. The Kinnara stood taller than most humans at a height comparable to a professional basketball player. Now bathed in sunshine, its smooth skin was iridescent and as sparkly as marble. Once again, presumably to show Calum its superiority, it unfurled its white wings as if they were large fans – although the pageantry of such a display was in sharp contrast to the stony expression on Klahan's face. Upon his head was a pointed, golden crown which gleamed ostentatiously, like a temple's ornate spire.

Suddenly jolted back to reality, Calum couldn't understand why there was no chorus of hysterical screams from the other holidaymakers at the sight of this fearsome monster. He spun around; people were continuing on their beach walks, oblivious to the mythical beast in their midst.

"They cannot see me," the creature explained, studying Calum with forensic interest. "I am only visible to you because you *expected* to see me." His voice was rasping; the words scoured Klahan's throat, challenging a tongue that hadn't been used for centuries.

"You speak English?" Calum gasped. He saw that the beast didn't cast a shadow and that there were no claw prints in the sand.

"Of course I can speak English," it replied, haughtily. "Also Dutch, Portuguese and Siamese. When we last met, I took every scrap of information from your underused brain and loaded it into mine. I have access to everything you have ever seen, read, or heard. Your pitiful memory will have forgotten most of it, of course."

"I do know that you are an avian humanoid," Calum declared, hoping to curry favour by showing a degree of familiarity with the species.

"Oh, am I now?" the beast sneered, seemingly unimpressed.

He had an ethereal quality and continued to study Calum as if he were conducting some silent experiment. His lips were mossy green, like algae on the exposed hull of a boat. Calum surprised even himself that he was no longer in the least bit scared of this winged phenomenon. Unbeknown to him, though, holidaymakers were pausing to stare at the crazy English guy who was having a deep discussion with the ocean.

"Do you have a name?" Calum asked.

"I do. It is Klahan Kinnara." As Klahan said this, he

jutted out his jaw, almost as if striking a pose. Then he approached Calum in the manner of a horse whisperer and placed his mother-of-pearl fingertips on top of his head, as if he were blessing him.

Klahan's tigerish eyes gave no indication of his temperament or his intentions. They recalibrated their focal length like the zoom lens of a camera, shifting between neutral and sullen, depending on the type of data he was receiving from Calum's mind.

Becalmed by Klahan's mesmerism, Calum was happy to allow the archives of his mind to be accessed but also struggled to come to terms with the contradictory principles of Klahan's manifestation. The creature hadn't left a single mark in the sand, and yet the hand that was placed upon his head felt solid. Also, Klahan had emerged from the sea bone dry but still had a damp, pungent smell about him, like a pond that had been recently dredged. In addition, Calum seemed to be the only person who could see him.

"If you were capable of understanding my ability to bend time, or were cognisant of the science behind the conversion of matter, then I would gladly explain it to you," said Klahan, reading Calum's last thought before removing his pearly hand.

Calum was only too willing to put up with condescension, hoping that Klahan's supernatural powers might hold the key to reversing Sawat's paraplegia.

It suddenly dawned on Klahan that much of the bitterness he felt towards humans was being misdirected at this wingless fool, and that this was overshadowing the joy that he should have been experiencing. Much to Calum's surprise, Klahan released a deep, palliative sigh and broke down, burying his tearful face in his large hands.

Calum was taken aback by this sudden display of emotion and instinctively sought to comfort the Kinnara, but his hand passed right through Klahan's crystalline arm. *Sawat's instincts were right,* thought Calum, *for some reason this sea ghost has also been suffering.*

Klahan continued to howl. His hoarse sobs similar to noises made by a startled goose. Then, when he eventually regained his composure, his eyes were no longer hostile and he seemed much less aloof.

"Calum Armstrong, without realising it, you have released me from an eternity of damnation, and for that I am in your debt."

"So how *did* you come to be on the bottom of the sea?" Calum asked, amazed that it was so easy to have an informal chat with a supernatural being. Unfortunately for him, at that moment, his conservation was interrupted by two male, beer-bellied, middle-aged English tourists who were bemused by Calum's solo performance:

"Mate, who're you talking to?" said the first one, mocking him.

Calum regarded their Beavis and Butt-head grins and resisted the urge to punch them both in the face. "Look, guys, I'm just here doing my own thing. I'm no bother to either of you, so could you please just leave me in peace?"

"But there's no one there," said the other one, stating the obvious, whilst sliding a hand under his man boobs to wipe away some trapped sweat.

Calum glanced at Klahan, who seemed to be intrigued by the dynamics of the situation. Beavis and Butt-head started to chuckle like village idiots and, given the momentousness of his situation, Calum's limited store of patience ran out. "Look, why don't you two dickheads just piss off and leave me alone?"

"Whoa! … OK fellah," Beavis gasped, backing off, alarmed at the intensity in the younger man's eyes. The two interlopers turned to waddle up the beach without another word.

Klahan shook his head in sorrow and offered an opinion. "This is the problem with humankind. Apart from very few exceptions, you cannot co-exist harmoniously."

"As I was saying," Calum continued, with a trace of irritation still in his voice, "how did you end up at the bottom of the sea?"

"Two thousand years ago I made an error of judgement and, just like you, I stupidly resorted to violence. As a consequence, I was cursed to reside at the bottom of that sea for two thousand years." Klahan paused to allow the enormity of this penance to register in Calum's mind.

"Two thousand years?" Calum gasped. "You have been trapped in that same spot for *two thousand* years?"

"Yes, but your recognition of this time scale cannot give you any understanding of the torment I have suffered because, throughout this entire period, I have been away from my love partner, Anong." His eyes misted again. "Could you imagine being forced apart from Hannah Cunningham even for the duration of one human lifetime?"

Calum's overriding emotion was one of extreme pity but he knew that any sympathetic words would just seem trite, given the magnitude of Klahan's suffering:

"So, how have I freed you? I don't understand," Calum asked.

"It wasn't *you* as such. It was your friend Sawat. He found it necessary to forgive me though for what reason, I know not."

"He thinks that you are the cause of his paraplegia because he disturbed you on two occasions."

"Ha! Well, as grateful as I am for his nonsensical beliefs, he could not be further from the truth. Calum, you and I both know the *true* reason for his present difficulties, do we not?"

"Yes," Calum agreed, hanging his head in shame.

"But as I stated earlier I am in your debt so, on that basis, I am prepared to help your friend. But only if you are prepared to accept that there must be consequences for your own precipitous actions."

"Of course, I will do anything," begged Calum, thankful for any glimmer of hope that Sawat might be helped.

"Anything?" asked Klahan, doubtful that any human could be that philanthropic, "So, what would you be prepared to give up if I could completely cure your friend?"

"Oh, my God, I would give up my house, all the money I have … I would give up *everything* if Sawat could walk again."

"So, would you give up Hannah?" Klahan probed, fixing Calum with a cold, penetrative stare.

Calum looked shell-shocked. Rendered speechless, he looked into Klahan's inscrutable face. "What exactly do you mean by *giving up* Hannah?"

"Calum, I have endured several centuries apart from my love because of my own hot-headedness so, surely, for the sake of your crippled friend, you could forsake your partner, and have no contact with her for say … six of your human months?"

"But why do you have to make the consequence so spiteful?" Calum complained. "I was about to propose to her. Could you not punish me in some other way?"

"Six months!" Klahan snorted. "It is a mere blink of an eye compared to the purgatory I have been put through by your kind!"

"Please, please, I'm begging you … please reconsider," beseeched Calum. He instinctively bowed and offered a *wai* which he held above his head.

"Do not test my patience. I have helped countless mortals like you, who have called out in their hour of need, whining, snivelling and grovelling – but look how mankind has repaid me."

"OK, OK. So how do I know for sure that you can cure Sawat?"

Klahan's nostrils flared in the face of such impudence. He crouched down and covered the blood-encrusted laceration of Calum's dog bite with the palm of his hand. Calum saw his own perturbed expression reflected in Klahan's golden crown and, within seconds, the wound had completely disappeared.

"Never again doubt me, human," hissed Klahan. "If you agree to my terms, your crippled friend will walk again within the hour. All *you* have to do is abandon your love partner, with immediate effect, without giving her the true reason. You must, thereafter, relinquish all contact with her for one hundred and eighty days. After this period, the curse will be lifted. You can resume your relationship, and Sawat will have the full use of his legs until the day he dies."

Calum's mind was in turmoil, but he knew he was fighting a losing battle and didn't want to provoke Klahan into rescinding his offer. Klahan, meanwhile, understood the human's uncertainty and offered some sage advice. "Calum, if the love that you both have can endure this, then believe me when I say that it is a love worth having."

Just as Calum prepared to make his decision, a young elephant tramped towards him, accompanied by its owner. Klahan's voice boomed with sudden urgency. "Your girlfriend is approaching. You do not have the time to dither. Make your decision!"

Calum was having palpitations and butterflies swarmed his stomach. This was a leap of faith from a skyscraper ledge to escape the blaze within. He scrunched his eyes and leapt: "OK, OK! I *will* finish with Hannah, but please, *please* do what you can for Sawat."

Satisfied with this covenant, Klahan imposed his curse

upon Calum and vanished in a kaleidoscopic cloud of pixels. A small pack of territorial beach dogs ran from the shade to bark at the elephant, who trumpeted them away.

"Calum! Look at the cute elephant!" shouted Hannah, momentarily distracted by such a sight. "Honey, I was so desperate to find you ... how are things with Sawat?"

Vertigo gripped Calum like a vice, the horizon curved like a convex lens and he felt as if he were plummeting down a lift shaft.

"Calum, are you OK? What happened?" She tried to pass him the bottle of water which she had carried from the hotel.

Calum couldn't bring himself to look at Hannah. He was about to betray her and yet, at that moment, he knew that he loved her more than ever. Suddenly his mouth felt as if it was filled with more than one tongue. "Hannah ... you and I ... it just isn't working out."

He heard the words tumble from his mouth and he could taste their poison. Hannah stopped in her tracks, astonished. Calum watched her smile melt like an ice cube.

"You are kidding, right?" she said, pushing her sunglasses on top of her head and placing her hands on her hips. She looked worried, but also annoyed.

"No, I'm deadly serious," he confirmed, drawing a semi-circle in the sand with his toes. He found it impossible to look into her eyes.

Hannah's jaw slackened. She was horrified by what she was seeing and hearing. "Calum, I appreciate that you're upset about Sawat, but whatever is happening I will support you every step of the way. In fact, while you were gone I'd already decided to use some of my savings to help him financially..."

"It's not that, Hannah. We ... we're just not right for each other."

"Not right for each other? How can two people be

any *more* right for each other? Please don't do this to me, Calum, please!"

Hannah's eyes implored him to change his mind. Tears cascaded down her distraught face. This wasn't the movie in her mind. Calum, filled with anguish, pulled at his hair and cried out like a wounded animal. As he turned to leave, Hannah tried to reach for his hand, but he swatted her away, leaving Hannah to crumple to her knees like a puppet whose strings had been cut. Her loud sobs were enough to cause the elephant to lumber over with a silent offer of comfort.

CHAPTER THIRTY-SEVEN

Resurrection

Because Klahan had extracted every bit of information filed within the registry of Calum's mind, he knew exactly where Sawat lived. Delighted to fly again he soared, unseen, in the skies above Patong, watching aeroplanes close up for the first time in his life. He even sat on the wing of one, just to see what it was like. Before Klahan could return to Anong he was obliged to complete one irrevocable task.

Touching down on the road surface of Soi Hwang he realised that he was hungry for the first time in two millennia, and that he desperately needed a scented wash to cleanse the grime from his briny body.

****

With Nok visiting the 7-Eleven store to top up her phone credit and buy provisions, Sawat was preparing vegetables in the kitchen. He julienned carrots and halved some shitake mushrooms, to save his mother time when she returned home. Suddenly, he felt the air around him change and then noticed a pungent, silty smell, which seemed to fill the kitchen.

He flinched and simultaneously yelped with alarm as a large invisible hand slid between his shoulder blades and rested against his spinal column. But his consternation eased as his mind and body were cocooned in an invisible bubble of tranquillity. His toes began to tingle and dormant leg muscles sprang back to life, expanding rapidly to fill his loosened skin with a succession of pneumatic creaks that continued into his hips.

Sawat suddenly saw his feathered saviour. He left his wheelchair and prostrated himself before Klahan, bowing his forehead to the floor as if he were revering a god.

****

As Calum once again rode pillion on Viset's motorcycle, he hoped to God that his appalling treatment of Hannah would prove to be justified.

When they slowed at the junction of Soi Hwang, a cluster of excited schoolgirls were huddled around Panit's stall, placing orders for his pineapple or banana pancakes. They wore the standard uniform; short-sleeved white blouses, paired with navy-blue skirts, their black hair cut into a regulation short bob. After they'd rounded the corner, Calum dismounted the bike while it was still coasting, because ahead he saw something unimaginable: Sawat was out in the street, surrounded by a group of astounded neighbours who couldn't believe what they were witnessing. They circled him as if they were watching an itinerant snake charmer, for he was stood bolt upright, energetically flicking his legs as if trying to shake off a pair of obstinate crabs.

Stupefied, Viset abandoned his bike in the middle of the road and walked towards this astonishing scene. Calum's chest involuntarily heaved as a paroxysm of sobs burst from his throat.

Sawat spotted his two friends. He already knew that

there must have been some cosmic connection which involved the Englishman, the sea spirit and his miraculous recovery. He called out to Calum and then fell to his knees in adoration as if the Englishman was a deity. The hushed crowd parted, enabling the three friends to join together for an exuberant group hug. Then Sawat shepherded Calum to one side, so he could talk in private, without Viset overhearing.

"*Khun* Calum, you spoke with the sea gho't, *na*?" he said. His trademark smile was as wide as the *soi*.

"Yes, I did," Calum confirmed. "But I had to make a deal and please do not say anything about this deal to *anyone*, not even to Hannah if you ever meet her."

"Oh no, *Khun* Calum, what deal you make? I worry you make problem for yourself."

"Sawat, there is nothing to worry about, but it is important for your recovery that nobody, I repeat *nobody*, knows about the sea ghost. Promise?"

"I promise."

News of a neighbourhood phenomenon spread like wildfire and within minutes a sizeable crowd of curious locals had congregated to marvel at Sawat's transformation. Everyone wanted to touch his legs, hoping that they might also become the recipients of such good fortune.

Calum continued to struggle with his conflicting emotions, knowing that Sawat's resurrection was wholly reliant on him ignoring Hannah for the next six months. "*Khun* Sawat, I don't have time to explain, but I have to leave the island immediately. I will come back, though, in seven months time."

"With *Khun* Hannah?"

"I'm not sure … I really hope so."

"*Khun* Calum, before you go, I want to thank you from me, my girlfrien' and my family, thank you from my heart. You gave me my life. You are more than frien', you are like my brother, *kap*."

"Thank you, *Khun* Sawat – that means a lot."

The two men hugged once more and then Viset started up his motorcycle, just as the blue sky darkened and the first heavy drops of rain spat against the dusty road surface.

Nok returned from the 7-Eleven before her fêted boyfriend had thought to phone her. When she saw the large crowd gathered outside Sawat's home, she was instantly fearful that he might have taken his own life. Dropping her carrier bag, she rushed towards the throng with an awful sense of dread and then, like everyone else who was present on that wondrous afternoon, she bore witness to something which was undoubtedly beyond any earthly possibility.

CHAPTER THIRTY-EIGHT

For the Greater Good

Fat droplets of rain, the size of plum stones hammered down on Calum and Viset as they rode through a torrential downpour. It was a deluge that required headlamps to be set on full beam, and which caused rivers of brown, sludgy water to spew from overwhelmed storm drains.

By the time he reached the hotel, Calum's sodden polo shirt was clingy as pasted wallpaper. After shouting out his gratitude to Viset through a wall of watery noise, he sprinted towards the plate-glass doors of the lobby, his flip-flops slapping noisily on the puddled ground.

Calum's drenched appearance was met with innocent chuckles by the white-gloved doormen who welcomed him in. Once inside, he carried his flip-flops, stencilling wet footprints onto the marble floor, all the way to the lifts.

****

As the storm raged outside, Hannah lay forlornly on the bed in their hotel room but immediately perked up when she heard the click of Calum's room card on the other side of the door. In readiness, she sat up with her legs crossed and hugged a pillow for comfort: she was mindful that Calum would need some time and space to get his mind right, then hopefully he might justify his irrational behaviour.

A fleeting glance was enough to tell Calum that Hannah had been crying since he abandoned her at the beach. At first she didn't speak and waited patiently to hear what he had to say. But Calum did not utter a single word and allowed his silence to pollute the room. He hurriedly towelled himself dry in the bathroom before slipping on a pair of jeans, a shirt and some trainers.

Hannah felt sick to the pit of her stomach and began to panic when he carried his wet suitcase in from the rain-swept balcony. "Calum, please ... what the hell is happening here? Please speak to me." Her voice was tremulous and broken.

Calum ignored her and continued like an automaton, detachedly packing the suitcase as if he were the only person in the room. Hannah slid from the bed and tentatively touched his back with her fingertips. "Honey, please, we need to talk. Have I done something to upset you? If I have, I sincerely apologise."

She felt him flinch under her touch. Rain lashed the glass panels of the balcony doors, gusted in by a wind that howled like a drowning man. Desperation took hold of Hannah's emotions and she snatched a T-shirt out of Calum's hand. She grabbed him roughly and spun him round. He stood passively, his gaze directed aimlessly across the ceiling.

"Calum, look at me! You are acting like a complete arse! I don't know what I've done to deserve this!" Her voice convulsed with emotion. For a split second Calum nearly broke his silence, but he reined himself in, mindful of the clear-cut terms of the agreement. After tearing himself loose, he punched a four-digit code to open the room safe. With cold efficiency, he removed his passport, credit card and a moderate amount of cash.

Hannah could not believe that the same considerate boy, whom she had known for almost half of her life, could behave so spitefully. "This isn't you, Calum and I know you well enough to guess that you're not doing this of your own free will. What the *hell* is going on?"

Her words fell on deaf ears; Calum maintained his grim silence, grabbed his phone and some other belongings from the dressing table, and made for the door. Hannah clung to him, as if her life depended on it. "Calum, don't do this," she beseeched, as he half-dragged her across the floor. "You're making me look a complete idiot. What am I supposed to tell my parents, my friends? Tell me Calum, what am I supposed to do?" She barely managed to utter these words before she collapsed in a heap, sobbing uncontrollably.

Seeing her anguish tore Calum apart: it took all his willpower not to lift her up and let her know that everything was going to be just fine; to tell her he wanted to marry her and that he wanted to spend the rest of his life with her. Instead, he knew that he had to escape. Pretty soon he was pressing buttons in the lift, closing the doors as Hannah lunged towards them.

As soon as he arrived at the ground floor, Calum made for the hotel entrance. The brisk thump of his suitcase wheels on the marble surface alerted Nuay, who was disconcerted to see one of his favourite guests hurrying through the lobby with a thunderous look on his face.

"*Khun* Calum, is everything OK, *kap*?" he asked, wringing his hands and furrowing his brow.

"Could you call me a taxi, please?" urged Calum, displaying none of his usual easy charm. Nuay instantly sensed that something dreadful had happened between Calum and his beautiful girlfriend so, without prying further, he marched straight over to his lectern and made the call.

Inevitably, Hannah charged into the lobby, her tormented face attracting the attention of every person present. Calum heard her call out to him and gazed up at an enormous crystal chandelier, trying not to burst into tears. Nuay and one other bellboy stood half-poised, unsure if they should still attend to his taxi, which had rolled up outside.

Abandoning all self-respect, Hannah made a last-ditch attempt to stop Calum from leaving and flung her arms around him, imploring him to stay.

"Calum, please, please I'm begging you. I will do anything … please, you're breaking my heart!"

The bustle of the foyer ground to a standstill as everyone stopped to gape at this distressing display of raw emotion. Nuay could not believe his eyes when Calum callously ignored Hannah's hiccoughing pleas and left her crumpled in a tearful heap. As a matter of principle, Nuay didn't bid the Englishman a cheery farewell. Without saying a word he held the door open, astonished at the disgraceful way in which Calum had treated his girlfriend. Meanwhile, two female receptionists had abandoned their posts and were rushing to her aid, their slender heels click-clacking as they ran. The girls shepherded her into a back office, where they doled out tissues and offered soothing platitudes in an attempt to console her.

The taxi's tyres splashed along the watery road beyond the security gate. Calum's driver was too preoccupied with the treacherous weather to notice the bonfire of his passenger's tortured emotions. The cabbie drove with his eyes myopically close to the windscreen. Through necessity he had pushed his chin and shoulders up against the steering wheel as the frantic wipers struggled to maintain any worthwhile visibility.

Within this cauldron of stormy noise, Calum wept silently to himself and his rain-battered taxi was chased all the way to the island's airport by a stampede of thunder.

****

Hannah spent the evening alone in their room, too upset and embarrassed to call family or friends. When the bedside telephone rang, she answered it calmly, hoping that it would be Calum announcing that he had finally banished his demons.

"Hello, room four-zero-six," she answered, keeping her hoarse voice as composed as she could.

"Hey, *Khun* Hannah! *Sawasdee kap*. It Sawat here, so good to finally speak with you."

"Sawat, is, um, Calum with you?"

There was a pregnant pause on the line as Sawat gathered his thoughts. "So, he not with you at the hotel?"

After this, the only thing that Sawat could hear was the sound of Hannah's tears as she broke down, unable to sustain her fragile composure any longer.

"*Khun* Hannah, please not cry, what happen?"

"I'm all on my own," she croaked between sobs, barely able to speak.

"Okay, I come to see you. Meet you in the lobby, eigh' o'clock, *Kap*?"

****

When Sawat strolled into the hotel wearing the most casual of clothes, the doormen weren't anywhere near as obsequious as they would have been had he been a rich *farang*:

Hannah was sitting in the centre of a commodious sofa which faced the entrance. She immediately recognised Sawat from his photograph. What she absolutely didn't expect, though, was for him to come striding into the lobby like an Olympic gymnast.

Sawat intuitively guessed which one of the assembled guests was Hannah and greeted her with a *wai* and a solicitous smile as he walked towards her. "*Sawasdee kap*, *Khun* Hannah, so happy to meet you."

Hannah didn't reply; instead she stared at Sawat in disbelief. She imagined that Calum, for some unfathomable reason, had concocted the whole elaborate tale about his friend's disability, and that this cock-and-bull story bore some relevance to his abrupt disappearance.

"OK, Sawat, let's get right to the point," she stormed, jumping to her feet. "I was led to believe that you had a terrible injury, and that you were in a wheelchair. Am I missing something?"

"Please, *Khun* Hannah, sit down maybe I can help you understand, *kap*?"

"No, I won't sit down! Why has Calum lied to me? Why has he made me look a fool?" Hannah snorted, her sadness turned to anger.

"*Khun* Calum, he never tell lie to you. What you say is true, I *am* paralyse … cannot walk for long time. I have wheelchair for many month."

"So are you seriously telling me that you were paralysed and in a wheelchair, and now you can run around as if nothing had happened? I'm sorry, but that is ridiculous."

Sawat could see the hurt in Hannah's eyes, he would have loved to ease her torment, to explain the day's extraordinary events but he had promised Calum that he wouldn't tell a soul. Furthermore, his friend had made it perfectly clear that this rule applied especially to Hannah.

"Where you think *Khun* Calum is now?" Sawat asked, desperate to offer some help.

"Well, as far as I know, he's at the airport or he's probably already on a flight to Bangkok. He left me here without any explanation. He said he doesn't want to see me anymore."

Sawat was increasingly worried about the deal that Calum must have made with the sea spirit. When his English friend mentioned leaving the island *immediately*, Sawat assumed it was just a figure of speech. And he certainly hadn't expected Calum to leave his girlfriend behind.

"Please, *Khun* Hannah, I want you to listen to me. *Khun* Calum, I know he have some problem that he cannot say. But I know he love you from all his heart, please believe me. Something really good happen to me today but I think something very bad happen to him."

"But what exactly *did* happen to him today? Why is everything such a big secret? I just don't know what to think any more."

Sawat held Hannah's hands and looked deep into her sad eyes. "*Khun* Hannah, you already know that *Khun* Calum is a good guy, kap?"

"Yes, of course."

"So, today he do something that not in his nature, *na*? But please know this, he is still the same guy and when he fix this problem, he will come back to you."

Despite her desolation, Hannah could sense that Sawat was a genuine person and his soothing words thawed the ice of her loneliness. "Thank you, Sawat. I really do appreciate you coming to see me this evening. I still haven't the faintest idea about what's going on but you have helped me enormously."

"I give you my number, *kap* and alway' remember that you have a new frien' on Phuket island ... and already today *Khun* Calum say that he would like to come back again *with you*, *Khun* Hannah."

"He really said that?" she asked, the faintest of smiles reaching her lips.

"I promise you, he say exact' that ... he *love* you, *Khun*

Hannah, no matter what happen."

CHAPTER THIRTY-NINE

Paradise Regained

The universe allowed Klahan to bend two thousand years of time and so he travelled back through the centuries, arriving in the airspace above the Swan Kingdom on the same day that he was originally banished by Prarachar, the Swan King.

After descending through a wisp of cirrus clouds, he flew at great speed above the canopy of the forest. The balmy scent of tropical pine began to revive his senses and an uplifting chorus of birdsong welcomed him home. His heart began to pound even faster than his wings as he swooped towards the lake because, on its far side, he saw his beloved Anong, for the first time in eons.

In the shade of a large fan palm, on a soft blanket of grass, Anong played an emotive tune on a bamboo flute while her sisters serenaded her, each one singing like a nightingale. Their carolling was a deliberate attempt to distract her, as she was so desperately anxious to learn of Klahan's fate, acutely aware that today he could be brutally punished for killing that human. She hadn't seen Klahan since first light that morning, when he was precipitously summoned to appear before the swan king. She already knew that King Prarachar was intolerant whenever one of his own subjects disobeyed a royal decree – and especially if such an act threatened the harmonious relationship that existed between the Kinnaree and their human neighbours.

All at once, Anong sensed Klahan's presence and spotted him above the northern end of the lake. The distance reduced him to the size of a dragonfly. He flew low, his wings clipping the glassy surface on their downward beat, causing sunlit jewels of water to spray out from the rear of his fast-moving shadow. Anong heard the *thwoom-thwoom, thwoom-thwoom* of his feathers as he neared the shoreline and then there was silence as he hovered above the ground before her.

Disturbingly, as soon as Klahan touched down, he knelt onto one knee and then sobbed noisily into his hands – something she had never seen him do before. Anong leapt up and rushed to console him. His appearance gave her further concern – he looked and smelled as if he had recently fallen into a swamp.

"My darling Klahan, what has happened?" she asked, sudden panic rising in her voice. She immediately looked for any wounds that might be concealed by the patina of ingrained dirt that encrusted his skin. Klahan enveloped Anong in an impassioned hug, relieved that she was back in his arms once more. And she, without knowing the cause of his distress, pressed against him, allowing him time to regain his composure.

Her dumbfounded sisters kept a respectful distance and huddled together like doves in a storm. All three were perplexed by Klahan's unkempt physical state, and also by his heightened state of emotion.

As soon as Klahan was able, he relinquished his impassioned grip and a relieved smile appeared on his tear-streaked face. Looking directly into her curious eyes, he held one of Anong's alabaster hands and pressed it firmly against his cheek. Because of this connection, he was able to transmit every heart-breaking detail of his solitary existence directly into her mind.

The shock of this was almost too much to bear for Anong, who was immediately beside herself at the flagrant unfairness of his sentence. "Oh, Klahan, my love, your suffering was beyond cruel!"

As she continued to see his lonely torment in her mind's eye, her own tears streamed down the contours of her naked body before dripping off her hip feathers like raindrops from banyan leaves.

****

As the setting sun dropped behind the twilight whisper of the coconut palms, Anong cleansed Klahan's grimy body in the shallows of the lake with lavender flowers that she had mixed with crushed almonds; at the same time, her sisters scrubbed at his soiled wings until his feathers were the colour of the moon. No sooner had the night cast its black cloak than the solidity of the forest receded into a depthless mural of silhouettes.

After sipping bowls of chrysanthemum tea, Klahan gorged on mangoes that were drizzled in honey. Together they revelled in the novelty of their recently-shared knowledge. Klahan recited Shakespeare, while Anong gabbled excitedly about the Eskimo people and giraffes, but also about space rockets and skyscrapers.

Under a galaxy of stars, the lovers kissed unashamedly, each time receiving boisterous vocal applause from an unseen audience of noisy tree frogs. Gradually, Klahan drifted into sleep for the first time in two thousand years. He melted into Anong's arms, allowing her love and companionship to soothe his resentment. Then, just as a final wave of heavy-lidded tiredness washed over him, Klahan attempted to focus on Anong one last time, as if he needed to reaffirm her actual existence. He saw her gaze up at the pearly light of the moon, stretching out her fingertips, as if to touch it.

"Are not mortals amazing?" she enthused, now furnished with the knowledge that humans would one day walk upon its surface.

Klahan was far too exhausted to dispute this point and instead fell into a deep, curative sleep.

CHAPTER FORTY

The Vamp on the Rank

Once Calum had cleared immigration at London Heathrow Airport, he reluctantly switched on his phone, which pinged like a pinball machine under an onslaught of text messages. Waiting to transfer to the off-airport car parking site ten minutes from the terminal, he grimaced as each text drilled through his heart:

> *Calum, what on earth is going on? One minute you're about to propose, and the next you've abandoned Hannah in Thailand! She deserves so much better than this. Plz call me when you get the chance. Sophie.*

> -

> *Cal, what the hell buddy? Sophie has called me to say that you stormed off, leaving Hannah alone at the hotel. This just isn't you. I'm worried for both your sakes. Ring me soon, yeh? Leo.*

> -

> *Darling, I really don't know where you are, or what is happening. I'm worried about you, could you at least let*

me know that you're safe? If you don't want to speak to me, please just text, Love Hannah xxx

-

Calum, just because you don't want to be with me right now doesn't mean that I'm going to stop trying. God knows why, but I'm prepared to ride out the storm. I love you. Hannah xxx

-

Then there was one exclamatory text that corroborated the reason he had committed such a monstrous violation in the first place:

Heyyy Calum i am so happy!!! thank you for my legs walk again!!! You are my best friend! i saw Khun Hannah, she sad but ok i think. Not tell her anything. But I do tell her that you love her.

****

In the subsequent weeks, because Calum had blocked all calls from Hannah's phone, Sophie acted as an intermediary on her behalf but she was exasperated by the vagueness of Calum's assurances:

"Calum, it's not enough for you to say that you love Hannah, when all you do is ignore her. It's not enough to ask her to believe in you, when you won't even pick up the phone. You need to make your mind up, one way or the other. The poor girl is in bits and she's done nothing wrong!"

Similarly, Leo's attempts to decipher his friend's baffling about-face bore little fruit. Even when he was burdened with the unenviable task of retrieving Hannah's possessions from Calum's house, Leo could only tell her lamely that Calum *did* still love her, and that one day, apparently, this would all make sense. There soon came a time when Leo didn't dare broach the subject in front of Calum, sensing the turmoil that his best friend was trying to muzzle.

Mindful of the curse, Calum went to extraordinary lengths to avoid bumping into Hannah. Because she also worked part-time at the sports centre, he handed over the teaching of his karate classes to his friend, Naz. In addition, because he knew that Hannah would eventually turn up at his house, he peeked through an upstairs window when anyone rang his doorbell. On one such occasion, he looked out with deep dismay to see his beautiful girlfriend standing stoically in a deluge of rain, like a Victorian ghost. After a torturously long time he heard something clatter through his letterbox, and then he watched the lights of Hannah's car disappear in the direction of Unthank Road.

He rushed down the stairs to discover an envelope, upon which she had written his name above an inky love heart that had been blotched by rain. He slid the letter out and read it whilst his heart thudded against his ribcage.

My darling Calum,
It's been several weeks since you left me in our hotel room in Phuket, and I'm still no nearer to finding out what has happened for you to snub me without any explanation.
Somehow, something has darkened your beautiful soul and forced you to behave in this way. But I know what a wonderful person you are, and I know that you wouldn't do something as unfair as this without a perfectly good reason.
We've known each other since we were kids, and there is no way that the Calum who I've grown up with would behave this cruelly to anyone, least of all to someone who loves him with all her heart.

So, the only thing that I'm able to do is to read between the lines, and I sincerely hope that the secret which you daren't speak of will be revealed to me in time.

It pains me so much to say this, but I am going to give you all the space you need, in the hope that you will come back to me again, one day. I have too much pride to embarrass myself by chasing after you. The ball is firmly in your court.

In the meantime, I will keep up the pretence of being a single, independent woman … but know this, Calum, you will always have my heart and I will wait for you no matter how long it takes.

Yours, forever,

Hannah xxx

****

Only two nights later, when Calum's doorbell rang, he raced up the stairs but was surprised to see Hannah's father standing as immovable as a rock face on the chequered tiles of his front path.

When Calum opened the door, moonlight cast a sheen on the dark skin of Marvin's impassive face. The big man moved one step forward, closing down Calum's personal space. Calum noticed the deadpan expression, but also the tight black leather gloves that could barely contain Marvin's enormous hands.

"You told me that you would make my daughter happy. I told you that I would love you like a son. I kept *my* side of the bargain." His flat tone contained an undercurrent of menace.

"Please, Mr Cunningham, come in…"

"I'm just fine where I am."

Calum heard Marvin's gloves creak and half-expected a heavy punch to be thrown any second. "I know how things look, Mr Cunningham, they look bad – real bad – but I want you to know that I love your daughter with

285

all of my being and one day you might all understand the crazy predicament that I'm in."

"So talk, tell me about this *crazy* predicament."

"I can't. As stupid as it sounds, I just can't!"

Calum felt as if he'd been forced into a corner and to be on the receiving end of a hostile punch would at least have provided him with some welcome relief. Words, though, were so much harder to deal with. He knew that if he offered any kind of explanation, it would just seem cryptic and completely ludicrous in the eyes of Hannah's remarkable father.

Marvin was unprepared for the tears that he saw in the young man's eyes:

"So what is it? Is it drugs? Another woman? Are you being blackmailed? Whatever it is, we can help you. It breaks my heart, Calum, to hear my daughter crying alone in her bedroom night after night."

Calum's tears escalated into choking sobs, and even Marvin became misty-eyed. "Look, Calum, you're a good kid. I got mixed up in all kinds of crazy shit when I was a boy. You've still got feelings for Hannah, I can see that so, once you get rid of this problem, we will all be there for you. But we won't wait forever, you get me?"

"I appreciate that, Mr Cunningham, I really do. I promise you that I will do everything in my power to restore your faith in me and I can assure you that I don't want to lose the love of your daughter."

Marvin took one last look into Calum's wet eyes and saw the sincerity, there. "Whatever this is, get it sorted, yeah?" With this final instruction, he ambled to the gate, turning to close the latch with a dexterity that belied his size. Then he fixed Calum with a penetrating stare. "Like my own son ... just you remember that, Calum."

****

Feeling like a gooseberry, Calum dined at Jamie Oliver's Italian restaurant with Leo and Tilly, who insisted that he needed to get out of the house:

By the end of the evening, Calum was profoundly grateful for their social intervention. Good food, some Chianti and their company had a restorative effect on his soul and the three friends tumbled out of the restaurant and into the Royal Arcade in a haze of boozy conviviality.

"You guys are just the best," Calum slurred, draping his arms over both of their shoulders. "Hey, isn't this pretty?" he said, flapping his fingers at the Art Nouveau tiling and the stained-glass windows.

As they walked to the taxi rank on Guildhall Hill, Calum broke away from Leo and Tilly, leaving them to stumble along like contestants in a three-legged race.

"Oh, my God, look who it is!" Leo shouted, pointing towards Imogen Gibson who was standing in the taxi line. A push-up bra and a low-cut dress made her look like a modern day Moll Flanders.

"Hi, Imogen" Leo cheered, raising one arm like a Chinese waving cat. "Crikey, if Hooters restaurant were ever to start recruiting in Norwich, you'd be a shoe-in."

"Ha-bloody-ha," Imogen replied, cupping an elbow with one hand and holding a lit cigarette with the other.

"So what are you doing out on your own?" Calum asked, unconcerned about the ignominy of their break-up and that the last time he saw her she was red-faced and stark naked.

"Well, I've just walked out in the middle of a dinner date at the Wine Cellar," she clucked, nodding towards the restaurant and puffing smoke sideways from one corner of her glossy lips. "Good-looking guy, plenty of dosh, but he continued to talk whilst stuffing his face – I cannot tell you how disgusting it was to see undigested food tossing around his gob like socks in a tumble drier."

"So, how did you end the date?" Leo asked, intrigued.

"Just told him he had the table manners of a pig, then got up and left."

This revelation caused Calum, Leo and Tilly to break into peals of laughter; even Imogen forgot her vexation and allowed herself a smoky chuckle.

"Imogen, this is my wife, Tilly" Leo said. "Tilly, this is Imogen, Calum's ex."

"I guessed that," Tilly smiled, shaking Imogen warmly by the hand.

"Calum, is it true that you and Hannah Cunningham aren't seeing each other anymore?" Imogen quizzed, arching her eyebrows mischievously, hoping that an opportunity had fallen into her lap.

"Don't want to talk about it," Calum said bluntly.

"Well, let's put this another way," she continued, running a shiny nail down the front of his shirt and into his belt. "We're both without a date for the night, and you know that my flat is only a ten-minute cab ride away."

"It's not going to happen, Imogen," Calum said, flatly.

Unfortunately, before he could remove Imogen's intrusive fingers from the waistband of his trousers, Hannah and Sophie came past, unnoticed, in a taxi.

CHAPTER FORTY-ONE

Misapprehensions

Hannah reluctantly accepted that seeing Calum out on the town with Imogen Gibson was the wake-up call she needed. In that shocking moment, the pain of being apart from her boyfriend was supplanted by the cold, hard realisation that she had been a fool for continuing to believe in him. Every day, for more than a month, she clung to the mistaken belief that Calum might sort out whatever nonsense was flapping around in his head, and would come scuttling back to her with an explanation and a cluster of heartfelt apologies. Instead, he evidently preferred the proficient porn-star skills of slutty Gibson.

How could I have been so stupid? Hannah reflected. *And how could Leo and Tilly be part of such a betrayal of trust?*

None of this made any sense. In all the years that she had known him, Calum had always been caring and considerate. Similarly, Leo just wasn't the kind of guy who would usually behave in such a deceitful way – especially since he had convinced Hannah of Calum's continued love for her only two days previously.

Because news of Hannah's separation had spread throughout her Aviva workplace, there was no shortage of uninvited offers to go on a date, including one from Hamish, in corporate pensions, whose halitosis was noxious enough to fell a rhinoceros. In the light of her recent discovery, Hannah conceded that she ought to put Calum to the back of her mind and start to move on with her life.

****

It didn't go unnoticed by the ladies in Hannah's Step Aerobics class that the handsome American with the athletic physique couldn't take his eyes off her.

Brett Carter was a logistics officer working at the US Air Force base in Mildenhall, a one-hour drive from Norwich. His film-star good looks caused a salacious stir among the sweaty women of the Legs, Bums and Tums group, and each of his hip thrusts prompted a string of lip pouts and lusty looks behind his back. Brett stood six feet tall in his Reeboks; he had a Hollywood smile, ocean-blue eyes and black hair brilliantined to such an extent that it resembled patent leather. Unsurprisingly, he was the main topic of conversation amongst the ladies as they showered and changed in the locker room.

"God, if I wasn't married I'd be all over him, like a rash," enthused Megan, the libidinous redhead from Thorpe End. "In fact, sod my husband, I'd happily risk divorce for one smutty afternoon with him in a Travelodge."

"Why just settle for a Travelodge?" Hannah grinned.

"Oh, he could do me in a bus shelter if he wanted," Megan chuckled. "Besides, we all know who he really has the hots for, don't we Hannah?"

"Mmm, he is quite easy on the eye," she admitted. "But I definitely need a break from men for a while."

"Nonsense! You need to get back on the horse and, oh, *what* a horse!"

Immediately afterwards, as Hannah was visiting the

sports centre's café for a latte and a Danish pastry, she was greeted by Brett and his persuasive smile. "Hi, Hannah, mind if I join you?"

"Um, yeah, sure," Hannah responded, moving towards a vacant table.

"We haven't properly met. I'm Brett. And as you can probably tell, I'm an American…"

"Yeah, I got that," she chuckled, shaking his hand and finding his enthusiasm comical. "How long have you lived in Norwich?"

"Oh, I live in Mildenhall," he replied.

"Mildenhall? Don't they have step classes in that neck of the woods?"

"They do, but then I heard that the instructors are so much prettier in Norwich."

"Well, aren't you a charmer?" smiled Hannah, breaking off a bite-sized piece of pastry.

"Gee, how do you stay so slim eating stuff like that?"

"Are you for real?" she laughed. "You sound like an American boy scout."

Brett was captivated by Hannah; she, in turn appreciated some harmless flirting. Continuing to make conversation, he withdrew some black-rimmed spectacles from a leather case and buffed them with a lens-cleaning cloth. He offered them up to the light, slipped them onto his head and then corrected them with a finger prod:

"Hey, I don't want to tread on anyone's toes … like, is there a jealous boyfriend on the scene who would want to knock my block off for talking to you?"

"There isn't," Hannah replied, hesitating. "I've just come out of a steady relationship, and, just so you know, I'm not looking to start dating yet."

"Oh, me neither," said Brett, looking as if such an idea couldn't have been further from his mind. "Like I said, I'm just aiming to make new friends."

"OK, friends it is," Hannah agreed, raising her coffee cup to meet his bottle of mineral water.

Then, Hannah's extrasensory perception kicked in. To the right of her line of vision, she spotted Calum, no more than ten agonising metres away. Calum looked at her, and then at the guy who returned his stare with a toothpaste smile. The man, he noticed, was probably in his late-twenties. *Looks like Clark Kent,* he thought, regarding his clean-cut appearance. Even at a distance Calum could tell that Hannah's Mister Perfect companion seemed overly-pleased with himself. Plus, he was a little too groomed. In short, the man had the sort of smug face that Calum would have loved to smash his fists into.

Hannah caught Calum's gaze for the first time since Phuket and tried to convey a reassuring message with her eyes. She saw the tension in his jaw. Calum shook his head, turned on his heel and walked out of the cafeteria.

"So that guy was your ex?" Brett guessed.

"Correct."

"Seemed somewhat intense."

"He's got his demons. In fact, I'm not completely sure we've even officially split up."

"How so?"

"Well, one minute we're happily in love on a carefree holiday in Thailand and the next he's abandoned me and flown home to England."

"No way! So, for what reason?"

"I honestly don't know … and the sad thing is, I really do still love him."

"Jeez, he did that to you, and you still love the guy. That's a powerful love."

Brett decided not to pursue the subject further. He saw the sadness in Hannah's beautiful eyes and wished that he was the recipient of her affection. "So, what kind of stuff does Hannah like to do when she's not teaching aerobics?" he asked, trying to lighten the mood.

"O-kay, well I like listening to music. I love to eat, I like walks on the beach, my family and friends are very important to me. Do you really want me to bore you with this?"

"So, hey, here's a proposition. It's Sunday tomorrow and as far as I know you don't have any classes?"

"No-o," said Hannah, hesitantly, worried about what was coming next.

"Maybe I'm being too bold, but how about a Sunday morning walk on a beach, followed by a pub lunch?"

"Um, that all sounds perfect, Brett, but I'm not quite ready for that kind of thing just yet … I'm sorry."

"Hey, don't be sorry. Like I said, I'm not looking to date either. It would have been a friend thing. Walk, lunch, home. End of."

Hannah sensed that Brett wasn't harbouring a hidden agenda and the image of Calum and Imogen canoodling on the taxi rank suddenly invaded her mind. "OK, let's do it," she confirmed, slapping her hands on the table.

"I could pick you up from your home, say ten thirty?"

"Ten thirty it is," Hannah smiled while delving into her bag for a pen and paper to scribble down her address.

****

Calum returned home, consumed with anguish. He tried to reassure himself by re-reading some of Sawat's recent emails, but now his own life was spiralling cruelly out of control. Calum stared with longing at a photograph which Sophie had taken of Hannah during the Foo Fighters gig at the Reading Festival; just as she did at school, her eyes were crossed and her tongue was impishly pointed towards the camera. More than anything, Calum missed her playfulness. He hadn't bargained on each joyless day lasting an eternity, and there were still almost five months left to endure. He found the ceaseless gnaw of separation almost too much to bear, and in desperation he called out to Klahan, hoping to God that he could hear his pleas and that he might reconsider the inhumane terms of their deal.

****

While carefully harvesting almonds in the branches of a tree, Klahan heard Calum's plaintive cries as they echoed through the centuries. Initially, he huffed contemptuously at the thought of this wretched human failing so miserably in such a brief time span but Anong urged him to relinquish his punitive command.

"Klahan, has not the mortal suffered enough? Should his place not be beside this woman whom he so clearly loves?"

In his heart Klahan knew this to be true; besides, his own return to normality had induced him to shed most of his hostility like a snake discards its skin.

"Please do not allow yourself to think as they do, Klahan. Show mercy."

They sat together and kissed on the bough of the almond tree. Klahan finally agreed to prepare for the onerous journey to visit the human.

****

Teleported through a cosmic wormhole, the universe granted Klahan the power to travel forward in time, turning decades into minutes and miles into centimetres. He traversed international date lines, watching day and night flash on and off like a stroboscope. He soared high above mountaineers in the Himalayas, bending time with each wing beat. Ice crystals formed on his eyelashes and in his nostrils. At times he was so cold he felt that his blood might congeal. He hurtled above India and Pakistan and in the time that it would take to butter a slice of toast, babies wriggled from their mother's wombs and then died of old age, their bones quickly crumbling to dust. He decelerated over the Caspian Sea and into Europe, reaching the year 2013 in the skies above Holland.

It was three o'clock in the morning and drizzling heavily when Klahan made his descent into Norwich. He landed weightlessly on Dover Street in a triangular confluence of two roads where the Mad Moose public house stood. The moon hung, anaemic, in the blue-black sky, and the wet pavements reflected squiggles of light from streetlamps. Klahan inhaled the damp night air which was infused with the smell of stale beer, cigarette butts and newly-painted railings.

At this hour, apart from the haunted plasma glow of an insomniac's television set, almost all of the tightly-packed terraced houses were plunged into darkness. Klahan passed through the Victorian red brick walls of Calum's property and stood by his bed as the human dreamt of his previous life filled with happiness.

He infiltrated Calum's psyche and, without speaking, conveyed words that fell about the young man's head like the casting of a net. Still fast asleep, Calum received this information in the form of a distinct dream. When his duty was fulfilled, Klahan disappeared into the night sky, keen to return to the warm, fragrant air of his ancient civilization.

Because the dream was so vivid, Calum woke with a jolt expecting the Kinnara would still be there, looming over him like a winged spectre. Instead he heard and saw nothing, except the distant rumble of a lorry on Unthank Road and the comfortless glow of his digital clock display.

The Kinnara's instructions seemed real enough though: Klahan had enunciated each word with precision and stood over the bed, glowing against the dark like the chiaroscuro of a Rembrandt portrait. Calum was advised that, in order to resume his relationship with Hannah without causing any harm to Sawat, he was to return to the same stretch of shoreline on Patong beach where he had summoned Klahan from his watery confinement. The curse could only be lifted at the scene of its conception.

Switching on his bedside lamp, Calum was annoyed that he had allowed himself to entertain such a preposterous idea. But then, in the lamp's glow, he discovered a large white feather nestled in a fold of his duvet.

This evidence was the authentication that he needed and with a glimmer of hope budding in his heart, he scrambled out of bed to search the internet for the next available flight to Phuket.

****

Because of the absence of traffic on a Sunday morning, Calum's taxi arrived at Norwich Airport in double-quick time. He had booked a morning KLM flight to Amsterdam's Schiphol Airport, from which he would fly long-haul to Phuket.

At the same moment that Calum's plane was preparing for its descent over the Hook of Holland, Brett arrived at Hannah's house in a customised 1970s' Ford Mustang that looked as if it might have once been driven through a stack of cardboard boxes on an episode of *Starsky and Hutch*. When the doorbell rang, Hannah was still getting ready and called down the stairs for her mother to let him in.

Despite opening the door to Brett's all-American smile, Sinéad wasn't overly impressed: *too clean-cut for my liking*, she thought. In addition, this guy hooked his thumbs into the front pockets of his jeans, something she loathed almost as much as when men turned their shirt collars up. In anticipation of the newbie's arrival, Sinéad had planned a bit of fun at his expense.

"Hello, Brett, I'm Hannah's mother. Now I'm afraid I'm a little precious about my carpets, so you need to take your shoes off and put these on."

Soon after, she brushed past Hannah at the top of the stairs, stifling a fit of the giggles and pointing in the direction from whence she came.

"Oh, Mum, what have you done now?" Hannah groaned, as her mother sat on the top step, trying not to squeal like a piglet. Brett stood patiently in the hallway with a resigned expression on his bespectacled face; on his feet was a pair of oversized, novelty hedgehog slippers.

"Hello, mister. Do you know where Calum is?" Marcus asked, suddenly appearing from the living room to interrogate Brett.

"Uh, I'm afraid I don't," Brett replied awkwardly, looking to Hannah for some help.

"He's my friend," continued Marcus, "but my sister doesn't know where he is."

"OK, Marcus, come here, big hug," Hannah interjected, taking her brother in her arms. "Me and Brett have to hit the road. We'll talk about Calum later, yeah?"

Upstairs, out of sight, her father watched from a bedroom window as the American boy ushered Hannah into his conspicuous car. *Huh, looks like Clark Kent*, he thought.

****

Hannah directed Brett to Happisburgh, the site of one of her all-time favourite beaches on the North Norfolk coast. They went via the market town of Stalham, driving past pancake-flat landscapes and the scenic waterways of the Broads. She felt that Brett would have loved her to gush over his macho left-hand drive American muscle car, but she deliberately didn't – precisely for that reason. In fact, when they were stuck behind a mud-caked lorry which had momentarily ground to a halt, she mischievously hoped that some of its load of sugar beet would tumble down onto his shiny bonnet.

Fending off questions from Brett, Hannah didn't divulge the name of their destination, preferring to retain some degree of control over the day's events. She only mentioned it once Happisburgh's name was in plain sight. "Now, you see that?" she said, pointing to its charming hand-carved village sign. "You will never, in a million years, guess how *that* is pronounced."

"OK, I'd say Happis-boro', Happis-burg ... something along those lines?"

"Nope ... it's pronounced *Haysbrough*."

"How the heck did they arrive at that?" he said, shaking his head but at the same time enjoying Hannah's playfulness. He found her closeness intoxicating and, without meaning to, he realised that he was falling in love with her.

Brett left his Mustang in a small car park within sight of a red-and-white striped lighthouse that resembled a barber-shop pole.

"Wow, it's simply breathtaking," he gasped, sniffing the briny air, able to see for miles in almost every direction. "Great choice. Oh, and by the way, I was born in Arkansas which, as you know, is also pronounced different to how it's spelt."

Hannah was glad she'd decided to take Brett up on his invitation. She'd spent most of Saturday night having second thoughts and very nearly phoned him to cancel. Now that she was here, she felt invigorated by their surroundings. Then, just as she closed her eyes to feel the North Sea's liberating breeze on her face, the ringtone of her phone announced a call: Leo's name was on the screen.

She pressed green to answer. "Hello, Leo," she said

curtly, still bristling at his recent disloyalty.

"Um, you OK, Han? You sound a bit off."

"Might have something to do with me seeing you and Tilly on a night out with Calum and Imogen," she said. There followed a moment of dumbfounded silence as Leo evaluated her statement.

"Oh, my God, you obviously saw us with Imogen at the taxi rank on Guildhall Hill. I swear we just bumped into her … in fact she did try it on with Calum and he wasn't having any of it. Hannah, he still loves you!"

Brett allowed Hannah the privacy of her phone call and walked towards the cliff edge to stare at the sea. Hannah knew Leo well enough to know that he couldn't lie to save his life, and instantly felt guilty for giving up on Calum so easily. Hope once again mushroomed in her chest and she listened intently as Leo continued.

"Look, Hannah, the reason I'm calling you is to say that Calum is on his way to Thailand to sort things out. Couldn't get much out of him, the usual secrecy, but he asked me to phone you, so you would know that he was trying to end this nonsense."

"But, Leo, I still don't know what this nonsense is."

"Well, it beats me too. I have never seen him like this before, it just isn't him."

"Thanks for phoning me, Leo, you've really made my day."

"That's great … don't give up on him just yet, yeah?"

"I won't," said Hannah, smiling into the phone.

"Tilly sends her love."

"Yeah, love you both back."

"Everything OK?" asked Brett, as Hannah strolled towards him through the straw-like grass.

"Big development on the ex-boyfriend front," she replied. "Seems he might be a step closer to losing his demons."

"But, you're not seriously thinking of taking him back after all he's put you through?"

"Why not? Like I told you, Brett, I love him."

Brett looked stunned. It was as if such an eventuality had never occurred to him. There was an uncomfortable silence in which he narrowed his eyes and stared at Hannah in utter disbelief. Then he spoke: "*Liebe macht blind.*"

"And what does that mean?" Hannah asked, forcing a smile whilst jigging up and down on the balls of her feet, hoping to keep the mood buoyant.

"It simply means *Love is blind,*" he explained coldly.

"O-kay…" she quavered, surprised that his mood had shifted so dramatically. "So you speak a little German, then?"

"Oh, more than a little," he said, pointedly. "I grew up in Germany, on an American Air Force base, and then I enlisted … again working in Germany, before I came over to the UK."

"Well, I am extremely impressed," exalted Hannah, trying to remain upbeat despite the change in his demeanour. Seagulls mewed noisily as they wheeled overhead. Brett's sudden frostiness was making her feel uncomfortable and Hannah, with the gift of hindsight, wished that she had stayed at home with her family. Then, almost as if he had flicked an internal switch, Brett was suddenly affable again, smiling like a politician and crinkling his eyes.

"Hey, look at me, being a real downer. What d'you say we finish our walk, have a drink in the pub and then head for home?"

"Music to my ears," Hannah chirped, relieved that Brett wasn't going to turn into some kind of spurned weirdo.

"Wow, just look at the erosion of these cliffs," he

marvelled, peering over the precipice.

"Oh God, be careful. I wouldn't dare stand that close. I'm not exactly good with heights."

"Aw, don't be such a scaredy-cat, I'll keep hold."

Hannah tiptoed as near as she dared. Brett surveyed the landscape; only a quartet of elderly ramblers was visible in the distance. Then, with one forceful shove he pushed her, screaming, over the cliff edge.

Almost immediately afterwards there was only the jarring noise of the gulls. He peered down at Hannah's contorted body, which had come to rest on a concrete rampart. A halo of dark blood slowly radiated from the stillness of her broken skull.

"Fucking bitch," he snarled.

****

At 12.43 p.m. Hannah was pronounced dead at the scene. One of the attending police officers rang the *In Case of Emergency* numbers that were listed in her phone. One of these was Calum's, whose mobile was switched off for the duration of his flight to Thailand. The other number was that of Hannah's parents.

The Mother Killer had committed his first mistake; he had killed impetuously, rather than dispassionately and despite his tearful account of how the perilous cliff edge gave way under Hannah's feet, he hadn't bargained on the agoraphobic old man who watched it all from his bedroom window through a powerful telescope.

CHAPTER FORTY-TWO

The Big Fish

Brett Carter knew that the game was up when extra police officers arrived on the scene and approached him with a look of disapproval on their faces. He deliberately annoyed them by smirking as his rights were read to him.

You hicks don't have a fucking clue what you've got, he thought, grinning from ear to ear.

They bundled him, handcuffed into the back of a police wagon and slammed the door extra hard for intimidatory effect.

****

Not long past midnight on the sixth of November 1984, while most of Arkansas was fast asleep, a baby boy was abandoned just two hours after his birth, swaddled in a chenille blanket on a cold doorstep at the Jacksonville Fire Department. The fire crew was alerted to his existence by a distraught call from a public phone. Through tears of heartache and anger, the baby's birth mother spoke of her rape by the stranger who had befriended her and announced that she did not want anything to do with the child that she had secretly carried for nine dreadful months. The phone went dead before any questions could be asked and the mother was never found.

The baby remained in hospital under the protection of the Department for Child Services, until he was placed into foster care. Eventually he was adopted by Robert Carter, an aircraft engineer at the Little Rock Air Force Base, and his librarian wife, Maria. They named the boy Brett in honour of the considerate adoption agent who helped them to become a family.

Robert and Maria were a churchgoing, equable couple, who managed to eke out the positives during even the darkest of times. They were desperate to produce children of their own but despite several expensive courses of IVF, they were unable to do so. Then, when this beautiful 8lb baby boy was offered to them, they thanked their God for taking the time to answer their prayers.

From an early age, though, it became apparent that their son had inherited some of the cruel characteristics of his rapist father. Robert and Maria were concerned to see that he derived sadistic pleasure from tearing off the legs of live crickets and they were horrified when his elementary school teachers told them how their son would strike out at any girl who chose to ignore him.

Robert hoped that a posting to a USAF base in Germany might help the family to regroup, but instead the problem worsened. A child psychologist diagnosed a narcissistic personality disorder. He said that the boy was highly intelligent but lacked empathy. Brett also held a disproportionately elevated view of himself and was contemptuous of others.

In the winter of 2005, Robert and Maria were discovered slumped and open-mouthed on the sofa of their living room in Kaiserslautern. Their death was caused by carbon monoxide poisoning; the flue of their gas fire had been obstructed by an eiderdown which someone had stuffed up the chimney. Investigators reached the conclusion that Robert had placed it there in the summer months to eliminate draughts, and, tragically, had forgotten to remove it when winter came.

****

"Cut the light conversation," Brett sneered, as his recorded interview got underway at the Bethel Street Police Station in Norwich. "You jerks need to wise up fast and listen to what I'm saying. And then, after checking out my story on Google, you can pat yourself on the back for catching the big fish."

"Oh, so you're a big fish are you Brett?" said one of the detectives sarcastically.

CHAPTER FORTY-THREE

Déjà Vu

The immigration area at Phuket's International airport echoed to the sound of Thai voices and unintelligible tannoy announcements.

Because he'd only travelled with hand luggage, Calum circumvented the baggage carousels and aimed straight for the green channel. Then, before leaving the cool of the terminal building he switched his phone on for the first time since Schiphol Airport, allowing it to search for a local network. After fleetingly regarding the sweaty heat of a Thai afternoon, he slid onto the back seat of the first available taxi.

His phone burst into life, announcing its presence with a series of immodest pings. There were a lot of texts from a variety of people. He selected one from his father, who urged him to call home as soon as possible.

"Where you want to go?" asked the driver as he pulled away from the kerb.

"Uh, Redford Beach Hotel," Calum said distractedly, as he phoned his father:

"Hi, Dad, you asked me to call you urgently?"

"Hello, son, are you okay to talk?"

"Yeah, yeah, has something happened? Is Mum OK?"

"She's fine Calum. Uh, I'm assuming you haven't heard yet … it's terrible news … um, oh God … Hannah, she's dead, son. I'm sorry, I just don't know how else to say it."

"Dead? … w-what do you mean, dead?"

"She's been murdered, some American guy who came to her fitness class. I am so sorry Calum, your Mum couldn't bring herself to tell you. Hannah's family are beside themselves. I wish it wasn't so, son…"

The taxi driver looked anxiously in his rear-view mirror as his young passenger began to break down behind him.

"Come home, son, just come home, we'll all be here waiting for you." His father's voice trailed off as he also was overcome by sorrow.

Calum was barely able to think, let alone speak.

"I'll, uh, get back soon, Dad," he sobbed, before dropping the phone onto the seat and holding his wet face in trembling hands. The driver continued the journey in silence, not wishing to intrude on the young man's despair.

****

By the time the taxi arrived at the Redford, Calum's pain had curdled into anger. After handing the cabbie a one-thousand baht note and not waiting for change, he strode through the lobby, heedless of the greetings that fluttered past him. The urgency of his headlong dash through the hotel unnerved a security guard, who scurried after him whilst gibbering into a walkie-talkie. Once outside, on the lawns to the rear, Calum stepped out of his espadrilles and made for the beach like a boxer heading towards a ring.

It took him only a few minutes to reach the spot where he first spoke with the Kinnara, and where the toxic curse was conceived. He stared out towards the shadow of dark water:

"Klahan!" he hollered out in anguish. "How much

more can you make me suffer?"

The sea remained indifferent to his turmoil and lay serene and undisturbed. Gentle waves lapped at Calum's toes, as if to mollify him. His rage came in spasms. "Come on! Fucking face me, you coward!"

At that moment, a young elephant trooped towards him, accompanied by its owner. A small pack of territorial beach dogs ran from the shade to bark at the elephant, who trumpeted them away. "Calum! Look at the cute elephant!"

When Calum's astonished eyes followed the direction of the voice, his heart turned a somersault. Hannah, larger than life, was strolling towards him, holding a bottle of water.

"Honey, I was so desperate to find you, how are things with Sawat?"

Calum ran to Hannah, flung his arms around her and then sobbed uncontrollably.

"Oh baby, don't be upset," she soothed, stretching the sleeve of her kaftan over her fingers to wipe away his tears. Then she noticed a smile appear across his face.

"Oh God I love you so much," he bubbled.

"And I love you too … but now I'm confused. How's Sawat?"

"I think Sawat's going to be just fine," he grinned.

The elephant made a beeline for Hannah and began to communicate with her via some gentle flourishes of its trunk. Its owner lifted the brim of his conical straw hat, amazed at their instinctive connection.

"The elephan', I think he know you in another life, Madam."

CHAPTER FORTY-FOUR

Das Unglückliche Ende
The Unhappy Ending

Patong 2017

Almost four years have passed since Calum orchestrated their special romantic dinner by the beach. Hannah, of course, dutifully pretended that his marriage proposal that night came as a complete surprise. What she hadn't bargained for, though, was the reappearance of a letter which she had sent him while they were still at school together.

Because of Klahan's manipulation of time, Hannah had never knowingly met, nor was aware, of the psychotic American who Calum had seen in the fitness centre's café. Calum thought it sensible to keep any knowledge of this to himself, but surreptitiously kept an eye on things, just in case the guy ever turned up to one of her step classes.

He was, however, forced to share his tale of the Kinnara with Hannah after she repeatedly badgered him about the unexplicably, unnatural disappearance of his leg wound. Astonishingly, Hannah believed every extraordinary word, immediately understanding the true reason behind Sawat's miraculous recovery.

After finally achieving her dream wedding to her teenage crush, Hannah made sure that their Year 2005 school photograph was afforded a position of prominence in the hallway of their new home. It gave visiting friends much to laugh about, especially when they spotted Mr Pugh's desperate attempt to hide his contaminated mouth. For Hannah and Calum, though, the photograph also served as a poignant reminder of the undervalued life of poor Mr Bingham.

****

And now, to celebrate their second wedding anniversary, they were back in Phuket, this time accompanied by their baby daughter, Celine, thus named after one of Hannah's favourite aunts in Jamaica.

As they played together on Patong beach, the family were joined by the other newly-weds, Sawat and Nok, who had brought enough food and drink for a satisfying picnic. As usual, the group laughed and chatted, blissfully unaware that the Mother Killer was only a short distance away.

****

Brett Carter sat on the sand and gazed upwards at the blue sky above Patong bay. He had, by this time, completely lost his mind and couldn't even string a few simple words together.

He was reported as being absent without leave and also missing from his living quarters at the US Air Force base in Mildenhall. He literally vanished from the face of the earth nearly four years ago, and no one had seen him since.

Brett scooped up a handful of wet sand from under

his feet and squished it between his fingers as a manta ray winged past his submerged head.

Insane and isolated, this is where he would forever remain, entombed by dark seawater, five lonely fathoms beneath the turquoise surface of the Andaman Sea.

Acknowledgments

I would first of all like to thank you for taking the time to read my novel.

I'd also like to thank 'Bad Cop' Karen Holmes, the editor at *2QT* publishing, for her diligent proof-reading, and Catherine Cousins, for her belief in me.

Hopefully my love for Thailand and its wonderful people is clear to see: I am extremely grateful to my many Thai friends, for their unfailing hospitality, and for helping me to learn their language and understand their culture.

I drew inspiration for Sawat's fictional struggle with paraplegia from Melanie Reid's real-life battle with tetraplegia. I would urge everyone to read her inspirational and candid *Spinal Column* online.

Lastly, I wish to publicly thank my wife, Julie, for exhibiting the patience of a saint whilst I commandeered our dining room for use as a writer's retreat. Although not customarily tolerant, Julie magnanimously ignored the screwed up balls of notepaper and the thesauri that lay strewn around my laptop for the duration (I really didn't want to use the cheerless little room in our house that she idealistically calls 'the office').

This armistice worked surprisingly well: Julie didn't murder me in my sleep, and I completed my novel without a murmur of marital condemnation.

She is also the first person I turn to for an honest, unvarnished appraisal of my work.

Julie, without your support, this book would never have got off the ground.

I love you.